AF067354

THE DEMON'S SHADOW

An Urban Fantasy Thriller (Myth & Magic, Book 4)

S. W. Millar

TAGLINE
PUBLISHING

Tagline Publishing

ALSO BY S. W. MILLAR

Myth & Magic

The Thief's Magic # 0.5 (FREE prequel short story)
The Witch's Revenge # 1
The Coven's Executioner # 2
The Fury's Vengeance # 3 [Novelette]
More *Myth & Magic* coming soon...

The Demon's Shadow: An Urban Fantasy Thriller (Myth & Magic, Book 4)

Copyright © 2022 by S. W. Millar

All rights reserved

Published by Tagline Publishing

https://swmillar.com

ISBN (eBook): 978-1-915192-06-6

ISBN (Paperback): 978-1-915192-07-3

Cover design by Damonza

Formatted using Atticus

No part of this book may be reproduced in any form or by any electronic or mechanical means, including information storage and retrieval systems, without written permission from the author, except for the use of brief quotations.

This book is a work of fiction. Names, characters, places and incidents are either a product of the author's imagination or are used fictitiously. Any resemblance to actual people living or dead, events or locales is entirely coincidental.

Contents

Is This Book For You?	IX
Dedication	X
Epigraph	XI
1. Summoning Dark Things	1
2. Chapter 1	8
3. Chapter 2	20
4. Chapter 3	31
5. Chapter 4	36
6. Chapter 5	40
7. Chapter 6	47
8. Chapter 7	50
9. Chapter 8	57
10. Chapter 9	64
11. Chapter 10	76
12. Chapter 11	86

13.	Chapter 12	91
14.	Chapter 13	96
15.	Chapter 14	103
16.	Chapter 15	109
17.	Chapter 16	115
18.	Chapter 17	122
19.	Chapter 18	126
20.	Chapter 19	138
21.	Chapter 20	148
22.	Chapter 21	154
23.	Chapter 22	160
24.	Chapter 23	165
25.	Chapter 24	173
26.	Chapter 25	177
27.	Chapter 26	187
28.	Chapter 27	195
29.	Chapter 28	201
30.	Chapter 29	206
31.	Chapter 30	209
32.	Chapter 31	215
33.	Chapter 32	217
34.	Chapter 33	221
35.	Chapter 34	229
36.	Chapter 35	231
37.	Chapter 36	236

38.	Chapter 37	240
39.	Chapter 38	247
40.	Chapter 39	251
41.	Chapter 40	255
42.	Chapter 41	263
43.	Chapter 42	269
44.	Chapter 43	276
45.	Chapter 44	283
46.	Chapter 45	288
47.	Chapter 46	293
48.	Chapter 47	298
49.	Chapter 48	300
50.	Chapter 49	311
51.	Chapter 50	315
52.	Chapter 51	321
53.	Chapter 52	326
54.	Chapter 53	330
55.	Chapter 54	336
56.	Chapter 55	340
57.	Chapter 56	350
58.	Chapter 57	353
59.	Epilogue	360
	Want More From The Myth & Magic Universe?	370
	Acknowledgments	372
	About The Author	374

Also By S. W. Millar

IS THIS BOOK FOR YOU?

This book contains adult themes, fantasy violence, and colourful language. Basically, all the fun stuff. I write using British English. Sound good? Then read on and enjoy!

For all the people who refuse to give up on their dreams.

"Most people can bear adversity; but if you wish to know what a man really is give him power."—**Robert Green Ingersoll**

SUMMONING DARK THINGS
Aidan

The sharp blade parts the skin on my palm like fabric scissors slicing through silk.

Shiny beads of crimson well up from the crescent-shaped wound, but in the candlelight—which casts sinister shadows across the barren walls—the viscous droplets appear black.

I hold my arm over the small bronze bowl at my feet, the dark blood collecting in the lines of my hand.

The four of us stand around the edge of a wide copper circle inlaid into the floor, each cradling a bloody pool in our outstretched fingers, each with a tiny bowl at our feet. The air is thick with the dark stench of death.

Belladonna.

Valerian.

Vervain.

Dark herbs to summon dark things.

Ground into a paste and dispersed into the four bowls.

An unholy trinity, if ever there was one.

It's fitting.

Tonight, we are doing an unholy thing.

My spine tingles with anticipation. "Time?"

Naomi checks her watch, using her free hand. Her dark eyes sparkle in the candlelight. "One minute to midnight."

My heart rate spikes, the silver crown atop my head growing heavy. I concentrate on that weight.

Show me.

The band of silver warms.

A harsh electric shock races through my body, and I cry out in pain.

Then—

Shimmering golden letters burst into existence, staining the air in front of me.

My eyes widen.

"What is it, Ade?" Eric asks.

I let out a long breath. "You can't see it?"

Chelle shakes her head. "See what?"

"The crown. It's showing me how to breach the Gates."

Naomi sports a wide grin. "This is it, my love. This is what we've been working for."

I return a grin of my own. "Let's do this."

As one, we clench our fists, carmine droplets splashing into the bowls below us.

The deathly mixture inside bubbles and hisses, and the candle flames flare.

Thank God I found the crown when I did and thank God it revealed its secrets and showed me the way. Fifteen years of waiting, and the moment is finally here.

"Chant after me."

The others nod.

I follow the golden words with my eyes, my voice low and haunting. My words echo from my comrades' mouths.

"*In tenebris hora, maleficatorium horae.*"

In the dark hour, the witching hour.

"*Vocamus ad infernales.*"

We call to the infernal.

"*Loquimur, et ita est.*"

We speak, and it is so.

"*Sicut supra, ita infra.*"

As above, so below.

"*Aperi portas, aperi portas, aperi portas.*"

Open the Gates, open the Gates, open the Gates.

The candle flames flicker and the stench of death makes my head spin.

Nothing changes.

Eric's head lifts. He lowers the hood of his scarlet robe and rakes a hand through his dark hair. "What's happening?"

The spark of hope in my chest gutters and dies, and my stomach sinks into my shoes. "I don't know."

Chelle arcs a flaming red eyebrow at me. "You said it was going to work this time. You promised—"

"I know what I promised." There's a harsh bite to my voice. Good. I'm feeling harsh. "We'll try again."

"Oh, what's the fucking point? I won't get my hopes up again, just for... for... this. I'm done." Chelle spins on a pointed heel and stalks towards the stairs leading out of the basement, the loud *click* of her footfalls echoing off the walls.

"Chelle, wait." Naomi turns to me, her tone calm. "Ade, maybe we all need to calm down, and—"

My fists clench at my sides, one tacky with congealing blood. I narrow my eyes at Chelle's retreating form. "Leave now, and you leave for good."

"Ade." Naomi shoots me a reproachful glare.

I ignore her.

Chelle freezes, one foot on the bottom step, knuckles white on the metal banister. She sinks in on herself, lowers into a seated position on the stairs, and winds a lock of bright red hair around her finger. "I'm sorry. I just... we've been trying for so long. It's hard, you know. I thought this time—"

"Remember what we said," I say. "Remember what we swore to each other."

She gnaws on her thumbnail. "Never give up."

"Never give up," I repeat.

Her eyes shine with tears. "I'm so tired."

I know what she means. There are moments—however fleeting—when a dark abyss yawns before me and threatens to swallow me whole, leaving nothing behind. On those days, I could happily crawl into bed, yank the covers over my head, and let sleep suffocate me.

Today is not one of those days.

When I speak again, my voice is firm. "We *will* find a way. I know—"

A tortured sound tears through the room, a malign amalgamation of thunder clapping, wolves howling, and people screeching in pain.

It's so loud, so invasive, it forces me to clap my hands over my ears and sink to my knees.

Anything to block it out.

The temperature plummets to below zero and my breath mists before my eyes. Goosebumps prickle my skin.

"What the fuck?" Eric shouts from his own cramped position, but his exclamation is barely audible above the banshee wail.

All at once, the terrible sound cuts off.

My ears ring with the sudden silence.

Naomi straightens, removing her hands from her ears. "What the hell was that?"

My head snaps left and right, scanning the room for threats. "I don't—"

The ground beneath our feet trembles.

Only one thing can make the ground do that.

Earth magic.

"We're under attack. We need to—"

Crack.

Chelle screams.

"Look." I point with a shaking finger.

In the centre of the copper circle, a crevice opens up in the concrete.

The room grows colder still.

My teeth chatter, the clacking sound reverberating around my skull.

An even more unpleasant smell replaces the pungent reek of belladonna, valerian, and vervain. A strange mixture of sulphur, decomposing meat, and something faintly sweet.

My stomach roils, and I gag, clamping a hand over my mouth.

Dense black smoke pours from the fissure in the floor. Inky tendrils swirl up and out, reaching for the edge of the circle but unable to breach it.

Something catches in my chest, dies.

Catches, dies.

Catches… dies.

A pilot light failing to spark the flame.

Hope.

"I—" I step back from the circle's edge, my shoe scuffing on the bare concrete floor "—think it's working."

The deepest, blackest area of smoke whirls, as if turning to face me. *Not quite.*

I flinch. I can't help myself.

The smoke spoke to me.

No.

That's not quite right.

It didn't speak so much as project the words straight into my mind.

My mouth drops open.

All these years, all our searching.

The legend is real.

Demons exist.

"Oh, my God," I say, my tone laced with unadulterated awe.

The heart of the smoke pulses, and a rough, scratchy chuckle scrapes around the inside of my skull. *Again, not quite.*

Eric's eyes widen.

Can he hear the voice, too?

Naomi wears a similar shocked expression. "You're a—a—"

Demon. Yes.

"Holy shit," Chelle breathes.

We can all hear the demon.

Just how powerful is—

Speaking of power, if you intend to summon me, you are going to need more of it.

A chill creeps down my spine. Is it—*he*—reading my mind?

No. I am not. It is more nuanced than that.

"I—" My voice cracks, and I clear my throat. "More power? We're four of the most powerful witches in the—"

I do not care whether you are on a first name basis with the elements themselves. You need a fifth. Another powerful witch. The most powerful you can find.

"But who—"

The wailing sound rips through the room again, and I grit my teeth against the grating sound. Above the agonised roar, the demon's voice is clear in my mind.

I cannot stay any longer. The pull of the Gates is too strong. Remember what I said. You need... you need...

The disembodied voice fades in and out now, but I catch the last word.

Another.

An unseen force sucks the onyx cloud of smoke back into the ground, and the crevice it emerged from seals shut.

My ears ring with silence for the second time in as many minutes.

"Holy shit," Chelle says. "What do we do now?"

"You heard what the demon said." I lower the hood of my robe. "We need to find a fifth."

Chapter 1
Christian

"Fuck off, mate." The bouncer shoves a meaty hand into my chest.

I stumble back, but keep my balance.

What an arsehole.

Where did they find this Phil Mitchell lookalike, anyway?

Stereotypes aren't really my thing, but he's your typical doorman.

Shaved head, piggy eyes, muscle turning to fat.

What isn't so typical is his outfit: biker boots, studded leather jacket, silver chain running from nostril to earlobe—connected by two hoops driven through the fleshy parts at either end.

The Pincushion is Daxbridge's number one goth dive bar.

Meat-hands here needs to look the part.

Nothing would give me greater pleasure than to use my magic to rip that chain from his face and watch him writhe around in agony, but that wouldn't win me any brownie points with my boss.

Unfortunately, there's this little thing called The First Law.

Never mix mortals and magic.

Never risk exposure.

"You deaf or summat?" Meat-hands barks.

Christ.

He even sounds like Phil Mitchell.

Why do I always get the cases that take me to the dodgy parts of Daxbridge?

Meat-hands grits his teeth. "I said fuck off. We don't want your kind in here."

My kind? I fold my arms and fix him with a glare. "What? Anglo-Spanish?"

"Comedian, eh?" He smirks at me, eyeing my suit, my white stiff-collared shirt, my brown brogues. "I don't give a shit whether you're black, white, green, or electric blue. You ain't coming in here dressed like that."

My eyes roll... hard. "I'm a goth on the inside, I swear." I go to push past him.

He bars my path. "Nice try. Now, piss off out of it before I lamp you one."

My blood boils, and a muscle ticks in my jaw. A quick fireball to the gut. That's all it would take to wipe the smirk off Meat-hands's face.

Never mix mortals and magic.

Never risk exposure.

Breathe.

The mantra calms me, but only a little.

I hold my hands up. "Fine. Whatever. Jesus."

I need to get into this pub.

My success in this case depends on it.

But, how?

I twist on my heel and stride away from *The Pincushion*, Meat-hands burning a couple of holes in my shoulder blades the entire time. I stomp past the outdoor smoking area—ignoring the catcalls of,

"Vanilla prick," and, "Stupid wanker,"—and round the corner. My car's parked across the road. When I reach it, I yank the door open, slide into the driving seat, and slam it behind me.

Detective Constable Henry Stone doesn't glance up from the book balanced in his hand. "So, Christian, how did it go?"

"Remind me why I rescued you from COVEN again."

He snorts, folds the corner of the page down—why do people do that? It's so fucking annoying—and throws the book onto the dashboard. "One. You didn't rescue me. You just told me the truth, and I did the rest. Two. When you offered me the job, you said, and I quote, I was, 'growing on you'."

"Layla was right," I grumble. "You grow on people like mould."

"Aw, don't be like that. This could be the start of a decent bromance."

That raises a chuckle from me, albeit a half-hearted one.

Stone's expression sobers, all levity leaving his voice. "Told you I should've gone in instead of you."

He's right. He's not a goth either, but with his dark hair, dark clothes, half-sleeve of black feather tattoos encasing his left arm, and his Sight-enhanced emerald green eyes, he'd have stood a better chance of getting past old Meat-hands than me.

"You're not ready," I say.

He clicks his tongue and stares out of the window. "You've got to take the training wheels off sometime. I was an executioner for the better part of three years, remember? I'm sure I can handle your mate Tally."

No.

He really couldn't.

"It's too dangerous."

"She's one person."

"I said no."

Besides, I wouldn't describe Tally as a person. Not anymore, anyway.

Poor Talitha.

My gut clenches and blood pounds in my ears.

If it wasn't for Dylan Carmichael, the ex-Director of COVEN, Tally's wife, Maria—my former boss—would still be alive. If it wasn't for Carmichael, Tally wouldn't have killed O'Hara, Henry's former coworker, or transformed into the monster she is today.

Tally has Fury Syndrome, which is an extremely rare condition that affects witches.

There are tremendous benefits, sure. Benefits I could leverage in my line of work. Super strength, speed, diamond-sharp talons, enhanced senses, and a sonic scream powerful enough to shatter brick, never mind glass.

The major drawbacks, however, aren't worth it. The compulsion to seek vengeance no matter the cost, the dampening of emotion, losing humanity.

No, thank you.

I'm a powerful witch, and I should be able to help her... but I can't. It's beyond even my power to turn her back into the witch she once was.

Knowing that makes me sick to my stomach.

What good is magic if I can't use it to save the people I love?

The people I love.

I have a habit of letting my nearest and dearest down.

My brother's face floats before my eyes.

John.

Where are you, buddy?

Are you okay?

I wish I'd never said those things to him.

Are you even alive?

I wish—

No.

I refuse to go down that road.

Not now.

Not in the middle of a case.

Stone turns back to me and catches my eye. "Hey, listen—"

"I'm fine."

He nods—even though I know he doesn't believe me—and asks, "How powerful can she be?"

In Stone's defence, he wasn't there when Tally launched O'Hara thirty feet across a car park from a fourth storey window, like he weighed the same as a bag of feathers. Or when the Supernatural Crime Scene Investigators had to scrape him off the crumpled bonnet of Kate's car.

A shudder goes through me. "You have no idea."

We sit in silence for a while, Stone tapping his foot the entire time.

Eventually, he sniffs. "So, how are you going to get into the pub now? The bouncer's seen you. He knows what you look like."

He knows what you look like.

A light flicks on. "That's it. Why didn't I think of that before?"

"Think of what?"

"I'll cast a glamour. He won't recognise me then."

Stone casts a dubious sideways glance at me. "It'll have to be a bloody good glamour."

"Come on. The guy's mortal. He'll be too busy thinking about updating his status on Facechat or Insta-snap-whatever-it-is to worry about me."

This draws a rare laugh from Stone. "Oh, my God."

"What?"

"You're not even thirty yet. Did you really just say, 'Facechat or Insta-snap-whatever-it-is'?"

"Whatever. I hate social media."

"Only because you don't have any friends."

"No one likes a smart arse, Stone." I keep my voice neutral, but I'm laughing on the inside.

My new DC reminds me of me.

I roll my neck and draw on my magic. The familiar buzz of pins and needles prickles over my skin, and I taste copper on the back of my tongue, revelling in the power surging through me. "*Dissimulato.*"

A shower of violet sparks engulfs me, sweeping from the crown of my head to the soles of my shoes and, when the light fades, a stranger stares back at me in the rearview mirror.

The 'vanilla prick' has vanished. I'm wearing a black AC/DC T-shirt, black jeans held up by a studded belt, and a pair of postbox red high-tops. My black, shoulder-length hair has a bright blue streak running down one side. Still missing something, though. I click my fingers and a silver bull ring appears in my nose, sticking out either side of my septum.

Stone shakes his head and picks up his book again. "Don't do things by halves, do you?"

"Where's the fun in that?" I shove the car door open. "Stay here. I don't want you anywhere near this."

His eyes flick across the page, but he doesn't answer.

"That's an order, Henry."

"Yeah, yeah. I got it."

I sigh.

That's as close to an agreement as I'm going to get.

I step outside and slam the door closed.

Right.

Let's try this again, shall we? Meat-hands still guards the door.

I make it to the front of the queue a second time.

He squints at me. "Hey. Don't I know you from somewhere?"

I shrug. "No, mate. Never been here before. Meeting a friend."

The bouncer sets his jaw. "This friend of yours. They a regular?"

"Yeah. Name's Talitha."

His eyes narrow to slits. "Don't know no one called Talitha."

"About this tall." I hold my hand up to my shoulder. "White hair. Crazy red eyes."

His expression clears. "Oh, shit. You mean Vex." He winks at me in a conspiratorial, Lads-Lads-Lads, sort of way. "That costume she wears... fuck me, I'd give my left bollock for a go on that one. Lucky bastard."

A go on that one?

Is this guy for real?

What an arsehole.

I sense now isn't the time to air my views on gender equality, so I force my lips into a lazy half-smile and say nothing.

Meat-hands laughs and claps me on the back like we're old pals, and waves me through.

I stride into the bar.

Inside isn't much better than outside.

Rough doesn't even cover it.

Suspect, rust-coloured stains mar the carpet, the faded wallpaper is peeling, and a barman tattooed from head to toe wipes a grimy pint glass with a grimier cloth. To top it all, despite the UK ban on indoor smoking, a group of mohawk-sporting head-bangers in the corner take alternating drags on something way too fat to be a cigarette.

For fuck's sake, Tally.

If Maria could see you now...

The crowd of Alice Cooper wannabes parts, and there she is.

Speak of the devil.

Literally.

It's been seven months since I last saw Tally, and—somehow—she's even more menacing.

Her hair's so white it's almost silver, falling down to her waist in thick waves, and her skin is corpse-pale. Even from this distance, I can make out her blood-red irises and claw-tipped fingers—the hooked talons catching the dim light like chips of obsidian. She's squeezed herself into a skin-tight pair of black leather trousers and a pastel blue corset, leaving little to the imagination.

Despite myself, I blush.

She's my friend, not some goth sex-symbol.

Tally's playing pool against a guy with cherry-red hair and pierced eyebrows. She leans over the table, potting one, two, three, four, five balls in quick succession. She's straightening up when every single muscle in her body pulls rigid with tension.

Then she stares right at me.

No, through me—or, more precisely, through my glamour—her aforementioned Fury-enhanced senses at work.

I freeze, ice-water running down my spine.

Her nostrils flare and, as if she can smell my fear, her lips peel back from her teeth in a wolf-like grin.

My pulse slams against my wrist like it's trying to break free, and I cross to the pool table, my leg muscle stiff.

When I reach Tally and the man with pierced eyebrows, she tells him to, "Leave the money on the table," in a monotone drawl that makes my skin crawl.

The man scrunches his face up. "You haven't won yet, darlin'."

Tally lets out a theatrical sigh and, in one long graceful movement, leans back over the table, positions her cue, and pots the remaining three balls with a single, stunning trick shot. "Money. On. The. Table." She smiles, so sweet it could rot teeth. *"Darlin'."*

With a face like thunder, the man slams a twenty-pound note down. "Fucking shakedown artist."

"No one likes a sore loser."

"Whatever." The man storms off towards the bar.

Tally rests the butt of the pool cue on the floor and leans her weight onto it.

"Tally." I can't think of anything else to say.

What's there to say? I need to bring her in. She might be a mate, but—whether she's under the influence of Fury Syndrome—she still murdered someone in cold blood.

I don't have a choice.

She cocks her head to one side, like a vulture sizing up its next meal. "Christian."

A woman with tattoos encircling her neck saunters past, sniffing with such ferocity I can practically feel the texture of the phlegm hitting the back of her throat.

My distaste must show, because Tally says, "This place wouldn't be my number one choice either, but looking like this, I doubt I'd blend in at *Patisserie Valerie*."

"Guess not."

She flicks her chin at the pool table. "Fancy a game?"

I rub the back of my neck. "It's not a social call. I'm taking you in."

She laughs, but there's no humour in it. "Good luck with that. The last witch who went toe to toe with me ended up splattered over the bonnet of Kate's car. Or had you forgotten?"

Bile rises in my throat, but I swallow it down. "You're a witch, too, Tally. You just—"

More of that toneless laughter. "Talitha's dead. It's Vex now. Get it? Vex, as in Vexed, as in furious, as in Fury."

I have to tense the muscles in my legs to stop my knees from shaking. "Clever."

She runs the tip of a black claw along the edge of the table, carving a deep scratch mark into the wooden surroundings. "I thought so."

My neutral expression doesn't change.

She pouts. "Oh, come on. You used to laugh at my jokes."

"You used to be funny."

"Jeez, lighten up, will you? Tell you what. Best of three. If you win, I'll kill you fast, so fast you won't feel a thing. If I win, we take things nice and slow."

I swallow, my Adam's apple bobbing.

"Wow. Tough crowd."

Something inside me snaps, furious rage melting the icy fear in milliseconds. I take a deliberate step towards the table, pitching my voice low. "You think this is funny? You murdered an innocent person. O'Hara didn't know what he was doing when he killed Ma—"

Her scarlet eyes flash. "Say her name, and I don't care how many mortals are watching… I'll snap your neck right here, right now."

It's only then Tally's ring catches the light.

Her *wedding* ring.

My boiling anger drains away as quickly as it came. "She was my friend. I miss her, too."

Her grip on the pool cue tightens. "Some friend. I heard about your promotion. Big congrats. You could've at least waited until she was cold."

The last of my rage dissipates, and guilt pinches my gut. Guilt and I are on first-name terms. Ever since Maria died, and I took over from her… "That's not fair."

She slams her hand onto the edge of the table, and a hairline crack appears in the wooden veneer. "You want to talk about fair? Do you think it's fair that my wife slaved away for the MID for fifteen years to get to where she was, and yet you got there in half the time? All because she died."

"Tal—"

"No. Do you think it's fair that Kate took you under her wing at the exclusion of everyone else? That my wife is rotting away in a wooden box while you parade around trying to fill her shoes? Don't talk to me about fair." The monotone drawl has disappeared. There's so much venom in Tally's voice, I'm surprised I don't get acid burns.

Heat races through my entire body. She's implying I got where I am because Kate plays favourites.

That's not true.

When I speak, I have to grind the words out between my teeth. "I got this job because I deserve it. Because I'm powerful. And if you don't come with me now, you'll find out just how powerful."

She laughs, high and cold. "Trust me. You're not as powerful as you think you are."

"Want to test that theory?" I challenge.

"Oh, please. I could swat you like a fly. Compared to me, you're about as powerful as a mobility scooter with a flat battery."

A hot blush creeps into my cheeks. "I don't want to hurt you, but I will if I have to."

She slinks around the table with an eerie, vulpine grace, pool cue still in hand.

My body tenses, and a bead of sweat trickles down my neck.

Tally halts two paces away from me, that rictus grin plastered back on her face.

"Too bad."

Oh, shit.

Her blood-red eyes harden, and her voice drops an octave. "Because I want to hurt you."

She's so fast I can't track her movements.

Thwack.

Sharp pain flares in my shins and my legs fly out from under me. My back slams into the floor hard enough to bruise.

Tally rams the butt of the pool cue into my stomach, and all the breath rushes out of me in one long wheeze.

Silence swallows the room, every pair of eyes glued to us, but no one moves to help.

She puts all her weight onto the queue and my stomach burns in agony.

Her alien eyes hover over mine. "It was fun catching up."

The pressure on my abdomen vanishes.

She chucks the cue aside, and it clatters onto the pool table. She gives me a little finger wave, turns and—without looking back—stalks towards a door at the rear of the pub marked *Fire Exit*.

I sit up, wincing when searing heat blazes through my stomach.

The fire exit door flies open and crashes against the wall.

A flash of snow-white hair, and Tally vanishes.

Bugger.

I have to stop her.

I can't let her get away.

CHAPTER 2
Christian

I haul myself to my feet and shove through the crowd, making a beeline for the fire exit.

Breathing hard, I jog down a short corridor reeking of stale piss and vomit. I shed my glamour spell, rush outside—a burst of muggy summer-night air swamps me—and emerge into a tiny, cobbled courtyard, sweat gathering in places I'd rather it wouldn't. My mouth drops open at the scene that greets me.

Tally stands in the centre of the courtyard, back straight, hands out, claws flexed.

Stone stands opposite her, sparks of green energy flickering up and down his arms. "Talitha Green-Hernandez, I'm arresting you for the murder of Anthony O'Hara. You do not have to say—"

She cuts across him. "Trust me, you don't want to play the hero right now."

"*Ignis.*" An emerald green fireball the size of an apple sparks to life in Stone's palm.

Tally purses her lips. "I'm warning you, witch."

He raises his arm, preparing to launch.

"Stone, no!" I shout.

But it's too late.

The fireball arcs from Stone's fingers, shooting towards Tally.

She braces herself for the impact, but she needn't have bothered.

The fireball makes it three quarters of the way there, then sputters and dies.

Stone hasn't quite mastered elemental magic yet.

"Shit," he says.

Tally glances at me over her shoulder. That wolf-like smile curves across her lips again. "Is this the best you've got?"

"Leave him—"

She sucks in a huge lungful of air.

I clap my hands to my ears just in time.

She shrieks, one long scream, shimmering waves of energy erupting from between her lips.

The ferocious sound-waves slam into Stone's chest.

He cries out, sailing backwards, landing in a pile of rubbish bags stacked against the far wall.

The earsplitting wail dies away.

"Tally, stop," I say.

Ignoring me, she bends into a low crouch and kicks off from the ground hard. She rockets high into the air. Up, up, up she goes, hair shining silver in the moonlight, rippling behind her like party streamers. She lands on light feet at the rooftop's edge, peering down at me with those dull red eyes. "Stop? I'm just getting started. Catch me if you can."

Then she disappears, footsteps racing across the roof.

Stone groans and heaves himself out of the rubbish pile.

A few bags have burst, leaking their fetid entrails, and the pungent scent of spoiled food fills the courtyard.

I march up to him, getting right in his face. "What the fuck are you doing? I told you to stay in the car."

"And you thought I'd listen? She killed O'Hara. I couldn't just sit there and do nothing."

I throw my hands into the air. "You are the most stubborn, pig-headed, belligerent twat I've ever met."

"Right back at you." His green eyes flick to the roof. "What now?"

I track his gaze. "Now, I'm going after her."

"But how—"

"*Caeli.*"

A powerful gust of purple-tinted wind sweeps through the courtyard, gathering around my ankles, travelling up my chest, and along my arms. The violet gust carries me skyward, the pub's wall flying past in a blur.

I clear the roof's edge.

Daxbridge spreads itself before me, a patchwork of old sandstone and modern glass and steel.

"Forgot you could do that," Stone says from below, an edge of envy in his tone.

I can't help but smile. I like it when people notice my power. "Portal yourself back to the MID."

"No way. I—"

"Go. Now. Or you're fired."

He grumbles, but seconds later, a harsh ripping sound tears the air and a bright green disc of light swallows him whole.

Good.

One less thing to worry about.

In the distance, a flash of white bounds from one building to the next.

I tilt forward so I'm horizontal, chest facing the floor, Superman-style. "*Volare.*"

I shoot forward like a champagne cork, cutting through the air with ease. Wind roars in my ears and my eyes stream with tears. I crow with joy. Can't help it. I love flying.

The white speck in the distance gets closer.

Narrowing my eyes, I flex my ankles so my toes point straight out behind me, and then I'm speeding across the night sky.

The city is a blur of beige and grey below me.

I want to stay up here forever.

Free of the pressure of work.

No worry.

No guilt over what happened to John.

No guilt over a promotion I rightfully deserved.

Pure freedom.

Free of everything.

Sadly, that's not happening.

I fly above Tally now.

She leaps from rooftop to rooftop.

Luckily, I'm up high enough she hasn't detected my presence.

How can she have fallen so spectacularly?

True, the Tally I know is fierce—so nothing's changed there—but she's also warm, and principled, with a heart of gold underneath all that snark.

The monster she's become...

I don't recognise her.

Not that it matters. I can't put this off any longer.

It's now or never.

I take a deep breath of the humid air, and dive.

My feet slam into Tally's back, the force of the blow causing her to stumble.

She trips, falls, rolls over her shoulder, and springs to her feet again.

I swoop over her, landing lightly on the rooftop twenty feet away. "It's over."

"Like fuck it is." Her face contorts into a mask of hate and rage, and she lunges at me.

I conjure a brilliant mauve fireball and whip it towards her.

She bats the spell aside, and it skitters off into the darkness.

What the fuck?

I'm so nonplussed, I don't even try to defend myself when she drives an open palm into my chest with the force of a battering ram.

I barely register the air rushing out of me and the blunt, deadening pain spreading through my torso, because I'm tumbling through the air. A moment of weightlessness, and then I crash to the ground, skidding right to the roof's edge and skinning my palms.

I black out for a split-second and—when I come to—she's striding towards me.

"Please, stop this," I say.

"Make me."

It hits me then.

The woman stalking across the rooftop isn't Tally.

The Fury's earlier words come floating back.

Talitha's dead. It's Vex now.

Tally's gone.

Vex has consumed her, and she's not coming back.

My fists clench.

I've had enough.

From my position on the floor, I fling out my hand. "*Fulgur.*"

A jagged fork of violet lightning streams from my open palm.

Vex takes a neat step to the side, and the lightning-strike whizzes past her. She laughs—one of those cold, cruel, unfamiliar laughs.

I roll to my feet, firing a death-strike in her direction.

She catches it—she actually *catches* it, like a ball.

"That's not possible," I whisper.

"Hot potato." Vex launches the death-strike back at me.

I dive to the side, avoiding the spell by a hair's breadth.

It passes so close, static tingles across my skin.

The death-strike explodes against the rooftop in a shower of sparks.

The Fury advances on me.

"*Eryx.*" Shining purple witch-gauntlets—magic gloving my hands from knuckle-to-wrist—enclose my fists, and I bring them up to my face in a boxer's guard.

Closer, closer, closer.

I swing at her head.

She ducks.

I crouch low and aim a sweep-kick at her legs.

She jumps.

Springing up, I snap a right hook clean across her jaw.

She doesn't even flinch. She just grabs my shoulders and slams her forehead into the bridge of my nose.

A wet crackle sounds.

Pain explodes across my face, stars dance in front of my eyes, and I cry out.

Vex shoves me away and I land in a heap on my arse, a blunt ache spreading through the base of my spine.

I taste iron at the back of my throat, hawk up the blood from my nose, and spit the gobbet on the floor. Dragging myself to my feet, I say, "Give it up. I'm going to stop you."

Those blood-red eyes sparkle like rubies. "I doubt that. You look exhausted, whereas I could go all night."

She's not wrong. I'm outmatched, and won't be able to last much longer. Which is why I need to end this.

Fast.

Something tells me I'm only going to get one chance. "I'm sorry."

"Sorry for—"

I reach deep inside myself—deeper than I ever have—and drain every drop of magic from my reserves, drawing it all from my chest, down my arms, and into my hands. The air reeks of ozone, the taste of old pennies on my tongue so vivid, and so vile, it almost chokes me. My arms shudder with the effort of marshalling so much magic at once.

Her eyes widen, not by much, but it's enough to tell me my power startles her.

She fears me.

I drink it in.

She sucks in another lungful of air, preparing to scream again.

I slam my hands together with a thunderous boom. "*Fluctus inpulsa.*"

The shock wave explodes from me with such force I stagger back, my feet inches from the roof's edge.

If Vex is a battering ram, my spell is a wrecking ball.

The spell catapults her off her feet.

She arcs high into the air—flipping head over heels one, two, three times—and crashes back to the rooftop in a crumpled, unmoving heap.

A wave of exhaustion washes over me and threatens to drag me under.

My leaden legs collapse beneath me, and I fall to my knees. My head spins, and a crushing weight settles on my shoulders, grinding me farther and farther into the ground.

With the last of my magic gone, I'm empty.

Ugh.

All I want to do is curl up on my side and sleep.

Right here. Right now.

But I can't.

I haven't finished the job just yet.

It takes everything I have—everything I am—to clamber to my feet and cross to where Vex lies.

Unconscious, head slumped to one side, she resembles a corpse.

I place two gentle fingers to her throat.

Her steady pulse thumps against my touch.

I straighten, the world tilting at an alarming angle, and extract my phone from my pocket. I punch in a number and bring the device to my ear.

A bored male voice answers on the second ring. "Operational Logistics."

"This is DI Winter. I need a portal now."

"You can't conjure one yourself?"

"I wouldn't be calling you if I could, would I?"

The tapping of computer keys filters down the line. "Location?"

"Um." I glance at the buildings on either side of me to get my bearings. "I'm on the roof of—"

"Roof?"

I bite back a scream of frustration. "You heard me. Darlington House, it's an office block in the city."

"I know it. Stand by."

The line goes dead.

Thirty seconds later, the air in front of me rips apart and a shimmering grey portal swirls into existence.

With my last vestiges of strength, I stoop down, heave Vex's dead weight into my arms, and stumble through the portal.

I throw my hands out just in time to protect my already broken nose from the onrushing floor.

The scent of citrus cleaner and pine tells me I've arrived at the MID.

There's a muffled thud as Vex's limp body lands next to me.

I wriggle onto my back and struggle into a seated position.

The thunder of dozens of pairs of feet reaches my ears as a small army of MID officers pours into the reception area.

My boss—DCI Kate Denton—leads the charge. She jabs a finger at Vex. "Get that Fury collar on her now."

"Yes, ma'am." DC Layla Jabara—Stone's partner—dashes over to us, wrangles a thick silver band around Vex's neck, and snaps it into place with a sharp click.

While silver replenishes a witch's powers and heals any wounds, it has the opposite effect on Fury's.

Vex's scream, her strength, her speed—it's all contained now.

Layla catches sight of my nose and grimaces. "Rough night?"

"Ha ha." My voice comes out garbled because of my broken, blood-filled nose.

"Here." Layla slips a slim black case from her back pocket and passes it to me.

I flip the case open and tip the contents—a capped syringe filled with liquid silver—into my hand. Uncapping the needle, I jam it into the crook of my arm and force the plunger down. I go cold, then hot.

There's a sickening *pop* as my nose clicks back into place.

"Ouch—fuck!"

Vex stirs beside me. "Ugh."

Layla scuttles back, a yellow orb of light leaping into her hand.

Without missing a beat, the Fury flips to her feet, opens her mouth wide, and screams...

Well, she tries to, anyway.

All that comes out is a strangled wheeze thanks to the silver collar.

Vex's taloned fingers flash to her throat, the black claws scraping against the metal choker. "What the—what the fuck have you done to me?" She takes a deliberate step in Layla's direction.

Oh, no you don't.

Thanks to the liquid silver, I'm back to full strength.

I spin round on my arse, lash out low with my foot, and knock Vex's legs out from under her.

She crashes to the floor with a surprised yelp.

I roll to my knees, wrench her arms behind her back, snatch a pair of handcuffs from my belt, lock them into place around her wrists, and yank her to her feet. "Talitha Gre—" I stop myself from using my dead friend's name. "*Vex*. I'm arresting you for the murder of Anthony O'Hara. You don't have to say anything. But, it may harm your defence if you do not mention when questioned something you later rely on in a court presided over by The Witches Council. Anything you do say may be given in evidence. Do you understand?"

"Fuck you," she snarls.

I lean in close. "I'm sorry it had to come to this."

"Again... Fuck. You. You and the fucking white charger you cantered in on."

"Get her to the cells," Kate orders.

Layla grabs Vex's arm, leading her towards the custody suite. "Sure thing, boss."

Vex twists in Layla's grip, but with that collar round her neck, she's not strong enough to break free. "You think you can hold me forever? This isn't over, Christian. Not by a long shot."

I turn away from her.

"You hear me? I'll escape. And when I do, I'll kill you, you son of a bitch. I'll kill all of you."

Layla drags Vex through a door and, when it swings shut, her threats fade away to nothing.

I try my best to ignore the fresh pang of guilt chewing my stomach.

Tally's gone.

I need to remember that.

Kate marches over to me, lips pinched into a firm line. "If she wants to kill you, she'll have to join the queue."

"What are you—"

"My office. Now."

"Can I at least wash the blood off my face first?"

"*Now.*"

A few of my colleagues snigger and mutter behind me.

My face flames.

How dare she speak to me like that in front of everyone?

I storm after her.

Chapter 3

Christian

Stepping into Kate's office, I close the door behind me. "I don't know what this is about, but—"

Kate—now standing behind her enormous mahogany desk—spins around to face me, russet eyes blazing. "What part of, 'Henry Stone isn't ready to go into the field,' didn't you understand?"

My face falls. "He told you what happened when he tried to confront the Fury?"

She makes a sound—halfway between a snort and a chuckle. "He didn't have to. When he got back here, he was regaling all and sundry about how you both tackled her."

I tip my head back, shut my eyes, and pinch the bridge of my nose. "Let me exp—"

"I'm not finished. Whose name's on that sign?" She jabs a crimson-painted fingernail at her office door. "I'll give you a hint. It's not yours."

I grit my teeth, a vein in my neck bulging. Kate never speaks to me like this, and I don't like it. "I'm not having this conversation." I turn away, preparing to leave.

"Yes, you bloody well are."

I spin back to face her, the dried blood crusting underneath my nose cracking against my skin. "You humiliated me in front of the team. There was no need to call me out like that."

Kate's nostrils flare. "Call you out? You're lucky I'm not kicking you out."

Heat races up my neck. "What?"

"I told you Henry was there to observe, not get involved. I let you get away with a lot of shit when you were in the lower ranks, but you're in management now. Everything you do reflects on me. How do you think it looks when you ignore a direct order?"

I take a step towards her, fists clenched. "How do you think it looks when you chew me out in front of everyone?"

She ignores my question, ploughing on like I never spoke. "I'll tell you how it looks. It looks like we're divided. It looks like we don't have a clue what we're doing. And it looks like you can't control your staff."

My cheeks burn like she slapped me.

She's right.

That's exactly how it looks.

As a Detective Inspector, it's my job to lead my team.

To gain their respect.

To be in a position of power.

Now, I'm in a position of weakness.

I hate feeling weak.

Vex's earlier words resurface.

You want to talk about fair. Do you think it's fair that my wife slaved away for the MID for fifteen years to get to where she was, and yet you get there in half the time? All because she died. Do you think it's fair that

Kate took you under her wing at the exclusion of everyone else? That my wife's rotting away in a wooden box while you parade around trying to fill her shoes? Don't talk to me about fair.

That's the crux of it.

I'm trying to fill Maria's shoes, and I don't know if I'm up to it.

What is the truth, anyway?

If Maria was still alive, there's no way I'd have this job.

Maybe Kate only chose me because she had no choice.

Maybe I'm second best.

I clear my throat and, when the words come, they sound flat and pitiful. "Maybe you promoted me too soon."

Kate's expression shifts as her hard resolve cracks. She strides round her desk and perches on the edge. "I'm not saying that. Honestly, you've got all the qualities of a great DI, but you have to maintain control. They'll run rings around you if you don't."

I cross my arms. "Doesn't excuse the way you spoke to me out there."

She smiles, not unkindly. "That was necessary. I had to take you down a peg. People would question my authority if I hadn't. They'd start asking questions about why I'd gone easy on you, and why I promoted you. I can't treat you any differently to anyone else, Christian. Just have a word with Henry. Get him to toe the line."

I click my tongue. "Have you met Stone? That's easier said than done."

Her brow furrows. "Want me to reassign him to someone else?"

"Ha! Wouldn't wish that on my worst enemy. Besides, he reminds me of me."

"Christ in a kayak." Kate kneads at her temples. "One of you is bad enough, but two—"

A knock on the door.

"Come in," Kate says, raising her voice.

Stone pokes his head into the room. "Got a minute?"

My eyes narrow to slits. "This is a private—"

"Make it quick," Kate says.

He slips into the room and closes the door behind him, then scratches at one of his feather tattoos. "Just wanted to say it won't happen again."

"What won't happen again?" Kate's tone is firm.

He holds Kate's steely gaze with one of his own. "I'll do what Christian says."

My eyebrow quirks. "So, next time I tell you to stay put?"

He shrugs. "I'll stay put."

It might be a trick of the light, but I swear the ghost of a smile crosses Kate's lips. "See that you do. You're dismissed, DC Stone."

Stone turns and places his hand on the doorknob.

"Henry, before you go," she says.

He pauses, the muscles in his shoulders pulling rigid.

"Disobey me again, and I'll put you on desk duty from now until the end of time. Understand?"

"Ma'am."

My eyebrows raise into my hairline.

Ma'am?

Stone doesn't show deference to authority figures often.

He leaves, and the door clicks shut.

Kate's flinty stare rests on me. "Same goes for you."

The corner of my mouth tugs upwards. "So, we're good, or what?"

"We're good. As long as you can get it together."

I hold up the first three fingers of my right hand. "Scout's honour."

She shoots me a sceptical look. "If you were a Scout, then I'm Mother Teresa." She sits behind her desk, shuffling papers. "Any plans for the weekend?"

Plans?

You bet I have plans.

Tomorrow is date night.

My small smile stretches into a wide grin. I can't help it. "Nothing much."

Kate smirks. "How are things going with you and Tori?"

I tap my nose. "Keep that out of it."

She holds up her hands. "Don't do anything I wouldn't do."

"Doesn't leave me with many options."

"Cheeky bastard. Go on. Get out of here before I change my mind about kicking you out."

"Right you are, boss."

When I leave the MID five minutes later, I'm still grinning.

Chapter 4
Christian

The powerful aroma of fresh tomatoes, white onions, and roasted peppers fills the kitchen.

I stir the simmering arrabbiata sauce on the stove, breathing through my nose to take in more of the rich scent, carried on the steam rising from the pan.

The wooden spoon slips in my sweat-slick hand.

I take a deep breath, get a firmer grip on the spoon, and keep stirring.

Tonight's the night.

It's a year to the day Tori and I got together, and I'm going to ask her to move in with me.

My stomach rolls. What if she says no? What if she throws the key back in my face? I don't think she will, but you never know. What if—

No.

I can't think like this. Things are good between us, and we love each other, so there's no reason she won't move in.

I nod, as if that settles the matter, and reach for the volume control on the old-fashioned radio I keep on the kitchen windowsill. *Stereophonics's* Have A Nice Day blares from the speakers. A sign, perhaps?

That's how I'm choosing to take it, anyway.

I stop staring and wipe my hands on a clean dishcloth. "Hot sauce." I scour the cupboards for the elusive pot of Tabasco. "Where's the hot sauce?" Reaching right to the back of the cupboard, my hand closes around a small bottle. "Got you." I pull my hand out.

Not hot sauce.

Soy sauce.

My breath catches.

I hate soy sauce, and not just because it ruins the taste of food for me and turns it into a salty mess. I hate this bottle of soy sauce, in particular. Why is it still here? Why hadn't someone got rid of it? I'm unable to stop myself. My eyes flick to the spot on the label just below the generic Chinese logo. The neat, rounded letters make the back of my nose sting.

Mitts off. This is MINE!

It's John's handwriting.

My throat closes, and my chest aches. The last words my brother and I yelled at each other are fresh in my mind.

I want the pain to stop.

For fuck's sake, John. Stop being a twat and grow up.

What did you just say to me?

All this bullshit—the drinking, the drugs—it's tearing Mum and Dad apart.

You don't give a shit. Nobody gives a shit about me. It's all right for you. You got your magic. You always get everything you want, and—

Oh, here we go.
I just want the pain to stop.
Don't we all.
Don't.
We.
All.

Those were the last three words I said to my brother before he disappeared. Before I found the blood-stained knife on the bathroom floor, but no sign of John. I was a DC at the time and, with Kate's help, we launched a full-scale enquiry into his disappearance. We found nothing. It's like he vanished.

Mum and Dad didn't touch his room when he went missing, and I haven't been in there to this day. The door stays closed; the memories sealed inside.

Well, mostly.

I still find the odd thing—like this godforsaken bottle of soy sauce—that stops me dead in my tracks and brings the guilt rushing back. It's here now. The guilt. Gnawing away at my stomach like a savage beast and prowling at the edges of my mind, threatening to pounce. I'd give anything to take it back.

Don't we all.

My hand shakes, the near-black liquid inside the bottle sloshing around violently. Everything blurs as tears cloud my vision.

All the while, Have A Nice Day carries on playing.

I close my eyes and take a deep, cleansing breath. And another. And another. Eventually, my hands stop trembling, and I dump the soy sauce in the bin, turning my attention back to the bubbling arrabbiata.

I let the familiar routine of cooking lure me back to normality, my thoughts returning to the task at hand.

Stir the sauce.

Taste.

A pinch of salt.

Stir again.

Easy.

The track changes.

Muse's cover of Feeling Good starts up. They sing about new dawns, and new days.

A small smile caresses my lips. You never know what's round the corner. Tori will be here soon, and hopefully we can start our new dawn together. She's good for me. Fierce, and brave, and kind. She's—

The doorbell rings.

Shit!

She's here.

I lick a drop of spilled sauce from my thumb—savouring the chili heat that blisters my tongue—and stroll out of the kitchen and down the hallway until I reached the front door. I pull it open. "I was just thinking about—"

My mouth drops open.

It's not Tori stood on the doorstep.

"Hi, Chris."

Chapter 5
Christian

Hi, Chris.

My heart slams against my rib cage.

Hi, Chris.

I'm breathing hard, close to hyperventilating.

No one calls me Chris, except—

Hi, Chris.

Except John.

But the man standing on my doorstep can't be John.

The John I know is a wasted skinny thing, with sagging yellowish skin, his lanky blonde hair hanging in greasy tails to his shoulders—where it isn't falling out in clumps.

No.

This man can't be John. Not with his neatly cropped hair, or his bright blue eyes, or the well-tailored clothes he wears.

The man speaks again. It doesn't even sound like him. His voice, once slurred and cracking on every other word, comes out clear, rich, and resonant. "Are you going to let me in?"

Dry-mouthed, I back away, turn, and retreat into the kitchen without answering him.

He doesn't look like John.

But it's him.

Hi, Chris.

He looks so well. Healthier than me, even.

All these years of stomach churning worry.

The nightmares.

They were all for nothing.

He's fine.

I'm too hot.

Too cold.

Too dizzy.

I grab the bottle of pinot noir—intended for my date with Tori—off the side, and point at the cork. "*Aperta.*"

Faint traces of misty purple light trail from my fingertip and surround the neck of the bottle.

The cork frees itself with a wet, sucking *pop*, landing in the sink with a clatter.

I snatch a clean wineglass off the draining board, relishing the rich-sounding *glug, glug, glug*, as it fills with dark wine. I drain half the glass in one gulp, the complex blend of sweet cherry, tangy raspberry, and bitter earth coating my tongue.

Damn.

I wish I had something stronger.

I throw back the rest of the wine and pour again.

This can't be happening.

It can't—

The front door closes with a soft click.

John's here.

He's in the house.

Where the hell has he been all this time?

My knees tremble a little.

The sound of footsteps muffled by the thick carpet come closer.

Closer.

And closer still.

They halt, and the air turns stuffy and close.

I don't turn around, but I know he's there, his new—shiny-bright—eyes burning twin holes into the back of my head. I take two long drafts of the wine, a warm, blurry feeling spreading through my chest.

What is going on? Have I finally snapped? Has the guilt driven me to imagine things that aren't there?

For years, I've wanted my brother to come home. Wanted it more than I've wanted anything else in my entire life. And now that he's here—with his smart clothes and carefully styled hair—the warm feeling transforms into something hot, bitter, and caustic.

My grip on the wine glass tightens.

"Say something," John says.

Oh, I'll say something, all right.

I pivot slowly on my heel, and offer him the wine bottle. When I speak, my voice is razor sharp. "Not your usual tipple, I know, but you're welcome to help yourself. I'm sure you won't be able to resist." It's cruel, but I don't care.

I aim to shock.

I want to wound.

Much to my surprise, John's expression barely changes, but I detect a flicker of something.

Hurt?

Remorse?

Guilt, even?

Good.

He should feel guilty after everything he's put me through.

After everything he's put Mum and Dad through.

His eyes flick to the bottle, and away again. "I don't anymore, actually."

He doesn't.

He's sober… but how? Last time I saw him, he was a wreck.

"Right." I keep the hard edge in my tone. "Well, I'm fresh out of heroin, but I'm sure your old dealer's still in business."

Too far.

That's a step too far.

What's wrong with me?

Why am I behaving like this?

He's home.

I should be bouncing off the walls… should be.

No emotion crosses John's face this time. "I deserved that."

"You think?" I take another generous sip of wine.

"You must have a lot of questions."

Until about five minutes ago, he would've been right. I would've had thousands of questions, millions. Probably more than he would've been able to answer.

I've imagined this moment so many times, but I've never pictured this.

A John who's whole.

In my version of our reunion, he's still the broken thing that fled up the stairs after our last row.

I just want the pain to stop.

The acidic heat tearing through me reaches a boiling point. "Four years. Four fucking years. I haven't had a decent night's sleep in four fucking years. Want to know why? Because of the nightmares. Every time I close my eyes, there you are. Scraping by on the streets. Being held captive—or worse—buried in an unmarked grave somewhere."

"Chris—"

"Don't you dare fucking *Chris* me." I take a step towards him, shouting now. "I've only got one question. How can you be such a self-centred prick? Do you have any idea how much pain you put us through? Me? Mum? Dad? They're not even together anymore because of you."

He glances down at his feet. "I didn't know. I thought—"

"You thought what? You could stroll back in and act like nothing happened? We thought you were dead, John. Christ, they can't even bear to set foot in the house anymore. Dad just cries, and Mum moved back to Spain because she couldn't stand to be anywhere near the place. Not that you give a shit."

John's eyes harden, glinting like chips of ice, and a muscle in his jaw ticks. "That's not fair. I do—"

"*Liar*!" I slam my empty glass down on the countertop, surprised it doesn't shatter. Then I rake my gaze over him from head to toe. "Looks like you're doing pretty well for yourself. If you care so much, why didn't you contact us?"

"I..." His hand goes to a thin gold chain hanging around his neck.

I hadn't noticed it before.

John's slim fingers trace the tiny links until they find the pendant—shaped like a dragon's head—dangling from it. He runs the pendant back-and-forth, and it rasps along the chain.

My brow creases into a deep scowl. "That wasn't a rhetorical question."

He squeezes the pendant in a tight fist. "I wanted to, but the thought of coming back here scared me."

"Scared you?" My voice is thick with derision.

He nods. "Yeah. Scared of this place, of what it might mean if I came back too soon. It's hard being here. Reminds me of who I used to be. I can't be that person again, Chris. I won't."

Something inside me snaps like an elastic band stretched beyond breaking point. "You selfish little bastard."

"You need to understand—"

"No. *You* need to understand. We broke when you disappeared. Scared? That's always been your problem. Constantly thinking about what you need. What about what we needed? Ever think about that?"

"Of course I—"

"More lies."

Heavy silence settles over the room, save for the sound of my harsh breathing and the blood pounding in my ears.

I empty the last of the wine into my glass, fill it right up to the top, and bring it to my lips.

"Don't you think you've had enough?" John asks.

His words are like a lit match set to petrol.

I place the glass down with deliberate care. "How dare you say that to me? I've lost count of the amount of times I sat up all night with you to make sure you didn't choke on your own vomit. I'm not the one with the problem."

"Yeah, well. All problems start somewhere."

"Sanctimonious little fucker." My arm rises of its own volition and, before I know what I'm doing, I launch the empty wine bottle at John.

It shoots towards him, spinning end over end.

I could stop it with magic, but the wine makes my head foggy, and I 'm not thinking straight.

It's going to hit him smack in the face, and—

John's hand flashes out.

The wine bottle slaps into his palm, and he snatches it from the air.

I blink once, my eyelids coated in syrup. "You—you can't catch for shit."

He lifts one shoulder and sets the bottle on the kitchen table. "Things change."

My rage drains away as quickly as it came, leaving something cold and barren in its place. A shiver creeps up my spine.

Something isn't right.

John's clumsy, literally the definition of two left feet. Safe to say, his hand-eye coordination leaves a lot to be desired. Back in school, he used to call in sick every Sports Day. No one ever picked him to play on their team. The one time his classmates chose him to play rounders, he didn't hit a single ball.

I can still remember the mocking laughter.

The pointing and baiting.

The way John sprinted off the field like death-strikes were chasing him.

A well of sour pity pools in my stomach.

Desperate for something to do with my hands, I yank the thin black band off my wrist, gather my hair into a knot at the nape of my neck and fasten it in place. I draw back a little. "What the hell happened to you? Where have you been? How can you afford those fancy clothes?"

His lips curve into a half-smile.

So calm and controlled.

So un-John-like.

The hairs on my arms stand on end.

"It's a long story," he says.

"We've got time."

He lets out a long sigh. "I don't know where to start."

"How about the beginning?"

He rubs the designer stubble bristling his chin. "The beginning. Right. Well, um—"

A key scrapes in the front door's lock, cutting John off.

Chapter 6
Christian

"Hey, gorgeous. Something smells great. I'm starving." Tori.

She appears in the kitchen doorway, fluffing up her Afro. She pauses, fingers still tangled in her hair, taking in the scene. Her eyes flick from me, to John, and back again. "Did I get my days mixed up?"

John chews on his lip. "Ah. No. Sorry. My fault. I should have called ahead."

"Or not called at all," I say.

He ignores me. "I was just leaving, anyway. This was a mistake."

I snort. "You think?"

John strides towards the doorway.

Tori blocks his path. "Hang on… you look familiar. Have we met?"

"No."

"I swear I know you from somewhere… wait. There's a photo of you in the living room." Her lips part. "Oh, my God. You're John."

For the first time tonight, John looks awkward. He shuffles from foot to foot. "That's me."

She laughs—a light, musical sound. "Christian... isn't this amazing? It's a miracle."

"It's something, all right," I say.

Tori shoots me a strange look and turns back to John. "I'm Tori, Christian's partner. Sorry. Shit. Sorry, I don't mean to stare, but this is insane. Christian's told me so much about you."

The corner of John's mouth twitches. "I'll bet he has."

I grit my teeth. "You're such a—"

Tori raises her voice. "It's great to meet you."

John holds out his hand. "Same here."

She ignores his hand, sweeps forward, and throws her arms round John in a tight hug. "Insane."

John's eyes widen in shock, then his face splits into a wide smile, and he hugs her back.

Why's she hugging him?

A hot coal singes my stomach.

Is this a joke?

"Listen, Tori, I really should—" John's entire body stiffens, and he draws back, holding her at arm's length.

What's he doing?

Why's he staring at her like that—mouth half-open, something close to awe on his face?

For fuck's sake.

He doesn't fancy her, does he?

A blush creeps into my cheeks.

Great.

That's all I need.

"You okay?" Tori asks him.

John schools his expression and releases Tori's upper arms. "Yeah. Yeah, I'm fine. I had a long journey, that's all. Please, don't let me spoil your evening." He goes to move past her again.

She blocks him a second time. "Don't go."

I clench my fists. "If he wants to go, then—"

"I think it's for the best," John says. "Besides, I booked a room at *The Royal Lorimer*, just in case." His eyes find mine. "If you change your mind about... anything, you can find me there."

Tori narrows her eyes at me. "What's going—"

"*The Lorimer*." My eyebrows shoot up.

When Kate sent me to track down King Arthur's crown last year, the case took me to the upmarket hotel. It's somewhere you need a second mortgage to afford.

I let out a low whistle. "Not cheap. Where are you getting the money to pay for that?"

Tori says, "Guys, can we—"

"I get by." John shrugs.

"Clearly." I fold my arms.

Tori brushes past John and strides up to me. "You won't make him stay in a hotel, will you? What's wrong with his room here?"

John shakes his head. "I wouldn't want to impose."

"You wouldn't be. Would he, Christian?"

I set my jaw.

Tori's brow creases. "John. Can you give us a minute?"

"Sure." He crosses to the kitchen door.

"Don't go far," she says.

For a moment, I think he's going to argue, but one stern look from Tori and he relents. "You got it." John ducks out of the kitchen, and his footsteps retreat down the hall.

Tori wears a mask of fierce determination.

Uh-oh.

Here we go.

Chapter 7
Christian

"What's going on?" Tori asks.

The wine is taking its toll, settling in my roiling stomach and smoothing the hard edges of my rage. "You wouldn't understand."

Her scowl softens. She takes a step closer and rests her hand on my forearm. "Try me."

I get a waft of her soothing scent, a sweet, fruity blend of coconut hair oil and mango body butter.

The knot in my chest loosens. "He looks well."

"And that's a bad thing?"

"No. Yes. I don't know. He looks really well. I think he got better a long time ago. So..." A weight crashes into my stomach.

She squeezes my arm. "Why didn't he come back sooner?"

Tears sting the back of my eyes. "He said he was worried about coming back in case he relapsed."

"And you don't believe him?"

"No, it's not that. But..."

"But?"

"It's not fair." The words taste bitter, curdling on the tip of my tongue. "He left. He left, and I had to deal with the fallout. I had to sit by and watch my parents suffer and try to pick up the pieces."

Tori's thumb makes tiny circles on my wrist, her touch tender. "I know."

I brush past her, stride to the centre of the room, spin on my heel, scrub a hand across my mouth. "I've been eaten up with guilt since the day he left because of the things I said to him. He... I thought he was dead. I thought—Jesus, I don't know what I thought. I mean, where's he even been?"

Tori stays quiet.

She knows I'm not finished.

"All this time, I've been stressing about him, and he strolls back in here looking like something off the cover of *GQ Magazine*." I slam my hand on the kitchen table. The empty wine bottle John left there jumps. "Fuck, fuck, fuck." I'm breathing hard, pulse pounding in my fingertips.

Tori approaches slowly. "I understand why he didn't want to come back."

I want my voice to sound angry, but when I speak, the words sound tired. "You're siding with him now?"

She wraps her arms around my waist and presses a gentle kiss to my shoulder, the heat of her lips burning through the thin fabric of my T-shirt. "It's not about taking sides. Think about it, Christian. Imagine what he's been through. From what you told me, he was so excited when he found out about his Manifestation."

That's true.

I remember the sparkle in his eyes.

His wide smile.

I was shitting bricks when my parents told me I was a witch.

Not John, though.

Tori carries on speaking, snapping me back to the present. "Then to have it snatched away from him like that."

I tilt my gaze up to the ceiling. "He cried for days. I thought he'd never stop."

"Exactly. Think about how hard that must've been for him."

My stomach churns, acid rising in my throat. "It was hard for all of us."

I just want the pain to stop.

"And to make it worse, his brother is a super powerful witch."

"It's not my fault if—"

"I'm not saying that. But you're powerful. He's not. You fit in with your own kind. He's shunned by them. Is it any wonder he started using? I might've run away, too, in his position."

I need to hang on to my rage—it's spiky and raw and comforting—but it melts away. I lean further into Tori's embrace, my back moulding to her chest, all the tension draining from my body and leaving me cold.

She's right.

I called John a selfish bastard.

Maybe I'm the selfish one.

Turning in her arms, I pull her close. "How did you get so wise?"

She chuckles against my chest. "I try my best."

A stinging realisation slaps me round the face. I swallow, hard. "Shit. Someone needs to tell Mum and Dad he's back."

"It's too late now," Tori says. "Call them tomorrow."

I release her, stepping back. "Want to know the real reason I'm mad at him?"

She waits.

"If he'd come back sooner, they might still be together."

She shakes her head. "You can't know that."

I untie my hair. Tie it up again. "I guess you're right."

"You'll let him stay?"

I rub my tired eyes. "I don't know if I can. He's so... different. And he won't tell me where he's been."

"He will, when he's ready."

I bite my lip, throat tight. "What if—what if he leaves again?"

"I'm not going anywhere," John says from the doorway.

I jump and spin to face him, heart thudding.

Jesus Christ.

How did he sneak in so quietly?

Normally, he stomps around like an elephant.

Normally.

Yet another difference.

I file that away for later and focus on what he said instead.

I want to ask him to promise, and I hate myself for it.

It's so weak.

I turn away so he can't see the tears brimming in my eyes. Voice hard, I say, "I don't trust you."

"I don't blame you."

"You need to tell me everything."

"And I will, but not tonight."

I wheel around. "Why not?"

"You're tired. I'm tired. Emotions are running high."

A flush creeps up my throat.

My emotions are running high.

That's what he means.

Ever since he set foot in the house, John's been cucumber-cool.

"If you don't want me to stay, I get it," he says. "I'll just—"

"You can stay." The words are out of my mouth before I can stop them.

John arches a blonde eyebrow. "Really?"

"Tonight, anyway," I say. "After that, well, we'll see how it goes."

He nods, the trace of a smile on his lips. "Cheers."

"Right, well," Tori says. "Now that's sorted, I think I'd better go."

"Don't leave on my account," John says.

"No, it's fine." She stands on her tip-toes and drops a feather-light kiss on my lips. "I'll call you tomorrow, gorgeous."

My heart sinks.

This isn't how tonight's supposed to go.

I'm meant to be asking Tori to move in with me.

She turns away.

I catch her wrist. "I was going to…"

John loiters in the doorway, looking awkward.

"You were going to what?" Tori asks.

I release her. "Never mind. It can wait."

"Okay." She smiles at me and crosses the room. Nodding to John, she slips past him and out into the hallway.

The front door opens, closes.

The following silence is oppressive and hot, smothering me like an electric blanket on a midsummer's day.

I rub the back of my neck. "So—"

"I—" John starts.

We both laugh, a little uneasily.

John's expression sobers. "Is my room… I mean the room I used to… is it still—"

"It's still the same. Mum and Dad didn't want to change anything."

"And you?"

"When they gave me the house, they told me not to touch it."

I don't tell him I didn't want to change anything about his old room, either.

He nods. "My toothbrush and stuff's at the hotel. I'll go grab it, then I guess I'll come back and get settled in."

I sigh. "There's a spare toothbrush in the bathroom cupboard, and you can use anything of mine you need for tonight."

"Cheers."

"Wait. How did you get here?"

"I rented a car."

"A car? How? You can't drive."

"I can now."

The uneasy feeling in my gut is back. "What happened to—"

"Tomorrow. I promise."

I open my mouth to argue.

Close it again.

Nod.

"Well. Night, Chris."

Chris.

That name again. It's been so long since I heard it, the single syllable winds me like an uppercut to the gut.

John leaves the room.

"Night," I say, long after he's out of earshot.

I stand, rooted to the spot.

Numb.

I'm not sure how long the dull sensation lasts, but when I come back to my senses, the air is thick with the acrid tang of burned tomatoes.

Shit.

I snatch the pan of ruined arrabbiata sauce off the hob, dump it in the sink, and turn the cold tap on full blast. A loud hissing sound fills the kitchen, thick steam billowing up from the congealed mess inside.

Congealed mess.

Like a metaphor for my life.

Something stinks, and it's nothing to do with the spoiled sauce.

John's story doesn't add up and, tomorrow, I'm going to get to the bottom of things.

Chapter 8
Christian

When morning rolls around, I'm slow to wake.

I blame the wine.

Thick fur carpets the inside of my mouth and, when I haul myself up—slouched against the headboard—my head spins like a manic carousel.

I gulp down the vomit rising in my throat and take a deep breath through my nose. My mind is foggy, and I sense I've forgotten something important.

What the hell happened last night?

Why did I drink so much?

I lean over and grab my phone off the bedside table.

It's eleven o'clock in the morning.

Shit.

I'm supposed to be on call today in case anything kicks off at work.

I scrunch my eyes shut against the sunlight streaming through the window—why did I leave the curtains open?—and painting the pale walls a harsh, deep gold.

Gold.

A memory struggles against the hangover, trying to wrestle it into submission.

Gold.

Why's gold important?

Finally, the memory breaks through.

His hand goes to a thin gold chain hanging around his neck. I hadn't noticed it before. His slim fingers trace the tiny links before finding the pendant, shaped like a dragon's head, dangling from it. He runs the pendant back-and-forth, and it rasps along the chain.

Who's hand?

Who's fingers?

What pendant?

I sit bolt upright.

The room lurches.

John.

"Ugh." I collapse back on the pillows. "Don't be stupid."

John's gone.

It must have been a dream: my brother showing up on the doorstep, healthy and well.

It's a new one.

Normally, my nightmares haunt me with images of John's blood staining the bathroom floor, sharp knives, and the echoes of my last words to him.

Don't we all.

My stomach spasms.

Fuck.

I'm going to puke.

I shove my phone into the pocket of my pyjama trousers and bolt out of the bedroom, along the landing, and into the bathroom. My knees strike the floor and I heave the contents of my gut into the loo, hot sick splattering the clean white porcelain. My throat burns, and the vile stench of vomit clogs my nostrils. I stagger to my feet and press the flush.

The yellow-brown liquid swirls away and I close the lid.

I brush my teeth with a generous dollop of toothpaste then, stumbling out of the bathroom, I catch sight of John's bedroom door, tightly shut as always. I cross to the door, brushing my fingers over the smooth wooden grain.

A mini-white-board still hangs from the door, John's handwriting scrawled across it.

Fuck off! I'm getting high. :)

No.
Wait.
The board.
It's clean now.
Clean?
That's not possible.
Unless... unless he really came home.
I remain glued to the spot.
My knees tremble.
Maybe it wasn't a dream.
Maybe he's back for real.
Heart thundering in my chest, I reach out and curl my icy fingers around the door handle.
Come on, Christian.
Get a grip.
It's not like I don't know what to expect.

John's unmade bed, the grey bedclothes tangled and rumpled. The perpetually closed curtains. The cloying scent of stale weed, body odour, and grime.

There'll be other things, too.

John's collection of vinyl records, scattered across the floor, some broken into minuscule sharp shards. The pin-up and band posters on the walls. The blocks of resin, teaspoon, and disposable lighter John hid in a hole he cut into his mattress.

He didn't think we knew they were there.

Get it together.

I shove the handle down and push the door open.

My lips part.

What the hell?

This is not what I expected.

The room is… clean.

Really clean.

Someone has stripped the grey bedclothes away, leaving the downy white duvet and pillows exposed, arranged neatly on the made bed. The curtains are wide open, sunlight spilling onto the bare white walls. The only sign they used to be covered in posters are the faint, greasy marks left behind by the *Blu Tack*. All the records are back in their cases and neatly lined up on the bookshelf, the floor clear of detritus. The windows are open, fresh air breezing into the room, cleansing the fetid stench from the space.

I take a tentative step into the room.

This is…

No way.

I cross the beige carpet in three quick strides and crouch down by the bed, flinging the bottom corner of the duvet aside and pinging off the fitted sheet. Sliding my hand into the hole in the mattress, I route around inside and find it empty.

My stomach drops, and I sink back onto my heels.

Shit, shit, shit.

I rake a hand through my sleep-mussed hair.

Last night was real.

"John," I croak. I clear my throat. "John."

No answer.

What if he's disappeared again?

I'm on my feet in a flash, bolting for the stairs. "John."

Still nothing.

I dash down the stairs and poke my head into the lounge.

Not in here.

I dart into the kitchen.

No sign of him.

My heart is in my mouth. "No, no, no. Not again."

Something moves in my peripheral vision.

My eyes flick to the window, looking out over the back garden.

The sun glints off blonde hair.

John.

A wave of relief washes over me and my shoulders sag.

He's still here.

It's strange I should feel grateful for that... especially after the way I'd behaved yesterday evening. But that was then, and I blame the wine, and the shock.

Something taints the gratitude, though.

There are still so many unanswered questions.

Questions I need answers to.

I cross to the back door on unsteady legs and step out into the garden.

It's only late morning, but the summer sun is already hot, warming my skin and burning away the faint wisps of white cloud scudding across the sky.

John stands stock-still with his back to me.

He's barefoot on the grass, wearing a vest and dark shorts.

What's he doing?

I don't have to wait long to find out.

He raises his arms high into the air, fingers stretched and back arched, before hinging at the waist. Bending down over straight legs, he rests his palms flat on the lush grass, nose almost touching his knees. His back rises to a ninety-degree angle for a few seconds. In one graceful—John, graceful?—movement, he sinks back into the forward fold, braces his hands on the ground, and steps back into plank position.

I'm mystified.

John and yoga are two words that don't go together.

In fact, John and exercise are two words that don't go together.

My brother twists his body through a variety of stretches and poses before he straightens, ending up back where he started, and lowers his hands to his sides.

I approach him—this stranger wearing John's face—with slow, careful steps. Once I'm close enough, I reach out and place a hand on his shoulder. "Hey—"

Thump.

Pain bursts through my stomach, all the air squeezed from my lungs in one long gust.

An iron hand closes around my wrist, and something hard strikes my legs, knocking them out from under me. The iron hand yanks my arm down and doesn't let go.

The world spins past in a kaleidoscope of blurred images.

I flip head over heels.

Ground.

House.

Sky.

Smack.

My back slams into the earth, and stars dance before my eyes. My already queasy gut swirls like a washing machine stuck in a spin cycle.

What in the name of—

A shadow looms over me, blocking out the sun.

CHAPTER 9
Christian

"Shit. Chris," John says.

I clutch at my chest, wheezing.

John's face appears above mine, plastered with a look of concern. "Are you okay?"

"Ugh... ugh..." That's all I get out.

"I'm sorry. I didn't hear you coming. You startled me."

I startled *him*.

John's hand appears from nowhere.

I grab it and let him pull me to my feet. Sagging forward, I place my hands on my knees and wait for my breathing to return to normal. I straighten, rubbing my sore abdomen.

The point of John's elbow caused the burst of pain I'd experienced driving into my stomach.

The kaleidoscope of images flying past me resulted from John flipping me over his hip.

"You okay?" he asks again.

"I'll be fine. Just a bruised ego." And a bruised stomach. And a bruised back, come to think of it. I wave him away, fixing him with a suspicious glare. "Where did you learn how to do that?"

He sniffs. Shrugs. "I picked up a couple of things while I was away."

I twist my back and am rewarded with a loud *pop*. "Clearly."

I can't help but recall the way John was before he left us.

His emaciated frame, his sallow skin.

I shake my head in disbelief.

He's strong now, his arms and legs corded with long, lean muscle, his bare skin brushed with a light, healthy tan.

Hang on...

Bare skin.

"What happened to your tattoos?"

He used to be covered in them.

John shrugs again. "I had them removed."

"All of them?"

"All of them." He doesn't meet my eye. Instead, he scratches at his neck.

My gaze tracks the movement, zeroing in on the thick band of pink scar tissue cutting across his left collarbone. "What happened there?" I point to the same spot on my body.

His deep blue eyes freeze over. He glances down and runs a finger along the edge of the scar. "Oh. That. Some guy attacked me."

"Attacked you? When?"

"About six months after I left."

I wait.

"I was sleeping rough," he says, the words halting, but steady. "Another homeless guy showed up and yelled at me. Turns out I was sleeping on his patch. I told him to piss off. He cut me."

It's strange. John doesn't display any telltale signs of lying.

I should know.

I've interviewed enough bullshitting suspects over the years.

There's no tremor in my brother's voice, and just the right amount of hesitation—being attacked is a traumatic experience, after all.

But there's something off.

Too bad I can't put my finger on it.

John walks over to the small patio table and sinks into a chair, his elbows resting on his knees.

I join him. "So, what? You went to the hospital?"

He snorts. "Couldn't risk it."

"What do you mean?"

"I was still... battling my demons." His mouth twists in disgust. "I couldn't risk being found."

Something slams into my gut, ten times more vicious than John's elbow. "Found by us, you mean?"

When he glances up, his eyes brim with tears. "I was—no, I *am*—so ashamed. Everything I put you through..."

I know he's telling the truth this time, the whole truth.

Tori's words from the previous evening come flooding back.

Think about it, Christian. Imagine what he's been through. From what you told me, he was so excited he found out about his Manifestation... then to have it snatched away from him like that... you're powerful. He's not. You fit in with your own kind. He's shunned by them. Is it any wonder he started using? I might have run away, too, in his position.

My own words follow, hot on their heels.

Self-centred prick.

Selfish little bastard.

That's what I called him.

My stomach pinches with guilt. "I didn't mean what I said. About you being selfish."

He laughs, but there's no humour in it. His fingers find the dragon's head pendant, and he brings it to his lips, mumbling against it. "No. You were right. I am selfish. Everything I touch turns to shit."

The pinch in my stomach intensifies. "I was pissed off, that's all. You know what I'm like."

"Humph." He carries on fiddling with the pendant.

"Where did you get that?"

John drops the dragon's head like it scalds him. "What? This thing? Flea market."

My scalp prickles.

There it is again.

That thing I can't put my finger on.

But it's more obvious now.

The way he jerked his hand away from the pendant when I mentioned it...

Flea market my arse.

He's lying.

"Where have you been, John?"

His lips form a thin line. "It's a—"

"Long story, I know. You said that last night. You also said you'd tell me what happened."

He lets out a long sigh. "I did, didn't I?"

I cross my arms and say nothing.

John stares into the distance. "That night in the bathroom... I tried to kill myself. Even slit my wrists the right way, and everything." He runs a finger along the pale blue veins lining the inside of his wrist.

The *smooth* skin of his wrist.

No tattoos.

No scars, either.

Apart from the one on his collarbone.

It makes little sense.

After a beat of silence, John continues. "I passed out on the bathroom floor and woke up about thirty minutes later. I'd lost a lot of blood, but not enough to... you know. Didn't cut deep enough, I guess."

The way he says it, so cold, so emotionless, unsettles me, because the tone is so un-John-like.

"It was like a second chance. I knew I'd never get better if I stayed. I knew I'd keep putting everyone through hell. So I ran. Climbed out the bathroom window—like we used to in school, remember? When we wanted to sneak out to parties." He smiles at me.

I don't smile back. "Where did you go?"

The grin slides off his face. "Caught a train to London. Had to be careful. I didn't have any money, but I dodged the conductor."

"And you got clean? Just like that?"

He shakes his head, shadows gathering in his eyes. "There were a lot of... false starts."

"You're obviously better now."

He taps his index finger to his temple. "Not better. Too much buzzing around in here. I'll always be an addict. But I'm sober, if that's what you mean."

"So, what changed?"

A sad smile curves his lips. "I ended up in a kind of halfway house, for people like me, who fall through the cracks. The woman who ran it took pity on me. She took me in when no one else would—" His voice cracks on the last word. "God knows why. I wasn't exactly... well, let's just say she didn't warm to me at first."

"No," I say in mock-surprise. "You shock me."

This raises a lighter smile. "She had a lot of house rules. Think I broke every single one of them. By rights, she could've kicked me out a thousand times over."

I quirk my eyebrow at him. "Why didn't she?"

He shifts in his seat. "I asked her that once. Know what she said?"

"What?"

"She said she could see a brilliant light inside me and, if I let go of my stubbornness long enough to get out of my own way, it would guide me through the darkness." He gives his head a little shake, fingers going back to the pendant. "I'm still not sure I believe her."

"This woman. She has a name?"

"Kalia—" his voice cracks, so he clears his throat and tries again. "Kalia Zhang."

I nod towards his fiddling fingers. "Did she give you that?"

He drops the pendant again, shutters coming down over his eyes. "No. Like I said—"

"You got it at a flea market."

"Yeah."

I grab the arms of the garden chair and squeeze tight. The colour leaches from my knuckles. I'm desperate to push him on this, but I'm also afraid that if I do, I'll push him away again. For now, I bite my tongue. Instead, I say, "She got you clean?"

He nods.

"How long did it take?"

John knows it's not an innocent question.

I can almost see the cogs whirring.

"A long time," he says, the words almost a whisper.

"How long?"

He licks his lips. "Eighteen months, give or take."

Eighteen.

Months.

He's been gone for more than twice that amount of time. He could've come home sooner, but he chose not to.

Tori was wrong about Mum and Dad.

Our parents split up two years after John's disappearance.

If he'd come home sooner...

He must read the hurt on my face, because he says, "I'm sorry."

I stand, pace back and forth, rub a hand across my nose.

I'm usually good at reading people, and I hate the way I can't get a bead on John.

I might be mad at him because of Mum and Dad, and how things ended up with them, but he's my brother, and I desperately want to believe him.

He's alive, and he's back.

That should be all that matters.

But...

There are too many holes in his story, too many inconsistencies. The amount of blood I found on the bathroom floor—he should've bled out.

And he's had martial arts training.

Who taught him?

Was it this Kalia woman?

Then there's that pendant.

Flea market...

Yeah, right.

But why lie?

Why?

That's not all, though.

There's the one-eighty change in his personality.

He's so calm.

And he's got shitloads of money.

Going from homeless and penniless to wealthy in the space of three years... not impossible, but irregular.

My spine tingles.

He almost seems... *powerful*, in his own way.

I hate to admit it, but John's transformation scares me a little.

He used to be an open book. Now, he's so full of secrets.

I hate secrets.

I hate lies.

John clears his throat a second time.

Despite myself, I flinch.

Why?

What's this thing gnawing at the back of my mind that I can't shake?

I shouldn't fear my brother.

There's nothing to fear.

I could take him out with a quick Latin phrase and a flick of my fingers.

But, still...

When John speaks, his voice is steady. "Did you hear what I said? I'm—"

"Don't." I hold up a finger to stop him. "There's something you're not telling me. What is it?"

His brow creases, like he's puzzled. "I'm not sure—"

"Don't lie to me. I need to know what—"

My phone rings.

Fuck.

Not now.

I consider letting it go to voicemail.

"Are you going to get that?" John asks.

I narrow my eyes at him and slide my phone out of my pocket.

Kate.

"Bugger. I need to take this."

"Go ahead."

"This conversation isn't done."

John doesn't answer.

I retreat to the bottom of the garden and answer the phone. "Winter."

"Christian? Jesus, are you all right? You sound like shit."

I squint up at the bright sun. "You got all that from 'Winter'?"

"What's wrong?"

Do I tell her?

I know the answer before the question's fully formed. "It's John. He's alive. He's back."

Nothing but the crackle of static answers me.

"Kate? You still there?"

"Yes, yes. I'm still here. I'm just... wow. That's... I mean, it's been so long. I thought—well, we all thought—you know."

My stomach writhes like a nest of vipers. "Yeah, I know."

Her voice brightens. "But that's brilliant news."

"Yeah, it is."

"Doesn't sound like it?"

"I'm adjusting."

John's standing stock still on the patio.

This is what I mean.

These are the things that make me uneasy.

He used to be a terrible fidget.

"Christian?" Kate says.

"He seems different, that's all."

"He's bound to be. I can't imagine what he's been through."

"That's what Tori said."

"She's right."

I tear my gaze away from John. "Anyway, that's personal. Why did you call?"

"Oh, it's about a case, but it doesn't matter. You need to be at home. I'll get someone else on it."

I have the sudden, overwhelming urge to get away from John. I don't know why, and I don't know where it's coming from, but I can't stand to be anywhere near him right now. "No. It's fine. I'll come in."

"No way, Christian. Your brother needs you. Anyway, this is an undercover case. It could take you away for days."

Take me away for days.

Take me away from the lies.

Maybe a bit of space is just what I need.

Time to quiet the thoughts swirling through my mind like a maelstrom. Time to figure out how to speak to John without getting angry or scared.

I make my decision. "He'll be fine. He'll understand."

She hesitates, then says, "Well... if you're sure."

"I am. Give me fifteen minutes." I disconnect the call before she can say anything else, trudging back up the garden until I stand opposite John on the patio.

"Everything all right?" he says.

"I—"

"Don't tell me. Work?"

I nod.

"How's Kate?"

I shrug. "She's Kate."

That raises a half-grin from John, but when he speaks, there's a hint of melancholy in his voice. "You have to go."

John's wounded tone cuts me like a blade, forcing my next words to pour from me like gushing blood. "We've got an enormous case on at the moment. They need me to come in. I tried to get out of it, but Kate didn't give me a choice."

Damn.

Those words blister the inside of my mouth, my gums, my tongue.

Who's lying now?

Hypocrite.

John holds up his hands. "It's fine. I get it. Besides, I know what you're like. If you're not there, and something bad happens, you'll beat yourself up over it forever."

"You sure? It's undercover. I'll probably be gone for a few days."

"Really. It's cool."

I nod, but the movement feels jerky, unnatural, and my mouth is as dry as sawdust. I head for the back door...

Pause.

Turn.

"John...?"

"Yeah?"

"I..." The words stick in my throat.

"What's up?"

"Nothing."

"No, go on."

A breath leaves me in one long gust.

Don't ask him.

Don't—

"You're not... you won't leave again?" My voice trembles a little.

I hate that tremble.

That weakness.

"I meant what I said last night. I'm not going anywhere."

I fight to hold my next question in, but I can't. "Promise?"

He smiles. "I swear."

I give a stiff nod, and turn to leave again, before an unwelcome thought barges its way into my mind. "Shit. Someone needs to tell Mum and Dad you're back."

For the first time since he came back, John's calm expression shifts to one of panic. "*No.*"

"John, we have to—"

"Not yet."

"You—"

"Please, Chris. I'll tell them eventually, but I'm not... it's not... shit. It's hard enough being here as it is. I'm not ready yet."

"Why come back?"

"What?"

"If you didn't want Mum and Dad to know, why come back? You didn't know they weren't here when you arrived. You clearly wanted to see them. To see me."

His next words come out slow. "Hindsight's a great thing. Like I said, being here is difficult... more so than I expected. I just need a little time. Please."

"You still haven't answered my question. Why come back? Why now?"

His fingers brush that damn pendant again, but he says nothing.

He looks so sad—hollow-eyed, his mouth turned down at the corners—my resolve cracks.

I can't push him.

Not now.

Not when he's like this.

I just need a little time. Please.

I let out a heavy breath through my nose. "We'll give it some time, but you have to tell them soon."

"I will. I promise."

"Fine. Look, I have to go—"

"Yeah. No. Go. Good luck. With the case."

"Thanks." I give an awkward knock on the door frame and retreat into the house, snatching up my car keys when I reach the hall.

Please.

Please let him be here when I get back.

CHAPTER 10
Christian

I'm at work fifteen minutes later, as promised.

Kate enters the briefing room.

All the assembled officers—including me—stand.

"Don't bother," she says.

We sink back into our seats.

She strides to the front of the room. "Okay, everyone, listen up."

Any last mutters fall silent.

Kate paces back-and-forth while she speaks. "Last night we received some Intel relating to an item connected to the Dylan Carmichael case."

Stone, who's sitting opposite me, pulls himself ramrod straight, his muscles tense.

Layla, perched next to him, reaches over and gives his hand a gentle squeeze.

If Kate notices Henry's reaction to hearing his former boss's name, she doesn't mention it. "For those of you who don't know, shortly before his arrest, Carmichael sold a crown. A crown stolen from Dr Thomas Ross's private gallery—"

"Stolen by these two." A junior detective nods at Stone and Layla.

I groan inwardly.

Some of my colleagues aren't happy about having the former COVEN Executioners on the team, and make no bones about it.

Stone braces his hands on the table and rises from his chair. "If you've got something to say—"

"That's enough." Kate's nostrils flare. "If anyone has a problem with 'these two', you'll have to take it up with me."

A hot flush creeps into the junior detective's cheeks, and he finds something interesting to look at in his lap.

With clenched teeth, Stone lowers himself back into his chair.

"As I was saying, Carmichael sold the crown to this man." Kate picks up a tiny remote control and presses one of its many buttons.

The beat-up old projector whirs to life with a clunk, and a click.

"Aidan Adedeji," Kate says.

The face staring back at us doesn't look like it belongs to a criminal.

Adedeji wears an affable grin that makes his wide brown eyes appear soft, like he's about to break out into a smile at any moment.

The MID has been keeping tabs on him ever since Stone told us he was Carmichael's buyer for the Cursed Crown of King Arthur.

Kate continues, "Adedeji, his wife, Naomi, and their business partners, Eric Jiménez and Michelle Rees, trade stolen goods at the Underground."

The junior detective lets out a low whistle.

It's easy to tell why.

People who trade in the Underground—the magical equivalent of the mortals' black market—are dangerous.

"They call themselves Pentacle," Kate says.

Wonder where that name came from? It sounds melodramatic as hell.

Kate steps in front of the projector, blocking the photo from view, and places her hands on her hips. "One of our Underground informants overheard a conversation about Adedeji and his crew. They were cagey on the details, but the gist is he's on the lookout for another witch to join Pentacle."

I lean back and cross my arms. "Why do they need another witch?"

"That, we don't know, but they mentioned the crown."

That bloody crown.

Figures.

The same junior detective from earlier pipes up. He's clearly over his embarrassment, a smirk now painting his face. "Is this King Arthur's crown we're talking about?"

A smattering of laughter drifts through the briefing room.

The corner of my mouth quirks. I can't help it.

That King Arthur existed, much less that this crown belonged to him, is laughable.

And as for the other stories of legend—demons exiled to Hell, and sorcerers guarding the Gates, keeping us all safe—it's ludicrous. If you believe that, you'll believe anything.

Layla flushes red.

No way! Does she think the legend's real?

Even Kate chuckles a little. "All right, all right. On a serious note, Adedeji must be interested in the crown for a reason. We assume it contains some kind of spell or power he wants. We also assume he needs a fifth witch to unlock this power. He's wealthy, well-connected in the Underground, untouchable. He has enough power already. The question is, why does he need more?"

A heavy silence falls while Kate lets that sink in.

The mood in the room grows sombre.

I clear my throat. "How's he going to choose this fifth witch?"

Kate smiles. "I'm glad you asked. Our informant tells us Pentacle's holding a contest to select their last member. Only the most powerful witches need to apply."

Stone's eyebrows tug low. "A contest? What kind of contest?"

"That's unclear," Kate says. "DI Winter will take point on this one."

"What?" Stone's on his feet again.

Kate's eyes flash. "You heard me, DC Stone."

His face falls. "I just thought..."

"You thought what?" Kate asks, tone sharp.

He holds her gaze, emerald eyes shining. "It's my fault Adedeji got the crown. I fucked up. I should be the one to put it right."

Kate's voice softens, just a little. "Ordinarily, I'd agree."

"Ordinarily?"

She counts on her fingers. "One. Adedeji beat you once before, and you're still learning elemental magic."

Stone's cheeks flush, the red glow bright against his pale skin.

"Two. DI Winter is more powerful than you."

He scoffs. "Debatable."

"And *three*. Adedeji's seen you. He knows who you are. There's no way he'll let you join his ranks."

Stone sniffs. "Fair enough."

I wait until he's seated again, then ask, "What do you need me to do?"

"Enter the contest. Win. Find out what Pentacle's plans are. Recover the crown."

She's not asking for much, is she?

I keep my expression neutral. "Fine. Where is this contest?"

Kate clicks another button on the remote control, and Adedeji's image flicks off the screen, replaced by a scrubby-looking warehouse surrounded by a deserted car park. Cracks split the tarmac, which desperately needs repairing.

Kate says, "Pentacle owns this building. It's on the outskirts of The Park End Industrial Estate. The contest is due to take place here at three o'clock today."

"Today?" I check my watch. "That only leaves me two hours."

"What about the rest of us?" the junior detective asks, a sullen look on his face.

I can't help my smirk.

Someone's pissed off they got cut out of the action.

After his earlier remark about Stone and Layla, I can't say I'm disappointed.

Kate continues, addressing the room at large. "Delve as deep as you can into Adedeji's background. I want to know everything. Family life, school, the works. If he eats overnight oats for breakfast, I want to know about it. Questions?"

No one says anything.

"Good. Now get to work."

I rise from my chair to the sound of shuffling feet as everyone exits the room.

"Christian," Kate says.

I halt, turning to face her.

"A word."

I hang back until everyone else has gone, then join her beside the projector. "What's up?"

Kate leans against the wall and folds her arms across her chest. "I should ask you that."

"I don't—"

"Are you sure you're up to this?"

I draw breath to protest.

She holds up her hand. "John's back. Are you sure this is the right thing to do?"

I perch on a table at the front of the room, close my eyes, and take a deep breath through my nose. "Honestly?"

"Of course."

"Being around him is… difficult. I need the space to get my head around it."

She gnaws on her bottom lip, considering her answer. Eventually, she says, "That's my point. Your head must be all over the place."

Heat surges through me. "It won't affect my work, if that's what you're getting at."

More lip gnawing.

More consideration.

She pushes off the wall. "Fine. But if I get so much as an inkling you can't handle this right now—"

"That won't be an issue."

"See that it isn't."

We're quiet for a moment.

Then Kate says, "Want to talk about it?"

I laugh, but it has a bitter edge. "Trust me, that's the last thing I want."

"Well, if you change your mind…"

"I won't."

More awkward silence follows.

Eventually, Kate clears her throat and says, "I've prepared an alias for you. It's one you're familiar with."

"Carl Weston?" I guess.

She nods.

Makes sense.

This isn't my first undercover operation and, over the course of my career, Carl Weston has built up quite the reputation.

Theft.

Extortion.

Murder.

He'll fit right in at Pentacle.

"Everything's sorted," Kate says. "Flat. Car. Passport. Your cover's airtight."

"Wouldn't expect anything less. One question."

"What is it?"

"If we know where Pentacle are, why don't we just storm their hideout and bring them in?"

"I wish it were that easy. Like I said in the briefing, Adedeji is well-connected in the Underground. I don't fancy starting a war between us and those traders, do you?"

"Good point."

"And you'll need to be careful. We'll have no way of contacting you once you're inside. I can't risk putting a tracking spell on you in case Adedeji or his crew detect it."

"I'll be fine, Kate."

She arches an eyebrow.

"Really," I insist.

Kate dismisses me with a wave of her hand. "Go on, then. Get ready."

I'm halfway to my desk when I realise the absurdity of her words.

Get ready.

That would be brilliant advice, if I had the faintest idea what I was walking into.

There's one thing I need to do before I leave, though.

Tori hadn't been in the briefing earlier.

I should fill her in on the case and let her know I'll be gone for a few days.

Thirty minutes later—having searched for Tori everywhere else—I enter the staff canteen, a large, square space reeking of fatty bacon grease and the pungent odour of singed coffee.

That smell always makes my nose wrinkle.

Tori sits at one of the small, round tables. She nurses a cup of the aforementioned plimsole-black liquid, and scrolls through her phone.

I stride towards her.

She glances up when I'm a few paces away. Her eyes widen in surprise. "What are you doing here?"

"Charming." I drop into the seat opposite her. "Great to see you, too."

She rolls her eyes. "You know what they say about sarcasm?"

I chuckle. "Kate called me in," I tell her, before filling her in on the Pentacle case.

Her forehead creases. "You're going undercover? Now?"

I shrug. "I'm the best person for the job."

"What about John?"

I can't quite meet her eye. "I cleared it with him. He understands."

She clicks her tongue. "You really think now is the best time to leave him?"

"I..."

"You're scared."

"No," I say, a little too fast. I rub the back of my neck. "Maybe."

"Why? He's your brother."

"I know, but he's so—" I break off, searching for the right word. "—different."

"We've been over this. He's been through a lot, and—"

"I get that, but I... it's hard to explain."

Tori's gaze sharpens. "Try."

I hesitate, take a breath, and when I speak again, my words come out slow and considered. "I don't know how to be around him. He's hiding things from me, and my instinct is to push. But if I do that, he..."

Understanding dawns on Tori's face. "He might leave again."

I bow my head.

Her hand finds mine across the table, her warm, gentle fingers squeezing mine. "Are you sure about this case?"

My eyes meet hers, and I nod. "I need a distraction. It's the only way to clear my head enough to get to grips with things. Taking on a case is the best way for me to do that."

She laces her fingers through mine. "Fair enough."

"You're not mad?"

"It's your decision. If this is what you need to do, then I'll back you."

That raises a small smile.

She really is wonderful.

The question I wanted to ask her burns a hole into my brain like a lit cigarette.

John's arrival had interrupted us.

I was going to...

You were going to what?

Never mind. It can wait.

"You've got that look."

Tori's voice jerks me back to the present. "What look?"

"Like you want to say something, but you're struggling to spit it out."

"I don't have a look."

She snorts. "If you say so."

Well, I can't ask her now. The moment's ruined.

Again.

"How long will you be gone?" she asks.

"Kate reckons it'll only be a few days."

She releases my hand. "Be careful."

"Always." I stand. "Wish me luck?"

"Ha! The day we rely on luck is the day the proverbial freezes over."

I chuckle. "True. See you soon."

Still regretting the question left hanging between us, I stalk from the canteen.

The quicker I finish this thing, the quicker I can ask Tori to move in with me.

Chapter 11
Christian

My brand-new *BMW*—on loan from work as part of my cover—pulls to a stop at the edge of the industrial estate, and I kill the engine.

I pick up the cardboard file folder on the passenger seat and flick through the files one last time. I know this alias like it's the back of my hand, but this last run-through before marching into the lion's den is a good luck ritual I can't shake.

It'll help me push all the questions about John out of my mind and allow me to focus.

Compartmentalisation is key.

My eyes track the lines of text, and I read aloud. "My name is Carl Weston. I'm twenty-nine years old. My mother is Sheila Weston. My father is Paul Weston. I grew up in Manchester. Moved to Daxbridge when I was sixteen. Since then, I've murdered seven witches and stolen over five million pounds. I heard about the contest through the Underground. My name is Carl Weston..."

I repeat these phrases over and over, like a mantra, until a soft calm washes over me.

I'm ready.

Let's do this thing.

I close the folder and pinch the corner between my thumb and forefinger. "*Ignis.*"

Whoosh.

A roaring purple flame engulfs the cardboard, devouring it in seconds. It leaves behind nothing but a puff of black smoke. The air is thick with the cloying scent of scorched cardboard and ash.

No one will find anything incriminating now.

I step out of the car into the blazing afternoon sunshine.

God, this place is depressing.

A smorgasbord of litter—crisp packets, fag butts, dirty polystyrene cups—blow across the cracked concrete. Here and there, withered brown weeds poke their heads through the cracks, battling the heat, and somehow hanging in there. All the buildings are the same. Brick boxes with huge, bird shit-smeared windows.

A few mortals dash about—either heading back into one of the monochrome offices or running for their cars.

Hamsters spinning a wheel.

I pity them.

How boring must their lives be?

One hamster, a young man with dirty blonde hair and clear blue eyes—who bears a striking resemblance to John—calls to a colleague across one of the featureless car parks.

She turns.

He smiles.

They chat—no, flirt.

So... normal.

They look happy enough.

Would John have been happy like them, if he'd been born a mortal? If vesseldom hadn't cursed him and left him with no power to call his own?

At least mortals were supposed to be powerless.

Would he have ended up in an office? Just another guy flirting with another girl?

Maybe.

Life would've been so different.

No drinking, no drugs.

Mum and Dad might still be together, they might—

"Want a picture or something, pal?" The smile has vanished from the young man's face. He's glaring daggers at me.

Lost in thought, I hadn't realised I'd drawn to a halt, watching the pair.

Idiot.

No use pining after things you can't have.

I am Carl Weston...

I duck my head, carry on walking.

If I get so much as an inkling you can't handle this right now...

I need to stay focused.

I am twenty-nine years old...

The job is what matters.

I am Carl Weston...

It's all that matters now.

I round a corner, turning into a disused part of the industrial estate, squeezing between two buildings. I inch my way along until I emerge in yet another deserted car park, sweat dripping down my back.

The Pentacle warehouse is up ahead.

Good.

Anything to get out of this blazing sun.

I take two more steps.

Everything falls silent.

My ears ring with the absence of sound.

It happened too fast to be natural.

It must be magic.

The skin at the nape of my neck prickles, my upper lip instantly clammy. It's the same feeling you get when you walk home late at night and you think someone's following you.

I spin round, raising my hand, preparing to cast.

There's no one there.

"Hello?" My voice sounds quieter than usual, a little distorted.

Someone's definitely cast a spell over this place.

"Who's there?"

Nothing.

I scowl into thin air. "Whoever you are, you're making a big mistake."

There.

That sounds like something Carl Weston would say.

I turn in a slow circle, the nape of my neck prickling.

The car park is empty.

Or is it?

I wave my hand through the air. "*Revelare.*"

Snap.

The air twelve feet in front of me shimmers, and a tall figure appears, swamped in a scarlet robe, the hood pulled up to hide their face.

I almost laugh.

Almost.

"Clever." The voice beneath the cowl is male. "No one else spotted us."

"You part of Pentacle?" I ask.

"All in good time."

My name is Carl Weston...

What would Carl do?

"Cut the cryptic bullshit." On instinct, I summon more magic, my hands flaring with violet light.

"I'd save your magic if I were you. You'll need it where you're going."

I answer him with derision. "Aren't you hot in that thing?"

When the man speaks again, there's a hint of a smile in his voice. "Ade's going to like you."

Ade?

Aidan.

He means Adedeji.

Whoever this man is, he's definitely from Pentacle.

I smirk at him. "I'm sure the Masked Magician routine is supposed to scare me, but—"

He laughs now. "Trust me, I'm not the scary one."

"What?"

"I am," a female voice whispers, her breath tickling my ear.

Her proximity makes me flinch.

Fuck.

I turn to fight, but it's too late.

A cool, slender-fingered hand closes around the back of my neck. "*Somnum.*"

I try my best to fight the sleep spell, but it's too strong.

My eyelids drift closed and I tumble into a sea of endless black.

Chapter 12
Christian

Wherever I am, it's dark and cold, and the air smells stagnant. I'm lying on my back, resting on something hard—the floor, maybe?—and my mind is a jumbled mess, thanks to the sleep spell.

They might be easy to cast, but they sure pack one hell of a punch.

Dust tickles my nostrils, and I sneeze.

I crack my heavy eyelids open and blink several times, allowing my eyes to adjust to the darkness.

The dense shadows around me take shape slowly.

The grey-walled room I'm in is small, square, and unfurnished.

I force my head up and off the icy concrete, my heart rate quickening.

Where the fuck am I?

Two more details emerge from the gloom.

There's a plain red door opposite me, and a blank plasma screen hung on the wall above it.

What the—

With great difficulty, I heave myself to my feet and shake off the lingering effects of the sleep spell. I work my way around the room, searching for an escape.

No luck there.

The door has no handle, and the walls are smooth and impenetrable.

There's no way out.

My mouth goes dry, my gut laced with the first twinges of panic.

No.

To hell with this.

Nothing and no one can hold me prisoner.

I raise an open palm and hold it level with the door, chanting in Latin. I'll blow the goddamn thing off its hinges.

Something catches the light, winking.

A thin silver band encircles my right wrist.

I examine the band, but—like the walls—it's perfectly smooth.

No catches.

No clasps.

Nothing to unfasten it with.

What is this thing?

There must be some way to get it off.

Perhaps an unlocking spell will do the trick.

I point at the band. "*Recludo.*"

Sharp pain explodes along my wrist, and I clench my teeth to stifle a scream.

My knees tremble and I stagger to the side, my hands slamming into the wall.

The pain travels up and down my arm and my chests screams with stabbing agony that leaves me panting.

I take long drags of air through gritted teeth. I don't know how much time passes but, eventually, the last of my pain fades. Breathing hard, I wait until my heart rate returns to normal.

What the hell?

Whatever this bracelet does, it can't be anything good.

What *does* it do?

Are Pentacle using it to track me?

To measure my magic?

To control me?

Something mechanical whirs above me.

My head snaps up.

They've fixed a security camera on the wall's apex, its green light winking.

My blood runs cold.

Someone's watching me.

Monitoring how I react, maybe?

Come on.

Snap out of it.

This is a contest, and—I'm one-hundred percent sure—it started the moment I opened my eyes.

I can't show weakness now. I plant my feet in a wide stance, draw myself up to my full height, throw my shoulders back, and glare at the camera.

My name is Carl Weston...

The TV attached to the wall flickers to life, and an inverted pentagram flashes onto the screen.

Here we go.

The pentagram fades, and four people in those ridiculous red robes appear, standing—straight-backed and imposing—against a black background.

I resist the urge to roll my eyes.

Talk about melodrama.

This set up is only some dry ice and funky disco lights away from becoming a cheesy eighties music video.

The foursome lower their hoods.

I recognise them instantly.

Aidan Adedeji.

Naomi Adedeji.

Eric Jiménez.

Michelle Rees.

Pentacle in all their glory.

Aidan raises his hands, opening his arms wide. He smiles then, a flash of bright white teeth. A shark who's caught the scent of bait. "Welcome to Pentacle."

I shiver.

He's not done. "There are five of you in the maze, but only one of you will become a member today."

Maze?

What the hell is he talking about?

"And for that lucky one among you, a fantastic prize awaits."

Jesus Christ.

Forget the cheesy eighties music video.

Looks like he's going full on nineties game-show host.

Next thing you know, they'll start wheeling out the luxury speedboats, twelve month supplies of chocolate, and all-expenses-paid trips to Benidorm.

What he offers turns out to be far more tantalising.

"Power."

The word makes my fingertips tingle.

"I know what you're thinking," Adedeji continues. "How will I prove myself worthy of such a great honour?"

No, actually. I was thinking, when the fuck are you going to climb down off your megalomaniacal high horse? I mean, who does this guy think he is? Voldemort?

"At the centre of the maze—if you make it that far—you'll find your prize."

If we make it that far?

The smile falls from Aidan's face, his voice hard as steel. "The contest has one rule. No killing. Pentacle stands for empowering witches who deserve it, not murdering those who don't."

Interesting.

So, Aidan wants to empower other witches.

What does the crown have to do with that?

"I've warned you."

The screen fades to black.

There's a loud click, the sound of a lock disengaging.

The red door swings open, revealing a dark hallway beyond.

This is it.

The contest has begun.

Chapter 13
Christian

I creep over to the door and poke my head out.

The hallway beyond forks off in a dozen different directions.

It's deserted.

I wait, heart thudding against my rib cage.

Everything's quiet.

Too quiet.

A maze.

That's what Adedeji called this place, and I can see why.

How am I supposed to work out which corridor to take?

I close my eyes, still hovering in the doorway.

Think, think, think.

I know a thing or two about mazes.

When we were kids, Mum and Dad took John and me to the sprawling hedge maze at Longleat.

John.

What's my brother up to now? I wonder if—

No.

John belongs to Christian.

I'm not Christian right now.

My name is Carl Weston...

I'm twenty-nine years old...

What was it Dad said again?

Always keep one hand on the wall. That way, you'll never get lost.

"One hand on the wall." I step into the hallway, fingers brushing the vast expanse of grey concrete. One tentative step at a time, I inch down the gloomy corridor. Each darkened corner I come to, I risk a quick peek, the sound of my breathing too loud in the silence.

The walls are like ice, freezing the tips of my trailing fingers. The temperature is in stark contrast to the broiling summer day outside.

Something scurries across the path in front of me.

I jump, biting back a yelp.

The small, furry thing skitters into the darkness.

My heart does a frantic jig.

A rat.

It's just a rat.

Get a grip.

My name is Carl Weston...

I'm twenty-nine years old.

My mother is...

The farther into the maze I travel, the colder it becomes.

A faint sound hovers in the distance.

The unmistakable *fizz-whoosh* of magic being unleashed.

Staying close to the wall, I drift closer to the sound on silent feet.

There.

Shimmering light around the next corner.

I flatten my back to the wall, sliding along it by crossing one leg in front of the other.

Toe to heel, toe to heel, toe to heel.

I'm almost to the corner—

A burst of pale pink fire roars past me, so close the heat singes the hair on my arms.

I drop into a low crouch, pulse hammering at my throat.

The last tongues of pink fire die away, leaving scorch marks on the wall opposite me.

That was close.

The sounds of battle continue.

Still crouching, I edge along the wall and peer around the corner.

Two witches circle each other, one male, one female.

The male witch flings out his hand and bellows a string of Latin.

A thousand pink pinpricks of light dart from his fingers.

The woman forms an X across her chest with her forearms. "*Obstructionum.*"

The swarm of pink lights surround her, each one pattering against her translucent, navy-blue barrier like rain drops.

Damn.

She's good. She must be, to react so fast.

The light fades.

She drops her barrier and, before her sparring partner can make another move, swings her arm up, fingers curled into sharp, glowing claws that rake the air.

The man flinches.

The air goes still, and the pair stare at each other, the woman breathing hard.

I frown.

Why's he just standing there?

I want to yell at him to move.

Has the woman's spell failed?

I'm about to take advantage of the confusion, rush in, and knock both of them out cold when it happens.

Gaping vertical lacerations split the man's throat apart, flesh sagging away from bone like paper steamed off a wall. The scarlet gouges unzip his chin, his lips, his nostrils. Thick, red-black blood pumps from the wounds and pours down his shirt-front.

I clamp a hand over my mouth to stifle a scream.

The man forces air from his mouth and it whistles through the tattered, fluttering remains of his lips. A bubble of blood forms at one shredded nostril.

It pops.

The man collapses to his knees and crumples to his side.

Dead.

Just like that.

A burst of static cuts through the cramped hallway, and Aidan's voice fills the space. "Attention. One of you has broken the rules and killed a fellow contestant."

Even from here, I can make out the female witch's eyes, as wide as dinner plates.

Aidan continues. "I warned you against this, and I will punish you in kind."

Punish you in kind.

Surely, he doesn't mean—

The woman squeals and clutches at the silver band around her wrist—a replica of the one I'm wearing. "No. No, please. I—ah—I didn't mean to kill him. It was an accident. I lost control."

"If you lose control that easily," Aidan's voice booms, "we don't want you, anyway."

She screams again. "Stop. It was an accident. Please don't do this."

The bracelet darkens to an unhealthy grey; the sheen wearing off the silver.

Her body shakes.

What the—

She stumbles into the wall, her back sliding down it until she's slumped in an awkward sitting position. Her body shakes so violently her head smacks against the concrete with a dull thud.

Shit.

She's having some kind of seizure.

I jump up from my crouch, race over to her, and crash to my knees at her side. "What can I do?"

She doesn't answer, her body still juddering.

I grab her hands, which are ice cold. "Can you hear me?"

Her eyes bulge and run with grey-streaked tears, but she doesn't make a sound.

"Shit, shit, sh—"

In an instant, her skin grows furnace-hot.

I yelp and snatch my hands away.

What the fuck is going on?

Thick, grey smoke—reeking of ozone and rot—pours from the woman's silver bangle in a noxious cloud.

I scramble back to avoid the foul smog.

The toxic substance sinks through the skin on her wrist, dying the blue lattice of veins beneath a bruised purple.

Her answering scream is so loud I'm forced to cover my ears.

The bruise spreads up her arm, and into her neck, the dark veins swelling, throbbing.

A wet rattle clicks in the woman's chest.

She coughs, and a fountain of tar-black liquid spews forth, spattering the floor and missing my boots by inches.

"Fuck." My voice comes out higher than usual.

The woman's body jerks once, and she pulls in a huge lungful of air, the muscles in her throat tightening. Her head flops to the side, more vile blackness leaking from the corners of her eyes. Then... she's still, and all is silent.

My skin erupts with goosebumps, and I hug my knees to my chest. My breath shudders on the way out. In all my years as an MID officer, I've never witnessed such a gruesome death.

It happened so fast.

And I was powerless to do anything to stop it.

What the hell kind of spell has Aidan cast on these bracelets?

One minute, two, three pass.

I'm cold all over, unable to tear my gaze away from the woman's bloodshot eyes.

Another burst of static cuts through the silence.

I flinch.

"We'll be watching you all closely," Aidan says.

More static.

Then there's nothing but an eerie quiet.

We'll be watching you...

Shit.

I can't stay here. I can't give in to the fear. Get up, keep moving, find the robe. I'm not Christian.

Five seconds.

Not Christian.

In five seconds, I'm going to move.

My name is Carl Weston...

Five.

The woman's dead-eyed stare glues me to the spot.

Four.

I'm twenty-nine years old...

Three.

The black ooze congeals around her on the floor.

Two.

My. Name. Is. Carl. Weston.

One.

I wrench my gaze away from hers, stand, and stalk away without looking back.

When I reach the end of the corridor, a mechanical whine comes from above.

My head snaps up.

Another security camera.

We'll be watching you...

Just like back in the room with the red door, now isn't the time to show weakness.

I shoot both middle fingers at the camera, place my hand back on the wall, and press on.

Closer to the robe.

To Pentacle.

Closer to power.

Chapter 14
Christian

The next person I come across—a man with spiky blue hair and a ring through his lower lip—slumps against a wall, eyes closed, his breathing deep and even.

Unconscious.

Odd red patches stain the pale skin on his hands, neck, and face.

I pause, bending over him to get a closer look at the florid splotches. From my new vantage point, I realise they're not splotches at all.

The angry scarlet marks form a pattern, like tree branches stretching towards the sky.

Tree branches.

Something tugs at the back of my mind.

Why are tree branches significant?

A light bulb goes on.

The marks are Lichtenberg figures, the result of lightning striking an insulated surface like wood or—in this case—skin.

They can't be natural.

They must result from someone striking him with lightning magic.

There are five of you in the maze, but only one of you will become a member today.

Two of my adversaries are dead.

This guy's unconscious.

That leaves one last opponent.

A powerful one able to use elemental magic, by the looks of it.

The nape of my neck tingles.

I need to be careful.

"*Invisibilia*," I whisper.

Magic rises inside me, pins and needles suffusing my entire body.

A cloud of shimmering violet light surrounds me and—when it fades—I know I'm invisible.

I don't want to show weakness, but strolling into an unknown space harbouring a lightning-wielding witch isn't a smart move.

Better to be safe than sorry.

Keeping my hand flat on the wall—my pulse pounding against the frozen concrete—I press on. I round one corner, and another, and another—

The short corridor ends in a set of wide double doors.

This is it.

This is the centre of the maze.

I reach out for the door, preparing to shove it open, but stop myself. There's a good chance the last competitor is right behind these doors.

We'll be watching you...

If Aidan's messaged played throughout the entire maze—which I'm confident it did—then my last opponent will have done the maths, too.

They will know there are only two of us still standing.

And the last thing I want to do is walk into a trap.

Backing away from the doors, I flatten myself against the wall and close my eyes.

My name is Carl Weston...

I take a deep breath and raise my hand.

It's now or never.

"*Dis*," I bark.

A bright purple orb of witch-light rockets from my out-stretched fingers and slams into the double doors, which burst open and smack against the walls on the other side with a loud bang.

A half-beat of silence.

That's all I get.

Then—

A fork of turquoise lightning flashes out of the darkness and streaks passed me, missing me by inches. The static raises the hairs along my arms.

As soon as the lightning dissipates, I dash into the room beyond.

It's cavernous, but beyond that, I register nothing else.

My eyes are too busy scanning for the threat of my adversary.

The room appears empty, but I know they're in here somewhere.

"Let me guess," a confident female voice says from the shadows. "Hiding behind an invisibility spell like a coward?"

Coward.

The word cuts me down to the bone.

No one calls me a coward.

I let the invisibility spell drop.

Another fork of blue-green lightning whizzes straight for me.

I dive out of the way just in time.

The lightning strikes the wall behind me, painting the flat surface with neon, zigzagging sparks before fading away to nothing.

I roll over my shoulder and spring to my feet.

"The Pentacle membership is mine," she says.

"I wouldn't be so sure. *Baculum*." A shimmering violet witch-staff—a fighting staff made of purple energy—appears in my hands. "If that guy out in the hall is anything to go by, you've been throwing out some powerful magic. How long do you think you can keep it up?"

A verdigris fireball blossoms to my left and darts at me.

I swing my staff behind me with one hand and summon a barrier with the other.

The lightning fizzles upon contact with my shield.

"A witch-staff and a barrier spell. At the same time. Impressive."

She's on my right now, circling me. Searching for weak spots.

Well, she won't find any.

"Who's the coward now?" I say. "Too scared to fight me at close range?"

She steps into the light, spinning her own witch-staff in tight circles. She's imposing, tall and lithe, short blonde hair swept away from her face. There's a determined set to her jaw and a steely glint in her eyes.

I'm reminded of the Valkyries of Norse myth.

This woman is a warrior.

"I'm not scared of anything." She takes a slow, deliberate step towards me.

I hold my ground. "That makes two of us."

Her lips peel back in a wolfish smile. "This is going to be fun." She darts forward, striking out with her staff.

I block... but only just.

Our staffs clash again, again, again, a shower of mauve and turquoise sparks raining down around us.

She lashes out with her foot and catches me on the shin.

I cry out and fall back, breathing hard.

She hasn't even broken a sweat. She swings her staff round and round in an elegant figure-eight pattern and laughs. "They only want powerful witches, right? What the hell are you doing here?"

Something in me snaps.

What does she know?

I took down a Fury single-handed, for fuck's sake.

She wants powerful, I'll give her powerful.

I fling out my hand. "*Crepitus est lux.*"

I shield my eyes against a blinding explosion of purple light.

She doesn't, clawing at her face and flailing around, firing lightning strikes blindly around the room.

I chuck my witch-staff away. It dissipates, and I drop flat on my stomach to avoid the woman's wayward magic. Then—spotting a gap in her assault—I leap to my feet and rush at her. "*Eryx.*"

My witch-gauntleted fist slams into her chin.

The punch knocks her off her feet, and she collapses to the ground.

She's out cold.

It's done.

Blood pounds in my ears and a giddy flush creeps into my cheeks.

The tannoy kicks in again. "Well done, Mr Weston," Aidan says.

"How do you know my name?" I ask between ragged breaths.

"I have my sources."

I inject steel into my voice. "Where's this prize?"

"Right here."

A spotlight set into the ceiling clicks on. Its harsh, white glow illuminates a scarlet robe floating in midair.

"Claim your prize," Aidan says.

"A robe."

"It marks your Pentacle membership."

"What about the power you promised?"

"All in good time."

I stalk towards the robe, reaching for it, my fingers inches from the velvety material—

Rip.

A white swirling portal spins into existence against the wall behind the robe, its light leeching the room of colour.

A portal?

The last thing I want to do is step into a portal conjured by Pentacle. There's no telling where they could drop me. I cross my arms and plant my feet, shouting over the loud hum of the whirling disc. "Where does it go?"

"You'll find out when you step through."

My eyes flick to the woman's body, still slumped on the floor. "What about the others?"

"What about them?"

"What happens to them?"

"Why do you care?"

"Answer the question."

"One of my people will erase their memories and leave them where we found them. As for the corpses... we'll dispose of them."

The way he says dispose of them makes my blood run cold. I clear my throat. "If you're powerful enough to work memory magic, what do you need more power for?"

A warning note creeps into Adedeji's voice. "You ask a lot of questions."

Shit.

I can't let him get suspicious. I set my jaw, snatch the robe from the air, and slide it on. "Whatever." I swallow—hard—and stride into the portal.

Chapter 15
Christian

When I emerge on the other side of the portal, having just left somewhere dingy, I'm forced to shield my eyes against a bright light that burns into my corneas.

"What the—" I sputter, fearing the worst.

An interrogation.

Torture.

Something—

A hand appears before me.

I lower the hand protecting my retinas from the glare. My gaze darts around the room, taking in the exposed brickwork and large sash windows, the low backed sofas and evenly spaced bookcases lining the walls. It finally lands on the dark eyes of Aidan Adedeji.

When Aidan speaks, his voice is warm. "Welcome to Pentacle, Mr Weston. My name's Aidan Adedeji, and I'm in charge here."

I grasp his hand in a firm grip. "Cheers. Oh, and call me Carl. Mr Weston is my father's name, and he's ancient."

He gives a sedate nod and a small smile. "You did well in the competition, Carl. Your command of magic is quite something."

"Humph."

My eyes flick to Michelle Rees. She's standing off to the side, her arms crossed and her lips pinched.

"This is Michelle Rees. We call her Chelle."

"My *friends* call me Chelle," she interjects.

I've heard her voice before.

Somnum.

She's the one who knocked me out with that sleep spell.

The self-proclaimed 'scary one'.

I offer her my hand. "Hello."

She deigns to regard my outstretched fingers like they're something contagious she's spotted under a microscope. She doesn't move to shake it.

Aidan winks at me. "Don't worry. She's not as bristly as she seems. It's the New Yorker in her."

Michelle mutters something that sounds an awful lot like, "Patronising ass-hat," but she says it with such fondness—no, admiration—that it sounds like a compliment.

Aidan moves to one side. "Let me introduce you to my wife, Naomi."

Naomi Adedeji steps forward, tucking one of her long dark braids behind her ear. She's all power and confidence. She moves with a sensuous, feline grace that's hard to ignore and, when she fixes her catlike eyes on me, I almost blush like an awkward teenager.

"Carl," she says in a voice as smooth and rich as sweetened mascarpone, "it's a pleasure to meet you."

"Likewise."

"To echo Ade, we're all really impressed with how you handled yourself in the maze."

Michelle lets out an irritated grunt. "Not that I don't love 'get-to-know-the-newb', but I haven't eaten since breakfast and I'm starving." With that, she turns on her heel and stalks off.

"She really is a pussycat deep... deep down," Naomi says.

"I heard that," Michelle calls over her shoulder.

Naomi chuckles. "I meant you to."

I crane my neck towards the high, cross-beamed ceiling, then glance over to the window.

We're four stories up, overlooking a long stretch of the Daxbridge Canal.

Someone has moored several lazy barges along the towpath.

"Like the view?" Aidan asks.

I turn back to face him and shrug. "It's all right. What is this place, exactly?"

"Our evil lair," Naomi says, deadpan.

I quirk an eyebrow at her.

Her full lips tug up at the corner. "Just kidding. We own the entire building. We live here."

Both my eyebrows shoot up now. "Wait... you all live together?"

Aidan steps closer to Naomi and tucks his arm around her waist. "It's practical. This way, we can move at a moment's notice, which is always a plus when the authorities sniff around."

At the mention of the word *authorities*, my chest tightens.

It doesn't matter how many undercover cases I crush—and I've crushed a lot of cases—moments like this make me feel like I've got Magical Investigations Department stamped across my forehead in big, bold letters.

I needn't worry, though.

Carl Weston has a criminal record as long as an octopus's tentacle.

Keeping my expression blank, and my voice neutral, I say, "And have they? Been sniffing around, I mean."

Aidan laughs, but there's a humourless edge to it. "Hardly. As I'm sure you're aware, given your... history, the MID aren't exactly quick on the uptake. It's embarrassingly easy to stay one step ahead of them. They're a joke, really."

His insult makes me bristle.

Aren't exactly quick on the uptake?

Embarrassingly easy to stay one step ahead of them?

A joke?

Well, the joke's on you, pal.

What a—

"Why so curious?"

I almost flinch.

Michelle must've ducked back into the room without my noticing. Suspicion creases her features.

Heart beating fast, I say, "Call me cautious, but I like to know what I'm getting into. If you've got coppers on your trail, I'd rather cut and run now. I don't know about you, but I don't relish the thought of Purgatory."

She's silent for a while, and I can practically see the cogs whirring while she mulls over my words. Eventually, she says, "Fair enough, I guess."

I hold back a sigh of relief.

She's bought my bluff.

For now.

Yeah.

I'm going to have to keep my wits about me around Michelle Rees.

Quick.

Change the subject.

I reach up and scratch the side of my neck. "Hey. Aren't there four of you? Where's the other guy?"

"Top marks for observation," Michelle says, with a not-so-subtle roll of her eyes.

"Play nice, Chelle." There's a note of warning in Aidan's tone.

"I'm only messing with him. Sort of."

He ignores her. "I sent Eric to wipe your fellow competitor's memories. He shouldn't be too much longer."

I tip my chin in assent and stuff my hands into my pockets. "So, what now?"

"Now," Naomi says, moving to my side and linking her arm through mine, "I'll show you round while Ade makes dinner. Chelle, why don't you phone Eric and see how long he's going to be?"

She phrases this like a question, but the steely edge to her voice makes it an order.

"Fine." Michelle tosses her long red hair over one shoulder and strides from the room.

Living under the same roof as Aidan and his cronies is going to cause problems, because it looks like I might be off grid for longer than Kate expected, and she needs to know.

The question is, how am I going to get out of here to tell her?

"Penny for your thoughts," Naomi says.

"Oh, it's nothing. It's just that if I'm going to be staying here, I'll need to go back to my place and pick up a few things."

Is it my imagination, or does her grip tighten on my arm, just a little? I suppress a shiver.

"Of course. Why don't you have dinner first? Then, when we're done, one of us will go with you."

One of us will go with you.

I force myself to stop my jaw from clenching. "There's no need, really. I can go by myself."

She smiles, but it's tight-lipped. "I'm sure Ade would rather you didn't, at least why you're... settling in."

Ade would prefer you didn't until we're sure we can trust you.

That's what she means.

Fuck.

There's no way out of this.

They'll never let me go alone, and I can't say I blame them.

I'd be keeping a close eye on the newb, as Michelle put it, in their position, too.

I have to warn Kate.

Maybe I can get a message to her somehow.

Maybe—

"Come on," Naomi says. "I'll show you your room first."

"Great," I reply, smiling wide enough to show all my teeth.

Just great.

I have a feeling dinner is going to be interesting.

Chapter 16
Christian

Tour complete, Naomi leads me back through the living space and into the clinical, white-walled kitchen.

A hulking, heavyset man—arms corded with muscle—sits at the sweeping breakfast island. He spins round in his seat.

Eric Jiménez.

"So this is the new guy," he says in a deep baritone.

Aidan turns away from the bubbling pot on the stove. "Ah, there you are. Eric, this is Carl Weston. Carl, meet Eric Jiménez."

Eric stands—towering over me—and sticks out a beefy hand. "Good to meet you, mate."

I slap my hand into his, and we shake firmly. "Same here, man."

He gives me an appraising look. "That was clever, what you did with the supercharged light spell in the maze."

Michelle, who stands to the right of Aidan—gnawing on a hunk of cheese—mutters, "Oh, please."

Hmm. Michelle doesn't trust me.

I'm going to have to address that.

Aidan shoots her a stern look.

I shrug, choosing for the moment to focus on Eric. "Thanks, but it was a pretty basic move. Most witches would've done the same."

"Don't sell yourself short," Naomi says, drawing herself up to her full height. "The ability to think on your feet in a challenging situation is rare."

"And talk about powerful," Aidan says, pulling knives and forks from a drawer and taking them over to the round table in the centre of the room. "You didn't disappoint on that score, either. Like I said earlier, impressive."

Michelle rolls her eyes, a now familiar expression. "Don't go overboard. He won't be able to fit his head through the door."

Aidan pauses by an open cupboard.

I spot a jar holding a handful of liquid silver syringes.

Hmm.

That could be handy in a pinch.

"Chelle..." There's a warning note in Aidan's tone.

This might be the perfect chance to break the ice with Michelle.

"No," I jump in. "She's right. I'm nothing special. Just used to getting myself out of tight spots, that's all."

Does her frigid gaze thaw a little?

"Humph," is all she says.

An awkward silence falls.

Eventually, Aidan reaches for the cutlery he'd dropped on the table, and carries on setting our places. Once he's done, he crosses back to the cooker and lifts the lid off the pot.

The rich, tangy scent of melted cheese wafts through the room.

My stomach issues a loud grumble.

It's been the better part of a day since I ate anything, and I'm starving.

"What's for dinner?" I ask.

"Carbonara," Aidan replies, giving the bubbling sauce a stir.

"I married Ade for his carbonara," Naomi stage whispers, a twinkle in her eye.

He chuckles. "I thought you married me because you loved me."

"That, too, I suppose."

Aidan shakes his head. "It's ready to dish up. Why don't you take your seats before I change my mind about feeding you?"

I'm nonplussed.

This display of familial domesticity isn't exactly what I'd expected to encounter.

In all my years with the MID, I've never come across a Supernatural Organised Crime Group that seems so... regular.

Seems being the key word.

I can't forget why I'm here.

Aidan has the crown, and it's my job to find it.

The question is, when I do, how the hell am I going to reach out to Kate?

My stomach rumbles again.

I'll worry about that later.

I stuff down my hundredth mouthful of pasta with gusto.

All I can say is, wow.

Naomi wasn't exaggerating about Aidan's culinary skills.

Hell, if the guy proposed to me right now, I'd probably marry him for this sauce, too.

Eric takes a slug of wine before turning his attention to me. "So. What's your story?"

Suddenly, the sauce loses all taste, and the texture of the pasta turns claggy.

My heart skips several beats.

Calm down.

I knew they were going to ask questions like these.

It's nothing I haven't handled before.

Chew.

Swallow.

Take a breath.

"How do you mean?" I ask.

Eric laughs. "Dude, relax. The interview's over. You're in. I'm just trying to get to know the new guy, is all."

"Erm—"

"I have a better question," Michelle says, running a scarlet-painted fingernail around the rim of her wineglass. "Why so defensive?"

Jesus.

This woman has it in for me big time.

Definitely need to watch my step.

I lean back in my chair. "I'm not being defensive."

"No?" She raises an eyebrow in challenge.

"No, but I'm not exactly used to opening up in my line of work, either."

She smiles at me, but it lacks warmth. "Oh, I know all about your line of work. I ran a thorough background check on you. What I don't get—"

"I think what Chelle's trying to say," Aidan cuts in, "is we're far more tight-knit than most of the groups you're used to working with."

"No," she says, without taking her eyes off me, an edge of sharpness to her tone. "What Chelle's trying to say is you've been out of the game for a while. Why the sudden jump back into the life?"

I bristle.

Naomi and Eric are watching me, waiting for my reaction.

I get the sense what I say next will determine how well I cement myself in Pentacle's ranks and, despite what Eric said about the interview being over, I have a feeling it's only just beginning.

Well, playing nice clearly isn't an option for dealing with Michelle Rees.

She's a bully.

And there's only one way to deal with bullies.

Fight back.

I lace my fingers behind my head and mimic Michelle's wolfish grin, taking up as much space as I can to show her she doesn't intimidate me. "If I'd known you were going to be part of *the life*, I wouldn't have bothered."

Eric snorts.

Naomi places her hand to her lips to disguise a smile.

A hot flush creeps up Michelle's neck and into her cheeks, standing out in stark contrast to her pale skin.

"Nice one," Eric says through a chuckle.

"Shut up," Michelle snaps at him.

Play it carefully.

I need to stand my ground, but I can't afford to alienate Michelle completely.

If what Aidan said is true about Pentacle being a tight-knit group, I'm sure her opinion holds a lot of sway with him.

I wink at her and inject more warmth into my smile to show her I'm only messing around.

"At least you give as good as you get," she says.

See?

What did I tell you?

Only one way to deal with bullies.

I take a sip from my wineglass before saying, "Truth is, the last job I was on paid really well, but the money ran out. I've got expensive tastes."

"You're not kidding," Michelle concedes. "That Beamer must've set you back some."

Shit.

The car.

I'd parked it on the edge of the industrial estate.

Kate will go spare if it gets damaged.

I clear my throat. "About that..."

"Don't worry," Eric says. "I drove it back here."

"You drove my car?"

"Relax. It's still in one piece."

"It had better be."

He just laughs.

I take another sip of wine, the dry sharpness dancing across my tongue. "Mind if I ask a question?"

Aidan sets down his knife and fork. "That depends what it is."

"No offense, the pasta's great and everything, but I came here because you promised power. Nobody's actually told me what this power is."

The smile slides off Eric's face.

Naomi's mouth tilts down at the corners.

Even Michelle remains silent for once.

All eyes turn to Aidan.

"That's not a question," he says, eyes glittering.

My gaze flicks around the group. "What? What did I say?"

Naomi reaches across the table and folds her hand over Aidan's. "It's your story to tell, love."

I stare at Aidan.

He stares right back. "You don't mess around, do you?"

"I prefer the direct approach." I lean forward a little.

Aidan wipes his mouth on the corner of a napkin. "I respect that. Let me be equally direct." He balls the napkin up and drops it onto his plate. "We're going to summon a demon."

Chapter 17
Christian

We're going to summon a demon.

I knew that's what he was going to say, but still... I can't wrap my head around the fact he believes in the King Arthur legend.

He's clearly intelligent. The way he talks, carries himself, and even his unquestionable leadership over Pentacle all points that way. So what drives a man like him to believe in some crazy myth?

"Demons don't exist." The words are out of my mouth, deadpan, before I can stop them.

A muscle in his jaw ticks. "No?"

"No. Everyone knows that."

Michelle glares daggers at me from across the table.

Naomi wears a disappointed frown.

Eric's gaze remains glued to Aidan and the twitch, twitch, twitch of that muscle.

Eventually, voice as firm as a steel blade, Aidan says, "Tell me. How much do you know about the King Arthur legend?"

I've strolled too far down the path of brashness to turn back now. "Enough to know it can't be real."

Naomi says, "Carl—"

"No." Aidan cuts across her. "It's fine." The tempo of the twitching muscle increases. "What makes you think the legend isn't real?"

I can't believe he's seriously asking me this question.

Pushing my plate aside, I say, "Honestly?"

Aidan takes a deep breath. "Honestly."

"Because it's ridiculous."

Michelle launches to her feet. "Is this guy for real? Listen. I don't know who the fu—"

"I said it's fine." Aidan's voice cracks like a witch-whip.

Michelle flinches.

"Sit down," he says.

She does as she's told.

Why do they all obey Aidan so readily?

Respect?

Admiration?

Fear?

Any of those labels would fit.

A little of all three, perhaps.

"Ridiculous?" He arches an eyebrow at me. "Explain."

I shift in my seat and place my hands on the table. "Think about it. It's impossible. Say demons and sorcerers exist. Where are they? Entire races of people don't just vanish off the face of the Earth without leaving a trace."

Eric stares at me now, eyebrows raised. "I thought you said you knew the legend. Demons were—"

"Banished, I know," I interject.

I'd read *Myth & Magic: The Truth About Sorcerers, Demons & the Legend of King Arthur* shortly after I Manifested, but my parents always told me to take it with a massive pinch of salt.

One particular passage comes back to me now.

> *Elaine, outraged by her brother's murder and mad with grief, demanded justice. She, along with those still loyal to Arthur, used their considerable powers to banish all demons to another dimension, which they named* Gehenna, *or Hell.*

> *The Gates of Hell—towering doors composed of human bones—were sealed for all eternity, the demons imprisoned behind them, unable to escape.*

"Well, there you are," Aidan says, breaking me out of my reverie. "That explains where all the demons went."

I shake my head. "Yeah, but what about the rest of it? What about the Gates of Hell?"

"What about them?"

"Surely someone would have noticed 'towering doors composed of human bones'?"

"Please." Michelle snatches up her plate and shoves her chair back with considerable force, rushing to her feet. "Use your brain. You're a witch. You know as well as we do that magic can hide things."

I have to concede she's right on that score.

"Fair enough. Maybe you can explain the disappearance of demons, but what about the sorcerers? Where are they?"

Michelle just rolls her eyes and stalks over to the sink.

The twitching in Aidan's jaw has stopped, and his mouth lifts at the corner—half grin, half sneer. "Let me guess, you read *Myth & Magic*?"

I shrug. "Yeah, so?"

"That's where I started, too. I've learned a lot since then."

"What do you—"

"Sorcerers withdrew from the world voluntarily."

I snort. "You can't know that."

"Like I said, I've learned a lot. Some texts say witches grew to fear sorcery. The sorcerers were worried they would suffer the same fate as the demons. The most powerful among them created Nexuses—dimensions that exist outside of time and space—where the Ley Lines intersect."

Nexuses?

Ley Lines?

What is he—

Wait.

"What texts?" I ask.

"Come with me," Aidan says, rising from the table and striding across the kitchen, towards the door.

Eric stands, too. "Want us to come with you?"

"No need," Aidan says. "Why don't you all clear up while I educate our new friend?"

I hurry to catch up with him. "Where are we going?"

"The library."

CHAPTER 18
Christian

Aidan leads me out of the living quarters, down a set of stairs, and up to a wide pair of heavy, wooden double doors.

He waves his hand over the handles and murmurs a string of Latin phrases, before working his fingers in a picking motion.

I realise then he's unpicking a witch-weave.

Whatever texts he's keeping behind these doors must be rare and valuable.

Aidan finishes unpicking the weave, and a dull *snap* cut through the silence.

He pushes the doors open, we walk through, and my jaw drops.

The library is enormous, the high ceilings supported by thick brick pillars. Mahogany bookcases line every single wall, each one crammed full of doorstep-sized, leather-bound tomes.

My nostrils flare.

The room smells of polish and the musty-sweet scent of old books.

Aidan chuckles at my shocked expression. "Impressed?"

"I'll say." I stroll across the room, my boots thudding across the floor, the sound echoing around the cavernous space. When I reach the first row of bookcases, I brush the tips of my fingers along the cracked spines.

The titles that leap out at me are foreign.

The Rise and Fall of Morgana le Fay: the Clairvoyant Enchantress.
Shadowmancy: A Guide to Demonic Power.
Curses & Gifts: The Abilities of Demons and Sorcerers.

I reach for that final tome.

Aidan clears his throat behind me.

My fingers halt, and I crane my neck to look at him. "May I?"

"Of course."

I slide the heavy book off the shelf.

The cover has a crack running down the centre.

I prise the cover open, releasing the strong waft of ancient paper and ink, and flip through the first few pages.

A particular section of text snags my attention.

> *Whereas a witch's power comes from within, demonic power comes from without. Demons—much like their counterparts, the sorcerers—possess the ability to harness the energy of the Ley Lines (the primordial force that gives life to the universe). When channeled by demons, the power of the Lines manifests as a dark shadow, hence the term shadowmancy. Demons can manipulate the Lines to produce various results (listed overleaf)—*

I tear my eyes away, and turn the page, my eyes instantly locking onto the aforementioned list.

Coercion: The ability to compel someone to take a certain action.

Possession: The ability to take ownership of a willing (or unwilling) host's body.

The Shadow-strike: A destructive force that can wound, maim and/or kill.

The Shadow-shield: A defensive (almost indestructible) barrier. Unlike barrier spells cast by witches, a demonic shadow-shield can defend against physical, as well as magical, attacks.

Telekinesis: The ability to move matter with one's mind.

Teleportation: The ability to move from one physical location to another in the blink of an eye, with no need for a portal.

Temporomancy: The ability to manipulate time, including slowing time, freezing time, and (in some extremely rare cases) reversing time.

Transference: The ability to infuse matter or energy with shadowmancy.

Curses: Only the most powerful demons are blessed with a Curse (one unique power only they can wield). Notable Curses include: Empathy, Immortality, Wish Fulfillment, Shape-shifting, and The Touch of Death [this list is not exhaustive].

I glance up from the page, mouth agape. "This is crazy."

"No." There's an impatient bite in Aidan's tone. "It's history."

I run my finger down the page again. "This says demons and sorcerers tap into the power of the Ley Lines. So... what? They have the same powers?"

Aidan shakes his head. "They share similar abilities, but it's a little more complicated than that."

I wait, confident he won't be able to resist the urge to explain.

I'm proven right a second later.

"The Ley Lines are raw energy. When a demon channels them, they produce darkness. When a sorcerer channels them, they produce light."

"What are you saying? Demons are evil and sorcerers are good."

He sighs, clearly frustrated. "Again, I don't think it's that simple. From what I've read, it's true that demons have a duplicitous nature, but I think it's more about balance. The universe is a place of light and darkness. One can't exist without the other."

"Two sides of the same coin, then."

"Something like that."

I close the book and place it back on the shelf. "Where did you get all this stuff?"

Aidan's almond-toed Oxford shoes tap across the floor. "This stuff, as you so eloquently put it, is my life's work."

"And you believe what this book says about Telekinesis, and Possession, and Curses?"

"I do."

I search his face, looking for any signs he's joking. Unsurprisingly, I find nothing.

"Demons don't exist," I say, repeating my earlier words from the kitchen.

Aidan's mouth pinches into a firm line. "Funny. According to mortals, we don't exist either. Yet, here we are."

I resist the urge to click my tongue. "That's different."

He places his hands behind his back and paces around the edge of the library.

I follow in his wake.

"Why?" he asks, all traces of his earlier irritation gone.

"Why, what?"

"Why is it different?"

"Because it is."

"Expand."

"Hiding ourselves after The Witch Trials was our only viable option. It was the only way to stop the killings."

Aidan waits. "Some humans still believe in magic. What's the difference?"

I roll my eyes. "They really don't."

He raises his eyebrows. "No?"

"No."

"I disagree. They celebrate Samhain, attend Tarot readings, visit mediums. Some of them even practise what they think is witchcraft."

"None of which is real magic."

"True, but why do you think they do these things?"

"I... I don't know."

"They pursue the occult, because deep down, they know magic exists."

"And your point is?"

"My point is, no matter how hard we've tried, we haven't erased the notion of magic entirely. We can say the same of demons and sorcerers. These books came from somewhere. Someone wrote them."

"Come on, it's just a legend."

He gazes around the library. "Aren't all the best legends true?"

I shake my head.

There's no reasoning with him.

He has too much faith in his convictions for them to be shaken.

We move further into the forest of bookcases, Aidan continuing his slow pacing around the library.

"So, you've dedicated your life to this, huh?"

He nods. "I have."

"What if you're wrong?"

"I'm not."

"You don't—"

"We met one."

A shiver runs down my spine.

We met one.

Despite myself, when I speak, my voice tremors a little. "You met one of what?"

"A demon." Aidan whispers the word with something akin to reverence.

I shoot him a look. "Bullshit."

"It's not. And I can prove it."

With each step I take, my throat gets tighter and tighter and tighter, the air becoming difficult to breathe.

He can't believe this, surely?

But he sounds so certain.

I can prove it.

"How?"

"With this."

We round the corner and enter a shadowy alcove, and there—sitting alone on a raised pedestal—sits the crown.

The crown.

The thing I've come all this way for.

Sitting right in front of me, there for the taking.

I'm tempted to just grab it and portal out... but I can't risk it.

Aidan's standing too close. Chances are, he'd stop me before I made my move.

Then I'd have a lot of explaining to do.

I keep my expression neutral. "What is it?"

Aidan narrows his eyes at me. "A crown. What does it look like? Can you guess who it belonged to?"

I don't need to guess. I know exactly who Aidan *thinks* the crown belonged to.

King Arthur.

But that's ridiculous.

Just like sorcerers and demons, King Arthur is nothing but a myth.

I shrug. "No idea."

"This," Aidan pauses for dramatic effect, "is the Cursed Crown of King Arthur."

I force a laugh. "Oh, come on."

He ignores my mocking tone. "Do you know why they say it's Cursed?"

"Enlighten me."

"When the demons succeeded in their plot to overthrow Arthur, with the help of Morgana Le Fey, the King's full-blood sister Elaine—"

"Tell me something I don't know."

This time, Aidan doesn't ignore my scoffing.

Instead, he lowers his voice and, with blade-sharp words, whispers, "Watch your tone."

I remain silent.

Eventually, Aidan says, "Elaine and the witches of Camelot banded together to banish the demons. Using a potent blend of portal witchcraft and sorcery, they created an entirely new dimension. They named this dimension *Gehenna*, or Hell."

I resist the urge to roll my eyes. One, I don't believe a word he's saying. Two, I have zero clue what this has to do with the crown.

"Alternate dimensions need to be anchored to a place or an object."

"A place," I interject.

He nods. "Take the Seven Wonders of the World, for example. Each of these acts as a Key to another dimension."

I shoot him the side eye. "You're shitting me?"

"I can assure you I'm not. The object Elaine chose as Hell's anchor was..."

"The crown."

"Exactly. The crown is the Key to the Gates, but it's also the Key to accessing demonic power and demonic Curses. Hence, the Cursed Crown."

"It's just a crown."

Aidan points a slim finger toward the pedestal. "See that symbol at the front?"

Again, I don't need to see this symbol—I've seen it before.

A golden circle divided into four sections by a vertical and horizontal line. Each quadrant houses a glyph. A pair of cupped hands, representing mortals. The golden sun, symbolising sorcerers. A pentagram, characterising witches. And, in the last segment, a razor-sharp crescent moon, delineating demons.

Aidan lowers his hand. "Each of the four symbols represents—"

"I know," I cut across him. "But it's just a story."

"No. Not a story. I'll say it again. It's *history*."

I scrunch my face up. "That symbol proves nothing. Anyone could've made this crown. There's no way to verify its authenticity, or to confirm it belonged to King Arthur."

"But I have verified it." Aidan's eyes shine with fervour. "Like I said, we've met a demon."

That odd shiver passes over me again, but I shake it off. "How? They were all banished to Hell, remember?"

Aidan steps over to the pedestal and lifts the crown into his hands.

The golden glyph shines as it catches the light.

Aidan says, "Every set of doors, once created, cannot exist without a key. It is the natural order of things."

He's quoting from *Myth & Magic*.

Oh, yeah.

According to Aidan, the crown is supposed to be the Key to the Gates of Hell.

As if reading my mind, Aidan says, "I put the crown on, and it divulged the spell."

"What spell?"

"The spell to unlock the Gates. The Key. We tried to summon a demon, but we didn't have enough power to pull him all the way through."

"Him?"

He bobs his head. "He appeared as this surge of thick, black smoke."

Thick, black smoke.

A line from *Curses & Gifts: The Abilities of Demons and Sorcerers* runs through my mind.

When channeled by demons, the power of the Lines manifests as a dark shadow, hence the term shadowmancy.

My mouth goes dry.

He's mad.

Aidan is off his fucking rocker.

There's no way...

"Who was he? This... demon?" I ask.

"He didn't give a name." Aidan's expression remains stoic.

I can't believe it.

He really thinks he spoke to a demon.

Bat-shit crazy.

I shift from foot to foot. "What you're saying is impossible. Demons don't—"

"He told us we needed a fifth. Another powerful witch to complete the summoning. That's why you're here."

That book—the list of demonic powers—mentioned something else.

Transference.

The ability to transfer demonic power from one being to another.

"You think this demon can give you—us—more power?"

So, the crown isn't a source of power. It's merely a gateway to the demon, and the power he can supposedly provide. Aidan's plan is ludicrous, but... what if there's a grain of truth to the King Arthur myth?

What if he pulls this off?

He seems so sure.

A sickly tingle spreads through my gut.

As if reading my mind, Aiden says, "I *think* nothing."

I know one thing about Aidan Adedeji.

He's charismatic.

That much is clear.

Charming enough to convince a group of people—his wife included—they spoke to a demon.

I'm not surprised.

After all, mortals have filled their history books with tales of magnetic leaders who've convinced entire nations to believe in their twisted ideals, to engage in abominable acts of violence.

Why should witches be any different?

But this...

Mental or not, I have to go along with his plan, at least until I can communicate with Kate and find out how she wants me to handle this.

When I speak again, I force false-awe into my tone. "It's... real." No, it isn't.

"As real as you and I."

Oh, Jesus. He's so full of himself, he hasn't registered my falsehood. "This is... incredible. What else did he say?"

"Nothing. The pull of the Gates dragged him back to Hell."

The pull of the Gates.

Please.

I can't believe I'm engaging in this.

What's he going to tell me next?

That Santa Claus dropped off his Christmas presents early, and he fed Rudolph a carrot?

Lunacy.

Regardless, I press on. "How did you get into this?"

Aidan runs his finger along one bookshelf, disturbing a thin layer of dust. He wipes his fingers on his trousers. "My father. This library was his, originally,"

My eyebrows shoot up. "Your dad?"

He shrugs. "He always believed the King Arthur myth."

"And he never attracted the MID's attention?"

A small smile crosses his face. "His collection was much smaller back then. Easier to stay under the radar."

I mull over everything Aidan has told me before asking the obvious question. "I don't get it. Aren't you strong enough already? The portals, the memory spells… what exactly are you going to do with all this power?"

Aidan's silent for a long time.

Seconds, minutes tick by.

I hold my body tense, sensing that what he's going to say next is monumental.

I'm not wrong.

Eventually, he says, "I'm going to destroy The Witches Council."

Chapter 19
Christian

The bottom drops out of my stomach.

Destroy the Witches Council?

What does he mean, he's going to destroy The Witches Council?

That kind of thinking is madness.

The Witches Council is a force for good.

After The Witch Trials in the 1500s, they helped hide us, helped us flourish in a world dominated by mortals. Their rules give us purpose and provide structure.

They keep us safe.

For what seems like an eternity, I stare at Aidan in open-mouthed shock. I try to respond, but my voice comes out as a dry croak. I clear my throat, and ask, "Why? Why would you want to do that?"

Aidan turns his back on me, pacing back the way we came.

I follow him, mute.

This can't be happening.

The way Aidan is talking is tantamount to treason.

I've heard a lot of crazy shit over the course of my career, but I've never heard something like this.

If he were to succeed in his plan to destroy the Council…

All the rules we live by, the checks and balances—not exposing our power to mortals who would do us harm, the threat of imprisonment for misuse of magic, the way our entire society not just functions… but thrives—gone forever.

It would be carnage.

A shiver runs the length of my spine.

It doesn't bear thinking about.

We're almost back at the entrance to the library when I find my voice again. "Answer me."

He whirls around, onyx black eyes gleaming like sharpened blades. "Trust me when I tell you The Witches Council is not what it appears to be."

An odd, tingling sensation spreads across the base of my skull, the skin on my scalp pulling tight.

Not what it appears to be.

What's he talking about?

"You're going to have to be a little more specific," I say.

The door, which Aidan must've left ajar when we came into the room, creaks open.

Naomi's concerned face appears in the crack. "You need to tell him."

A pained expression crosses Aidan's face, and he tilts his head down.

"Tell him about Jules," she presses in a gentle voice.

My gaze flits between Naomi and Aidan, and a crease forms between my eyebrows. "Who's Jules?"

Aidan takes a deep, steadying breath and, when he turns back to me, he looks a good ten years older. "My sister. She was my sister."

Was?

"She's..."

"Dead?" He gives a laugh so bitter it taints the air. "They murdered her."

I swallow, hard. "Who?"

"The precious Witches Council."

I stagger back like he shoved me.

They murdered her.

The Witches Council.

No.

That can't be true.

The Witches Council wouldn't do that. Their whole ethos is about protecting witches, not killing them.

Christ, they haven't issued a kill order in decades.

I don't know who put this idea into Aidan's head, but he's wrong.

I take a tentative step towards him, hands outstretched and palms facing down like I'm trying to placate a rabid animal. "Look. Obviously, I'm not the biggest fan of the Witches Council either—and I'm all for bending the rules—but what you're saying is insane. They don't kill people."

Aidan narrows his eyes at me.

Naomi wears a tight little frown.

"For someone who claims not to be a fan of the Council," Aidan says, steel in his tone, "you're doing a brilliant job of defending them."

Shit.

I'd let Christian slip through.

My name is Carl Weston...

I'm twenty-nine years old...

Recovering quickly, I roll my eyes and force my voice to come out sharply. "I'm not defending them. They don't kill people because they don't have the guts. I just—"

Aidan lunges at me, wedging his forearm beneath my chin and driving me back into a bookcase.

Pain shoots through my spine on impact and I have to grit my teeth to contain a cry.

He gets right in my face, so close I can see myself reflected in the white of his eyes. "You know nothing." The words are almost a whisper.

My mouth goes dry.

His mood changed so quickly.

Genial one moment, murderous the next.

"Ade." Naomi takes a step towards us. "Let him go."

Aidan's nostrils flare and, for a second, I don't think he's going to listen.

Then he backs away and says, "Do you remember the Siren Murders?"

Siren Murders?

Sounds familiar.

It takes a second to place the name, but I get there fast.

The Siren Murders happened long before I joined the MID, back when I was a kid.

I'd read the files as part of my studies at the MID training college. They began in the early 1990s and ended in early 2000. Over the course of a decade, a female witch abducted, tortured, and murdered fifteen mortal men in the most gruesome fashion.

They found one man beheaded, castrated, and left to rot.

The woman responsible—although she'd always maintained her innocence—took her life in her cell in Purgatory in 2010.

But that means...

"Shit," I say, pushing off from the bookshelf and fixing Aidan with a glare. "Jules? Your sister was Juliana Caldwell."

His fists clench. "Yes."

"But she committed suicide. The Witches Council didn't—"

"The Council might not have killed her with their own hands, but they might as well have. She was only in that foul place because of their lies."

That gives me pause. "Lies?"

"She didn't—" His eyes fill with moisture and his words choke off. "She wasn't…" His entire face crumples, and he lets out an anguished wail.

Naomi's by his side in seconds, folding him into her arms, and patting the back of his head like he's a frightened child. "It's okay. Hush now. It's okay. I've got you."

It seems wrong, perverse even, to witness Aidan's breakdown. I straighten my spine. "Look, I don't know what's going on here, but—"

Naomi fixes me with a hard stare. "Does the name Fabian Naismith mean anything to you?"

The room is suddenly hot.

Yes.

That name means something to me.

Fabian Naismith is the head of The Witches Council.

I've met him frequently, and he seems like a nice bloke. A bit of a fuddy-duddy perhaps, but nice all the same.

The words freeze in my throat, so I merely bob my head.

Aidan's sobs subside and he extracts himself from Naomi's embrace, crossing to one of the tall windows. He faces out into the city, silhouetted by the setting sun. "She was his assistant."

I know this.

It's all in her file.

"His assistant?" I ask.

He scrubs at his face and, when he faces the room again, his eyes are dry. "He told everyone he fired her for gross misconduct, that she snapped and went on a killing spree."

"That's what happened, isn't it?"

"*No!*" He jabs a finger at me, a dark shadow crossing his face. "That's a lie. My sister would never—she was the kindest, sweetest person I knew. She would never…" Just like before, back in the kitchen, a muscle ticks in his jaw, and I can tell he's close to boiling point.

I have to defuse this before it gets out of hand.

"Okay." I keep my voice level and calm. "Okay. So, tell me what happened then?"

Aidan snorts, loud and derisive. "That disgusting pervert Naismith was sexually harassing her. She knocked him back, and he fired her. He said…" He closes his eyes, takes a deep breath, his nostrils flaring. "He said that 'someone like her' should be grateful for his attention."

"What do you mean, 'someone like her'?"

"Take a wild guess."

I'm non-plussed. "Because she was his assistant?"

His eyes narrow to slits.

Understanding dawns.

"Because… because she was black."

He gives a tight, grim nod.

No.

I can't reconcile this.

Naismith might be a lot of things.

Old school.

Stuck in his ways.

Sure.

But this…

I cross my arms. "If that's true—"

"It is true."

It wasn't Aidan who spoke this time; it was Naomi.

Her features are hard and cold, like marble. She clenches her fists so hard her knuckles crack.

It is true.

The acid—the sheer venom in her words—is enough to curdle milk.

Tread carefully.

"Fine," I say. "But why didn't Julianna report him?"

Naomi tilts her chin at me. "You're bi-ethnic. Italian, Spanish maybe?"

"My mum's Spanish." I shrug. "So?"

"Have you ever experienced racism?"

I duck my head. It's not something I care to dwell on. "Once or twice."

Click.

Click.

Click.

It's the sound of Naomi's heels crossing the library.

When I glance up, she stands right in front of me. "Only once or twice? You're one of the lucky ones."

Aidan barks out a harsh laugh. "That's putting it mildly."

"What are you saying?" I ask.

"Jules did report Naismith," Aidan says.

"Then—"

He cuts across me. "Who do you think they listened to? The lowly black assistant, or the rich white lawyer?" He arches an eyebrow at me, waiting for an answer.

I can't fathom a response.

The picture he's painting of Naismith... it doesn't gel with the man I know.

And surely I would know.

Wouldn't I?

If he was racist—if he was some kind of sexual predator—I would know.

I would've picked up on it.

Spotted the signs.

I'd always felt included when he was around.

I'd never heard him utter a single slur.

Aidan must be mistaken.

"Jules wouldn't go quietly," Naomi says. "Naismith didn't know who committed those murders, and he didn't care. Didn't matter. He was smart enough to pin everything on Jules. All to protect his precious fucking career."

"Who told you this?" I asked, my voice quiet.

"Jules told me herself," Aidan says, a hint of challenge in his voice, daring me to refute his sister's account.

There's a snag though.

If Naismith framed Julianna, why didn't she expose him at her trial?

As if he can read my mind, Aidan says, "I know what you're thinking. The trial. She couldn't say anything."

"Why not?"

Aidan opens his mouth, closes it again, grits his teeth, and goes back to staring out of the window.

Naomi crosses to him and rubs a spot between his shoulder blades. "That bastard Naismith visited Jules in her cell one night. He threatened her. He told her if she implicated him, he'd make sure her entire family suffered."

They both speak with such vehemence, such utter conviction...

The smallest sliver of doubt works its way into my core.

Aidan strides up to me, his mouth set into a firm line. "Naismith and his precious Council are rotten to the core. They all played their part in Jules's death, and I'm going to bring them down." He slides a hand into his pocket, pulls out his wallet, and extracts a small square of paper.

"What's that?"

He hands it to me.

A photo.

A picture of Julianna Caldwell.

I've seen photos of her before, taken right after her trial.

In those pictures, dark circles ring her hollow eyes, her cheekbones are scythe-sharp, and someone's buzzed her hair close to her scalp.

She looks guilty.

Caught red-handed.

Surely, the woman in this photo can't be the same person.

Flawless skin.

Playful brown eyes.

Alight.

Alive!

Dark curls gleaming.

Shy smile threatening to break out.

She looks so...

Kind.

Sweet.

Innocent.

Words I never thought I'd associate with the infamous Siren.

"This is her," I say, with more than a little astonishment in my voice.

"You sound surprised."

"It's just... she's not what I expected, not after hearing the stories."

Naomi clicks her tongue. "Then Naismith did his job. I knew Jules almost as well as Ade, and I'm telling you, she was a good person."

"The best of all of us," Aidan murmurs.

Perhaps the look on Julianna's face at trial wasn't guilt.

Maybe it was something else.

Defeat.

But...

What they're saying can't be true.

I keep circling back to it.

The man they're describing isn't Fabian Naismith.

He's all about promoting an inclusive culture in the witching community. That's why we elected him. Naismith's the one who outlawed hate crimes against vessels.

Vessels like John.

Surely, someone who was trying to make life better for people like my brother wouldn't destroy Aidan's sister.

I can't stop the question that bursts from me. "What about the vessels?"

"What about them?" Aidan asks.

I reach up and tighten the band around the knot of hair fastened at the nape of my neck. "I'm just saying, if it weren't for The Witches Council—Naismith in particular—witches would still shun them."

"You seem to know an awful lot about how The Witches Council works," says a sharp voice from the doorway.

I turn.

Michelle.

Clouds of suspicion gather in her eyes. "Why would that be, I wonder?"

Chapter 20
Christian

Aidan and Naomi turn to me, both wearing expressions laced with suspicion, just like Michelle.

Heat creeps up the back of my neck.

Fuck, fuck, fuck.

I should never have opened my mouth.

I smooth my face into a blank expression. "I make it my business to know the law."

Michelle snorts. "Why?"

I give a louder snort of my own, mocking her.

Her eyes narrow and, if looks could flay skin, she'd be wearing mine like a onesie.

"Isn't it obvious?" I retort. "Knowing the law's the best way to get around it. You said you did thorough background checks on me?"

Michelle folds her arms and looks down her nose like I'm a steaming pile of dog shit. "Yeah?"

"Then you know the MID has never caught me. Why do you think that is?"

For once, Michelle keeps her mouth shut.

I've flummoxed her.

Good.

I march up to her. "It's because I stay one step ahead. I'm smarter than them because I know the law, because I know my rights, and because I know how to get away with pretty much anything." My voice drops a couple of octaves. "Including murder."

Two high spots of colour appear on Michelle's cheeks. "Is that a threat?" she hisses.

I've taken it this far.

May as well go the whole hog.

I step even closer to her, so we breathe the same air. "Let's hope you never have to find out."

My heart hammers in my chest.

My bluff has to work.

It has to.

If Pentacle rumbles me, then—

Michelle takes a step back and glances at Aidan.

I follow her gaze.

He's smirking.

But at whom?

Michelle?

Or me?

Silence blankets the room.

My heart beats faster, and faster, and faster—

Aidan laughs, a big hearty laugh, which bounces off the walls.

I flinch.

"I knew you'd fit right in," he says, wiping his eyes.

Michelle makes a huffy noise, spins on her heel and stalks from the room.

Naomi grins. "You handled that well."

"Thanks."

"Would you mind having a word with her, my love?" Aidan says.

"Of course."

Click.

Click.

Click.

Naomi's gone.

That leaves Aidan and me.

"Where were we?" he asks.

"Vessels," I reply, trying my best to ignore the stab of pain that goes through my stomach at the thought of John.

"Ah, yes." He taps a finger against the side of his leg. "What you need to understand is The Witches Council makes all the right noises and passes all the right policies. Why do you think that is?"

"Because they think they're doing the right thing."

Aidan smirk is back. "No. They do it to keep the witching community on side. To keep us in line. To stop a revolt."

The word *revolt* sends a static buzz from the crown of my head to the soles of my shoes.

Treason.

"Imagine it. If we all banded together, we could easily take them down."

Treason.

"Unfortunately," Aidan continues, "most witches worship them, treat them like gods. But they aren't. They're small-minded politicians who seek only to control us. They even dictate when we can and can't tell our children they're witches."

Treason.

Hearing Aidan talk like this—the full power of his charisma on display...

He speaks with such eloquence, such urgency, such authenticity.

I get why the others have bought into his vision for the future.

Speeches like this could bring the right sort of person round to his way of thinking.

I'm *not* the right sort of person.

Even if what he's saying about Naismith is true—and I'm not saying I believe him—there are better ways to handle it than staging a coup.

There should be an investigation.

The MID should arrest him.

There should be justice.

Aidan's a fanatic, nothing more.

And there's also a fucking enormous elephant in the room.

The fictional demon he thinks he can summon.

But...

I need to make out like I'm on board with him.

At least for the moment.

That's the hardest thing about undercover work.

Pretending to sympathise with criminals.

It doesn't sit well with my moral compass.

Then again, maybe it wouldn't be that difficult, after all.

Hasn't Aidan just given me the perfect opening?

A platform to integrate myself fully into Pentacle?

Sorry, John.

I hate to use his story to my advantage, but needs must.

"My brother's a vessel," I say in a quiet voice, dipping my head low.

Aidan's gaze sharpens. "I didn't realise you had a brother. It didn't come up in any of Chelle's background research."

"No." I give a hollow laugh. "It wouldn't have. He... He went missing years ago." Time to twist the truth, even though I know it'll be like twisting the knife into my gut. "My parents hated what he was. They treated him like shit. That's why he ran away. I couldn't stand being around them anymore, so I got out of there."

Sympathy softens Aidan's features. "I'm sorry he suffered."

"Me too." At least I can say that with sincerity.

John had suffered.

More than any of us realised.

Aidan does something that surprises me.

He walks over and enfolds me in a tight hug.

I shove down my inclination to blast him away from me with a burst of magic and return the embrace.

When he draws back, he says, voice almost gentle, "That must've been terrible for you."

"It was." The strain in my voice is real.

"Where was the Council then?"

Bitter water swirls in my stomach.

He has a point.

Aidan claps me on the shoulder. "See? All their proselytising about equality means nothing. The Council's corrupt. They need to be dismantled. Whatever it takes."

Aidan's earlier words from the competition float into my mind.

No killing. Pentacle stands for empowering witches.

"I thought you were all about empowerment," I say, "not killing."

He steps back and considers me. "I said we don't kill witches who don't deserve it. I said nothing about the ones who do."

His words leave me cold.

I clear my throat. "Say we do this. Say, by some miracle, we conjure a demon and bring down The Witches Council. Who's going to rule in their place?"

I have a feeling I already know the answer and, with his next breath, Aidan confirms it.

"Us, of course. Who else? Who better to rule than those of us who know what it's like to live in an unjust society? We will reshape our community. We will bring balance to chaos. And, above all else, we will bring justice to those who deserve it." His eyes shine with righteousness.

Wow!

He really believes he's doing the right thing.

My mind drifts back to all the ramifications of a life without The Council.

If Aidan's plan comes to fruition, the only thing he'll do is plunge the witching community into chaos.

Aidan crosses his arms. "The only question is… are you in?"

There's only one response I can give.

Only one answer he'll accept, if I want to keep my cover intact.

"I'm in."

Chapter 21
Christian

Early the following night, at ten minutes to midnight, Aidan calls everyone together in the living area.

He instructs us to wear our crimson robes.

I feel like a right gonk wearing mine, and tug at the heavy velvet sleeve.

Sweat pools at the base of my spine.

The summer heat and this outfit don't mix.

The material is too thick, and I'm sweltering.

Eric stifles a yawn. "What's all this about?"

Aidan has that familiar, fanatical light in his eyes. "It's time."

Michelle's gaze snaps to Aidan's. "You mean…"

"Yes." Aidan shoots us all a wolfish grin. "Today, we summon a demon."

I almost roll my eyes.

Almost.

Not long now.

Not long until Aidan and the others are behind bars.

Until I can get home and be with my brother, and work out where he's been all this time.

I clear my throat, and say, "You're going to summon a demon in the middle of your living room?"

"Not quite," Naomi says, her eyes sparkling with the same fervour as her husband's.

Aidan marches over to the back wall and places the flat of his hand against it. He murmurs a low string of Latin under his breath and, when he steps away a few seconds later, the bare bricks move of their own accord.

They twitch and shift and spin in place, each one moving over the other in an intricate, whirling pattern I can't keep track of.

An archway appears, shadows wreathing everything beyond the horseshoe curve.

A cool draft blows through the room.

Ice prickles my skin and, despite my earlier complaint, I'm grateful for the robe now.

"Where does it lead?" I ask.

The wolfish grin is back on Aidan's face, matched by those around me.

"Scared of the dark?" Michelle jeers.

"Screw you."

"That's enough, you two," Aidan says. "I've put up with your sniping for long enough. Not. Today."

Michelle finds something interesting to examine on the floor.

I don't look away.

Aidan's frown disappears. "This building has a sub-level."

With no further explanation, he wheels around and glides into the archway. He moves with an eerie calm now, smooth and sure. There's a serenity, a certainty about him.

I shiver again, but it's nothing to do with the cold this time.

He's so convinced this is going to work.

What if...

No.

I can't afford to be taken in by his games.

Aidan's just grasping at straws.

He wants revenge.

Revenge can lead people to believe anything.

Anything at all.

I follow in Aidan's footsteps, not trusting myself to speak.

The darkness of the archway swallows me.

"Keep your hand on the wall," Naomi says from behind me. "That way you won't slip."

Aidan guides us down a set of stairs that seems to go on forever.

Eventually, we reach the bottom and round a corner.

It's bitterly cold down here.

Far colder than it should be at this time of year.

Aidan flicks his hand and mutters, "*Ignis.*"

Blinding white flames burst to life at the tips of a thousand candles lining the walls.

Long, flickering shadows dance around the cavernous space, sinister in their twisting, serpentine movements.

Someone's set a bronze circle into the floor in the centre of the room.

Witches usually etch circles in chalk, or set them in silver. Either of these things creates a barrier that stops magical energy from escaping, which is why circles come in handy during a witch's Manifestation.

I've never seen a bronze circle before.

Aidan strides around the circle's circumference, halting when he reaches the other side.

There's a bronze bowl at his feet, and a harsh, herby smell rises from it.

Four more bowls line the circle at equidistant points.

Aidan turns to face us, the candlelight carving sharp angles into his face. "This is the moment we've been waiting for. Today, we take the first pivotal step towards defeating The Witches Council. We will make them pay for what they've done to us. We will have justice."

An eerie silence follows his words.

Static charges the air, like when a storm's about to break.

"Are you ready?" he asks.

Although this ritual is completely bogus, a heavy weight presses down on my shoulders.

It's all getting too... real.

What if Aidan's right?

Why's he so sure this will work?

What if he really has spoken to a demon?

No.

It's bollocks.

All of it.

But I have to ask.

"Have you thought about what could happen if..." My words trail off.

Aidan's inky eyes glint in the candlelight. "If what?"

The words jam in my throat.

"Speak."

"Have you thought about what could happen if this actually works?" I finish, forcing myself to keep my eyes locked with his.

"You still doubt it?" he scoffs. "After everything we've discussed, you're still calling me a liar."

His voice has dropped to a whisper.

It would've been less intimidating had he shouted.

My gut tightens. "That didn't come out right."

Aidan's nostrils flare. "Then explain."

"In all the legends, demons and sorcerers are infinitely more powerful than witches. What happens if the demon gets loose?"

Aidan's expression softens, just a little. "That's what this is for." He nods at the circle.

"No offence, but I've never seen a bronze circle before, and—"

"Copper."

"What?"

He sighs. "The circle. It's copper, not bronze."

My face scrunches up in confusion. "I don't see how that makes any difference."

Aidan's earlier tone of patience is wearing thin. "Copper is to demons what iron is to witches."

"They're allergic to it?"

"No shit." Michelle rolls her eyes.

I don't know whether it's the pressure of the situation, or the compound effect of Michelle's paper-cut like insults, but I snap. "What the fuck is your—"

"What did I say about your petty squabbles?" Aidan's voice echoes through the room and the candle flames leap towards the ceiling.

I shield my eyes against the blinding light.

When the flames settle down again, I blink blotchy spots from my eyes.

"Yes," Aidan continues, "demons are allergic to copper. Legend goes the witches of Camelot used copper to bind the demons, so that the sorcerers could banish them."

I scuff my shoe against the cement floor with a rough scrape. "And what are the bowls for?"

Aidan shrugs, as if it's of no consequence. "Witch's blood is required to bind the circle."

"Blood?"

A sliver of fear worms its way into my stomach.

Blood magic is no joke.

It's binding.

When we were hunting Dylan Carmichael down last year, we convinced Henry to sign a blood contract when we accepted him onto the team, with no little reluctance on my part.

His blood signature tied his life force to the contract.

Eric steps forward and claps me on the shoulder. "Relax. It only takes a couple of drops."

A couple of drops.

That's a couple of drops too many in my book.

One side of Eric's mouth slides into a half grin. "What? You didn't think we'd let a demon roam the streets, did you?" He laughs.

I give a half-hearted chuckle.

"We're summoning this demon to serve us," Aidan says, in a tone that brooks no argument. "We're using him for his power, nothing more. Once he's served his purpose, we'll send him back to Hell, where he belongs."

"Right," I say, with little conviction.

"I'll ask one more time. Are you ready?"

Am I ready?

Play along. Go through with this ridiculous ritual...

Kate's given me my orders.

I don't have a choice.

I step forward and say, "I'm ready."

This is so stupid.

It's never going to work.

I just need to remember to look disappointed when Aidan's plan fails.

CHAPTER 22
Christian

I stand at the edge of the circle and wait for Aidan to tell us what to do.

From his vantage point on the opposite side, he withdraws something from the folds of his robes.

My breath hitches, my heart dancing a wild little jig.

Aidan's holding the crown.

In this light, the glinting silver appears menacing.

He raises it.

"What are you doing?" I ask.

"You'll see."

My mouth is drier than sawdust.

He perches the crown atop his head, the golden symbol glimmering on his forehead.

My muscles have seized up, and a wooden, hollow ache has taken up residence in my chest.

I wait.

Wait.

Wait some more.

Nothing happens.

I scratch the tip of my nose. "What's going on?"

"It's the crown," Eric whispers. "It's showing him the spell to release the demon."

"I don't get it. Aidan said you've spoken to this demon before. He doesn't remember the Key?"

Eric shakes his head. "Part of the crown's curse makes the wearer forget the spell as soon as they take it off. A safeguard, I guess."

"But—"

A burst of static flies through the room, making the hairs at the nape of my neck stand on end.

My pulse pounds in my temples.

"Repeat after me," Aidan says, his eyes fixed on something only he can see.

What do I do?

Play along. Go through with this ridiculous ritual...

I hope you're right about this, Kate.

Aidan's next words come out low and slow. "*In tenebris hora, maleficatorium horae. Vocamus ad infernales. Loquimur, et ita est. Sicut supra, ita infra. Aperi portas, aperi portas, aperi portas.*"

In the dark hour, the witching hour. We call to the infernal. We speak, and it is so. As above, so below. Open the Gates, open the Gates, open the Gates.

I repeat the words in my own hushed tones; the incantation echoes from the others' lips.

"Now for the blood," Aidan says.

The blood.

I slide the wicked-sharp athame Aidan gave me earlier from the folds of my robes.

Naomi, Michelle, and Eric slice into their palms, their blood dripping into the bronze bowls at their feet.

The mixture hisses, its thick herbal scent growing so strong it almost chokes me.

I can't be a party to this.

If this works—

Michelle glares at me, her eyes narrowing. "What's holding you up?"

"I... erm..."

"Problem?" Aidan's question is keener than the blade clasped in my sweaty grip.

Fuck.

Play along. Go through with this ridiculous ritual...

I slice into my palm and grit my teeth against the harsh, cutting sting.

Bright red drops of blood well from the wound and pool in my hand.

Drip.

The blood spatters the herb paste in the copper bowl.

Drip.

The stink of herbs and death and blood clogs my nostrils.

Drip.

Belladonna.

Valerian.

Vervain.

The combination makes my stomach heave, but I hang on to its contents.

"Again," Aidan barks.

I flinch.

"Chant again."

The others close their eyes.

I follow suit.

"*In tenebris hora, maleficatorium horae.*"

We chant in unison now.

"*Vocamus ad infernales.*"

Our voices rise.

"*Loquimur, et ita est.*"

Getting louder and louder.

"*Sicut supra, ita infra.*"

And louder still.

"*Aperi portas, aperi portas, aperi portas.*"

Open the gates, open the gates, open the gates.

As soon as the last line of the spell leaves my lips, silence swallows the room.

Thump-thump, thump-thump, thump-thump.

My heart gallops behind my ribcage, and a bead of sweat drips down the side of my face.

The others stare at a spot on the floor in the centre of the circle, as if waiting for something.

I fix my gaze on the same patch of bare concrete.

And...

Nothing.

Nothing happens.

A relief so strong it almost buckles my knees washes over me.

Thank God.

I knew Aidan was barking up the wrong tree with this.

I told him there was no such thing as demons.

Now, I have to do what Kate said.

When it doesn't work, get out of there. Once you're safe, we'll pick all four of them up in one fell swoop.

That's my cue to leave.

I shake my head at Aidan, feigning disappointment. "Told you it was just a story. What a waste of time. I'm out of here."

I turn and head towards the stairs leading back up into the apartment.

"Wait," Aidan shouts.

Without breaking stride, I twist on my heel, walking backwards. "For what? It didn't work."

"Just wait."

I snort at him, pivoting to face the steps again. I've almost reached the bottom of the staircase when—

Boom.

A clap of thunder rends the air.

I freeze, my hackles rising.

What the fuck was that?

Chapter 23
Christian

"What the fuck was that?" I give voice to the words this time. They come out of me as a strangled cry.

The already chilly temperature plummets.

I exhale, and my breath mists in front of me.

Aidan spreads his arms wide like a priest at the pulpit, a huge smile splitting his face. "He's coming."

Another *boom* of thunder obscures my reply and, right in the centre of the circle—where the others had all been staring before—a deep crack opens in the concrete.

My heart hammers now, the laceration on my palm throbbing in time with my racing pulse.

This can't be happening.

It can't be working.

It can't.

I don't know what Aidan's playing at, but this has to be smoke and mirrors.

It has to be.

A moment later, thick black smoke pours from the crevice in the floor.

My mind is screaming.

Screaming at me to escape.

To run.

Deep in my bones, I know a predator is coming.

Try as I might, I can't make my body move.

Primal, ancient terror freezes me to the spot.

The heavy, pitch-dark smoke has almost filled the circle now, but it doesn't—no, can't, I realise—reach beyond it.

The copper line of the circle glows pearly white and the mixture of blood and herbs in the shallow bowls froths and spits.

What happens next will stay with me forever.

A voice—gravely and low, like stone grating on stone—speaks directly into my mind.

A voice of darkness.

Of pain.

Of death.

It says three simple words which chill me to the bone.

I am free.

The smoke grows darker still, shrinking in on itself. It becomes more and more dense with each passing second.

Then, it takes shape.

A distinctly humanoid shape.

Syrupy seconds pass, and the smoke coalesces.

Then it fades away to nothing.

It—*he*—stands with his back to me and, although there's a magical barrier between us, I can still sense his power.

It's nothing like my own.

My magic is all warmth, life and colour—familiar and comforting.

The energy rolling off the demon in heady waves that threaten to drag me under is alien to the extreme.

Cold.

Lethal.

Limitless.

The hairs on my forearms stand on end, my breath still emerges in fine white clouds, and my fingers go numb.

The demon's striking, even in profile.

He's tall and muscular. His cropped hair is as black and shiny as frozen oil. Though he stands stock-still—eerily so—his posture is that of a warrior. He's clad in dull black leather, and metal plates the colour of crow's feathers gleam at his shoulders.

Armour.

My hands tremble at the word.

Slowly—painfully slowly—the demon turns on his heel, with a sinuous, snake-like movement, until he's facing me.

Holy shit.

My throat goes tight, and my entire body stiffens.

His eyes are coal black.

No irises.

No whites.

Only two bottomless pits staring out from a heavyset, craggy, tanned face.

My heart rate spikes. I'm panting.

The demon smiles, if you can call it that—he draws back his lips from startlingly white teeth, bringing to mind images of hungry wolves catching the sight of prey.

Cold sweat peppers my forehead.

Aidan and the others lower their heads—a sign of respect, maybe?—but I can't wrench my gaze away from the nightmarish creature.

The demon points at me. "You."

I gulp.

His voice is a dry rasp.

I open my mouth to respond, but no sound comes out.

Demons are real.

The legends are true.

My thoughts come to a shuddering halt, and I'm unable to process anything else.

The demon blinks, and the darkness that swallows his eyes is gone, replaced by two human-looking brown eyes. "Are you mute, boy?"

"N—" My voice breaks like a snapping twig and, with considerable effort, I clear my throat and force myself to speak. When I do, my tone is firm—unlike my legs, which have transformed into mounds of quivering blancmange. "No."

He cocks his head to one side. "You are the one who set me free."

I pry my tongue away from the roof of my mouth. "Not just me. We—"

Aidan's head snaps up. "We set you free, my lord."

The demon spins to face Aidan, the movement a blur.

"*We*... ha! Such. Arrogance." The demon spits the word like venom before—in another flash of motion—he's facing me again. "Without his power, I would still be rotting in Hell."

"My lord, we—"

"Silence." The demon takes a step towards me.

The copper circle gives a faint pulse, bronze energy spilling from the metal ring and spiralling up to the ceiling.

The creature's beady eyes trace the line of the circle before his gaze lands back on mine. "What have they promised you, in exchange for my freedom, witch?"

I swallow, hard. "Power."

Another non-smile. "Indeed." He sniffs, a long pull of air. "You already have power. I can smell it. Yet you hunger for more?"

There's a challenge in the demon's tone, but I can't think of anything sensible to say.

"If I may, my lord?" Naomi says, with a slight quiver in her voice. "We plan to use your power for a specific purpose. It's a task we can't complete without your help."

Flash.

He stands before Naomi, stopping just shy of the pulsating circle.

She flinches back, her eyes going wide.

The demon regards her like an insect trapped in a marmalade jar.

A jar he's desperate to shake.

"Tell me…" He squints, and his eyes turn black again.

Icy power tears through the room.

Frost caresses my skin, and I shiver.

The demon's expression clears. "… Naomi Adedeji. Why should I give shadowmancy to you? Witches played a part in the downfall of my kind. I owe you nothing."

Across the room, Michelle's gaze sharpens. "We broke you out. We're entitled to—"

Flash.

He's in front of Michelle now.

To her credit, she doesn't flinch.

"*Entitled*. You are a fool, Michelle Rees. I should kill you where you stand."

She snorts. "You don't scare me."

The demon tips his head back, exposing his throat, a dry laugh scraping past his teeth. "No? Pity. Maybe I should find out what does."

Michelle's lips tug down at the corners. "What do you—"

The darkness swirls in the demon's eyes again.

The air pressure drops.

My ears *pop*.

Michelle draws away from the creature now, her breath escaping in sharp bursts.

The smile on the demon's face is genuine this time, and it's far scarier than the pseudo-smile he's been sporting until now. "You are afraid of being buried alive."

Michelle's lower lip trembles. "Stop."

The smile widens into a grin. "Imagine what it would be like down there, in the dark. All alone. Waiting to die."

Michelle lifts trembling fingers to her lips. "I said stop."

"What are you doing?" Aidan asks, his tone sharp.

The demon ignores him, his black glare still focused on Michelle. "You can feel it, can't you? Your life slipping away? Your lungs burning as they refuse to draw breath."

Silent tears poured down Michelle's cheeks.

"You scream, but nobody can hear you."

She collapses to her knees, hands clamped around her middle, and lets out an ear-splitting wail.

I can't stand this.

Michelle might be the world's biggest bitch, but whatever the demon is doing to her, it's barbaric.

I race around the circle and take a wide-legged stance between the two of them. "Stop it," I snap. "Whatever you're doing to her, just stop."

The demon's features resemble a granite mask.

"How did you do that?" Michelle croaks. "How did you know?"

Still glaring at me, the demon says, "I am an Empath. I can read your hopes and fears as easily as a fortune teller reads tea-leaves."

Something snags at the back of my of mind.

Empath.

Where have I heard that term before?

Wait.

My first day here, when Aidan showed me the library.

Only the most powerful demons are blessed with a Curse...

It's a line from that book.

Curses & Gifts: The Abilities of Demons and Sorcerers.

Empathy was listed as one of those notable demonic abilities.

"You're Cursed," I breathe.

I can read your hopes and fears as easily as a fortune teller reads tea-leaves.

My blood runs cold.

What would the demon's Empathy reveal about me?

As if he heard my thoughts, the demon says, "What about you? What are you scared of, boy?"

Aidan says, "Leave him alone."

The demon expels another harsh bark of laughter, guttural and low. "Why should I?" He narrows his eyes at me.

I know what's coming.

A wave—no, a tsunami—of coldness crashes into me.

I gasp at the otherworldly chill.

My hands tremor.

God, this is terrible... it's—

Oh dear, oh dear, the demon whispers into my mind.

Every muscle in my body pulls taught.

Someone has been telling lies. Can you imagine what they will do if they find out who you truly are... Christian Winter?

I swear my heart stops beating.

Sharp fear, hot and bitter, spreads throughout my abdomen.

"We have to send him back," I say to the room at large.

"No," Aidan says. "We need him."

The demon inches a step closer to me, causing the copper barrier to fizz and pop, and throw out tiny sparks of light. *If you so much as think about banishing me, I'll tell them who you are.*

My throat closes.

I wonder what they will do once they know the truth. A Detective Inspector from the Magical Investigations Department in their midst... the outcome will not be favourable.

My pulse thuds in my temples.

Another burst of icy power rips through me, and I stumble, but keep my balance.

So much fear behind that tough façade of yours. You worry about them, do you not? Kate, Tori... John. You should be worried. These people strike me as the sort who will seek vengeance.

My blood freezes in my veins. "Get out of my head."

I know your fear now, Christian Winter. This circle will not hold me forever. With everything I know about you, I could force you to break it now.

My entire body stiffens.

Luckily for you, I am not strong enough to stay in this realm without the aid of the circle... for now. Perhaps my first visit upon breaking free will be to your precious little brother.

I clench my trembling fists. "I said, get out of my head."

His mouth quirks at the corner, ebony eyes sparkling with glee. *As you wish.*

The demon's shadow pulls away from me, leaving me feeling sullied.

I wrap my arms around my chest and tuck my hands beneath my armpits to generate some warmth.

The last of the creature's power retreats, but not before his mental voice whispers, *I have warned you, witch.*

Chapter 24
Christian

I'm still shuddering when the demon says, "Nobody answered my question. Why should I grant you my power?"

Aidan steps forward. "It's my understanding that an early version of The Witches Council was formed—in part—to banish demons."

The creature's shrewd gaze goes to Aidan's. "Someone has informed you remarkably well. What of it?"

A spark of hope enters Aidan's eyes. "You're not the only one with an axe to grind. We want to use your shadowmancy to destroy them."

The demon runs his tongue over one of his canines. "You would do that? Turn on your own kind?"

Aidan narrows his eyes. "They took someone from me."

Another blast of the demon's foreign, devastating power tears through the room.

Aidan's entire body goes rigid.

"Ah, I see." The demon sniffs. "Your sister. You think destroying The Witches Council will bring you peace, help you lay the ghosts of the past to rest?"

"I don't *think* anything. It *will* bring me peace."

The demon taps his finger against his chin, meandering around the circle.

Round and round and round.

Eventually, he says, "I never thought I would say this, and least of all to a witch, but I can sympathise with your plight."

For the first time since the creature appeared, Eric speaks up, his voice tinged with longing. "Does that mean…?"

"Yes. I will help you."

Naomi breaks out into a wide smile. "My lord, we—"

The demon cuts across her. "The question is, what will you give me in exchange?"

The room falls silent, and we all exchange uncertain glances with one another.

Aidan nods once, like he's decided. "Your freedom."

My mouth drops open, and I stare at Aidan askance. "What? You can't."

"Ade," Eric says, speaking in a low, patient voice. "I want this as much as you do, but we can't promise that. We all agreed we wouldn't release him. Think of the damage he could do."

Aidan ignores his friend, his eyes fastened on the demon. "You won't help us otherwise, will you?"

The creature's smirk is answer enough.

I pace around the edge of the circle and place a restraining hand on Aidan's arm. "If you agree to this, thousands of innocent people will die. He'll kill us all."

Aidan shakes me off, a hint of iron in his tone. "No. He won't."

"Really?" the demon asks. "You sound awfully sure of that."

"I am." Aidan arches an eyebrow in return. "If we agree to your terms, you'll promise not to harm any witches once you're out."

It doesn't escape me that Aidan omits to include mortals in his demand.

Something tells me the demon won't have any reservations about killing non-magical folk if it suits his ends.

I can't let that happen, but I've got no idea how to stop this.

The demon laughs. "My, my, my... but you are a bold one. How do you know I will keep my promise?"

"Because," Aidan says, with a slight smile, "you're going to swear a Demonic Oath."

The Demon's mouth pinches, uncertainty entering his gaze. "How in the name of the Gates do you know about Demonic Oaths?"

Aidan's smile morphs into something cold and cruel. "I've been planning this for over twenty years and, like you said, I'm remarkably well informed."

The creature's Adam's apple bobs.

So, demons can feel fear, too.

Interesting.

What's so scary about this Oath?

Perhaps it's like a witch's blood contract.

Maybe the demon gives up has life if he breaks it.

Aidan takes a single, small step towards the barrier—a physical challenge. When he speaks, he echoes the demon's earlier words. "You really don't know what you're dealing with, do you?"

He's dispensed with the, "my lord."

Aidan means business.

The demon raises a clenched fist and pounds on the barrier.

A flash of bright light causes me to shield my eyes.

When I lower my hand, waves of bronze energy ripple around the copper circle.

The demon snatches his arm back, the skin on his knuckles singed and smoking. "How dare you?" His voice is a low, dangerous hiss.

"You are nothing compared to me. Were it not for this pathetic barrier, I would destroy you with a mere thought."

Aidan folds his arms. "True, but our 'pathetic barrier' has you trapped... until we say otherwise."

The demon's flint black eyes bore into Aidan's.

The corner of Aidan's mouth lifts. "But, of course, it's up to you... my lord."

Our captive's nostrils flare. "Fine. You have my word."

"The Oath?" Aidan counters.

The demon sets his face in a grim mask of hatred. "I swear that my hand will harm no witches, provided the five of you release me from this circle once I have help you complete your task. This Oath is binding and, should I break it, I will relinquish my life." He raises his hand and marks a cross over his heart with his index finger. Thick, black smoke pours into his chest, then fades. He lowers his hand, glaring daggers at Aidan. "Satisfied?"

"Very," Aidan quips. "Now, how about giving us a taste of this infamous power of yours?"

I shiver.

I've seen enough of this demon's power already.

Power is one thing.

I'm used to that.

But this... untamed and unlimited...

You should be afraid, Christian Winter.

The Demon's mental voice chills me to my core.

"Very well." The creature raises a finger and jabs it at my chest. "Him first."

CHAPTER 25
Christian

Ignoring the demon, I face Aidan. "Are you sure this is a good idea?"

The demon's laughter fills the room. "It might be a little late for that." Into my mind, he whispers, *Tread carefully. I will tell them who you are.*

I have to fight extra hard to keep the tension from showing on my face.

It's difficult.

Aidan places a warm hand on my shoulder. "It's the only way. We're doing this for people like my sister, like your brother. So they'll never have to suffer again."

An uneasy feeling worms its way into the pit of my stomach.

As much as I disagree with Aidan's methods, I can sympathise with the reason behind them.

He continues, "When we topple The Witches Council, we can build a truly fair society for witches."

I assess my next move.

If I act fast, can I take all of them down?

Can I defeat them before they realise what's happening?

If I can incapacitate them and call in the cavalry before the demon tells them who I am, then I can make this right.

I can do that, can't I?

Not before I tell them all about you.

My eyes snap to the demon's.

The redhead is already suspicious of you. I can tell. She fears involving an outsider in their plans. I could project your true identity into her mind before you could blink.

Even now, Michelle's eyeing me closely.

I don't have a choice.

As much as I don't want to, I'll have to accept one dose of the demon's power. If I don't, the creature will blow my cover.

Pentacle will seek revenge.

John.

Tori.

Kate.

They'll all be in danger.

I can't allow that to happen.

One dose.

That's it.

After that, I'll set up a rendezvous with Kate somehow, tell her about the demon, and work to send him back to Hell.

I wish you luck with that. You can hope all you want, but I am here to stay.

A sickening tingle spreads through my stomach.

No choice.

Press ahead.

"Okay," I say, my voice sounding far more confident than I feel. "Guess I'll go first, then."

"Smart choice," the demon says, with a slight smirk.

I'm not so sure about that.

I face the demon again. "How does it work?"

He holds up his hand and presses it toward the bronze barrier.

The shield ripples on contact, and he says, "Hold your hand up to mine."

"Why?"

"Just do as I say."

I gulp before tentatively raising my hand. Just before my fingers reach the barrier, I hesitate. "Is this going to hurt?"

A flash of the demon's teeth. "You know what they say. No pain, no gain."

Great.

Just great.

Well, here goes nothing.

My hand rests against the barrier's warm, fizzing surface.

The creature closes his eyes and a skein of black smoke curls from his palm.

I stare, transfixed, as the smoke seeps through the barrier.

That's not possible.

Magic bounces off a barrier.

But he's not using magic.

He's using shadowmancy.

The barrier twists and writhes, fighting the shadow's onslaught.

"Do you accept this power?" the demon asks.

Do I?

A profound sense of wrongness settles in my chest.

No.

I can't.

Oh, but you can, Christian Winter. Remember how high the stakes are should you refuse.

Kate.

Tori.

John.

My hand trembles against the barrier. "Yes."

"For the sake of clarity, you accept?"

"I accept."

The barrier yields a little.

The smoke breaks through the outer wall and meets my skin.

I suck in a huge breath, every single muscle in my body stiffens, and I'm forced onto my tip-toes.

The room disappears, and I'm swamped in a dark void.

Coldness like I've never experienced spreads across my entire body. It's like the demon's plunged me into a pool of ice-water, and I'm sinking... sinking... sinking... to the bottom. Icy, searing heat creeps up my arm, rounding the bend in my elbow. My veins twist beneath my skin, blood boiling. My muscles melt. The longer my hand rests against the barrier, the worse the pain gets. When the foreign energy finally seeps its way into my heart, I scream—loudly. The dark clouds dancing before my eyes are roiling and swirling and—

The shadows clouding my vision dissipate, and the room snaps back into focus.

The barrier relinquishes my hand and I crumple to my knees, my lungs heaving like I've just run a marathon.

As soon as I can breathe normally again, and the last of the dark agony subsides, the first thing I feel is... *energised*.

My blood hums with electricity.

Stinging heat—the kind you get when you step out of a hot bath—prickles my skin.

My muscles sing with power.

Closing my eyes, I take a deep, calming breath.

Holy shit.

It's like breathing after being submerged under water for a long time.

Every cell in my body ignites, the oxygen soothing my lungs like a balm.

The air enters my chest, circulates, and leaves my mouth again charged with static.

Someone's talking, but it sounds like it's coming from miles away.

Miles and miles away...

"Carl."

My eyes snap open, the voice yanking me back to my senses. The raw power still races through my system. I stand, the movement smooth and graceful.

Easy.

I pivot to face Aidan.

He sucks in a startled breath.

"What?" I ask, my voice echoing through the basement.

"Your... your eyes."

"What about them?"

When he speaks, Aidan's voice shakes a little. "They're—they're black, just like his." He points at the demon.

I find this hysterical. A warm chuckle bubbles up my throat. I laugh and laugh and laugh until tears stream down my face and my stomach hurts.

A mad hyena cackle.

I've never made this sound before.

That makes me laugh even harder.

"What the fuck have you done to him?" Eric asks. "Your power is useless if it makes you... well..."

"Inebriated?" the demon suggests.

"It makes you high." I collapse into another fit of giggles.

Damn.

I've never done drugs, but if this is what it feels like to be strung out, no wonder John enjoyed it so much.

The demon's speaking again. "There is no need to worry, Eric Jiménez. Over time, your pathetic witch bodies will acclimatise."

A broad grin splits my face in two. "I never want this feeling to stop."

"What's it like?" Michelle asks, her voice lacking its usual poison.

That's a hard question to answer, but I give it a go. "It's like... taking a bath... in syrup." I'm laughing again. The idea of taking a bath in syrup is ridiculous. "But..."

But...

There's something else there, too.

Underneath the warm, fuzzy coating of the demon's shadow—burning like hot coals—right in the centre of my chest.

My magic.

The borrowed power has made it something dark—a heady, smoky cocktail infused with twilight filling my chest.

I know the answer to Michelle's question now.

"Powerful. I feel powerful."

Aidan stares at me with wide eyes. "That's—"

I fling up a hand to stop him, my gaze fixed on the demon. "What can I do with it?"

The demon shrugs. "Anything I can do, you can do, too."

Anything I can do...

My mind conjures up the list of powers from *Curses & Gifts: The Abilities of Demons and Sorcerers*.

The Shadow-strike.

The Shadow-shield.

Telekinesis.

Teleportation.

Temporomancy.

What would it be like to move from one place to another without using a portal?

"How does it work?" I ask, my tone still laced with that deep, booming quality.

The demon smiles. "Shadowmancy is about intention. All you have to do is think the action into existence."

I blink. "It's that simple?"

The demon nods.

I shiver.

No wonder olden day witches were so afraid of demons.

I let out a long exhale. "Shit. That kind of power is…"

Unfathomable?

Dangerous?

Wrong?

The demon scoffs. "It is the type of power everyone wants. They just refuse to admit it to themselves." His voice pushes its way into my mind. *Even you, Christian Winter.*

Is that true?

Do I want endless power?

Your friend Talitha Green-Hernandez wanted endless power. That's why she became a Fury.

Tally.

Vex.

Her accusation on the night I arrested her slams into me like a wall.

Some friend. I heard about your promotion. Big congrats. You could've at least waited until she was cold.

Until she was cold.

Lancelot's voice enters my mind again, laced with a hint of smugness. *You understand that need, do you not? You stole your dead boss's job because it gives you power and influence. Shadowmancy is no different. You need power like lungs need oxygen. More than that. You crave it.*

Is the demon right? Am I that desperate for power?

You know the answer to that, boy. You know you want to try it. Just a taste.

He's right.

I hate to own up to it, but he's right.

The bastard.

A low chuckle bounces around my skull. *Show me what you can do.*

I focus on a spot over Eric's left shoulder. I want to go there. "So, say I wanted to—"

Black smoke—tinged with the violet glow of my magic—obscures my vision.

Someone drops me from a great height and my stomach fights to burst from my mouth.

When the smoke clears, I'm staring at the back of Eric's head.

"Whoa!" The word rushes out of me.

Everyone—apart from the demon—flinches and spins in my direction.

Eric lashes out like he's under attack, hand shooting out. "*Ignis*." A pale yellow fireball erupts from his fingers and rockets towards me with a roar.

Anything I can do...

Telekinesis.

I narrow my eyes at the oncoming missile.

Stop.

That's all it takes.

One simple thought.

The fireball skids to a halt in front of me.

"What the—" Aidan's eyes are wide.

The new power inside me doesn't respond well to threats.

Anything I can do...

Transference.

The ability to infuse matter or energy with shadowmancy.

Eric's magic is pure energy.

My next thought forms, almost unbidden.

Right back at you, times three.

My hand floats up, and a tendril of dark smoke rushes out to meet the fireball.

The shadow entwines with Eric's fire magic, and the spell grows in size, shifting and expanding into what I can only describe as a storm-cloud of fire. The cloud bursts outward, tongues of smoke-darkened flame shooting towards Eric.

"*Obstructionum.*" He conjures a barrier just in time.

When the corrupted fire strikes Eric's shield, it flashes and crumples like tissue paper. It spares him from being burned to a crisp, but he still gets knocked flat on his arse.

I laugh so hard I have to bend over and place my hands on my knees to support myself.

"What the hell, Carl?" Eric sputters, clambering to his feet.

"I'm sorry," I say, my tone light. "I was only defending myself."

"Incredible." Naomi turns to Aidan. "Think about what this means, Ade."

Aidan is gazing at me with something like awe. "Naismith won't stand a chance."

The demon clears his throat. "Do not get ahead of yourselves. Teleporting twenty feet across a room is one thing. Teleporting past The Witches Council's wards will be quite another."

Naomi bows her head. "I'm sorry, my lord—"

The demon tuts. "As much as I adore veneration, it grows tiresome."

Aidan says, "In that case, what should we call you?"

"By my given name. What else?"

"Which is?" I ask, still fighting against a fit of giggles.

"Lancelot," he says.

Chapter 26
Christian

The giggles burst from me in one long rush. "You're taking the piss."

The demon—Lancelot... fucking *Lancelot*—fixes me with a hard stare. "You find my name amusing, witch?"

I don't, but I can't stop laughing. "You can't... you don't mean Knight of the Round Table, Arthur and Guinevere—that Lancelot."

He rolls his eyes. "I am thrilled my reputation precedes me."

"Jesus fucking Christ."

The others' faces are stony.

"Guys. Are you hearing this? Lancelot."

Nothing.

Jeez... tough crowd.

When Aidan speaks, his voice comes out firm. "You're Lancelot?"

Lancelot sighs. "The only thing I find even more tiresome than veneration is repetition."

Aidan's expression is murderous.

"Who pissed in your porridge?" I ask.

Aidan's flinty gaze snaps to mine. "I thought you'd read *Myth & Magic*."

"I have… a long time ago. What's that got to do with anything?"

"The Fall of Camelot," Michelle breathes.

The base of my spine tingles. "What are you talking about?"

Naomi clears her throat, her voice carrying to the corners of the basement. "Unknown to King Arthur, one of his most trusted knights, Sir Lancelot—a skilled demon Cursed with the power of Empathy—his demonic brethren, and Arthur's half-sister—the Clairvoyant sorceress, Morgana Le Fey—were plotting against him."

Aidan takes over from his wife. "The evil pair killed the king and queen in a bid to take the throne for themselves. And they would have succeeded, if not for the quick thinking and decisive action of Arthur's full-blood sister, Elaine Pendragon."

Lancelot snorts. "Please. Elaine Pendragon was a tyrant."

Eric's eyes go wide. "You're a monster."

The demon narrows his eyes at Eric. "You should not believe everything you read."

"Are you saying you didn't kill King Arthur?"

"Would you believe me if I said no?"

Silence spreads through the room.

"Humph. I thought not," Lancelot says.

Michelle says, "Ade, maybe we should—"

Aidan cuts across her. "This changes nothing. We still need his help."

"Yes. You do." Lancelot carries on as if the revelation about his identity never happened. "Like I said, mastering shadowmancy takes time, but I can teach you how."

Aidan nods. "How long before we're ready to challenge the Council?"

"How long is a loop of intestine?" Lancelot asks.

I shudder, the vulgar turn of phrase cutting through the syrupy softness of the shadowmancy.

The demon laughs. "A few weeks, maybe."

Naomi's face falls. "Weeks? I thought… I thought it would be quicker."

Aidan moves to his wife's side and takes her hands in his own. "We waited twenty years, my love. What's another few weeks?"

"True," she says, but there's an edge of melancholy in her voice. Her attention goes to the fallen knight. "When do we start?"

Lancelot cocks his head to one side. "Small steps, Naomi Adedeji. Small steps. I will transfer increasing amounts of power to you over the next several days. Once your systems have adjusted, you will learn control."

I will transfer increasing amounts of power to you over the next several days.

A delicious tingle brushes my skin.

Despite myself, I want more of this power.

Electricity in its purest form.

It makes me feel alive.

It makes me feel…

Invincible.

I know, on some level, I should try to fight against the longing, but my sluggish mind can't quite remember why.

Power isn't the reason I'm here.

I came to do something.

To stop something…

No.

It's gone.

My need for power is all that remains.

What was it Aidan had said back at the competition?

As the fifth member of Pentacle, we can promise you power the likes of which you've never known. Nobody will ever be able to control you again. As the fifth member of Pentacle, you will be part of the most powerful Coven in history.

I hadn't believed him.

I sure as hell believe him now.

The last thing I want is to be controlled.

To be contained.

No.

I want power.

The next few days are... trippy.

Lancelot's true to his word.

He gives us more and more power, leaving us all in a state of entropic bliss.

Time passes in a hazy blur.

My entire world shrinks to the size of the demon's lair.

There's nothing outside of it.

Shadowmancy courses through my veins.

Every so often, my mind snags on that thing I should be remembering.

The reason I'm here.

The real reason.

But I have no inclination to explore further.

I sense that just beyond the veil of shadowmancy lie shame, guilt, and fear.

Shame.

Guilt.

Fear.

Three things I'm not interested in right now.

Because now I'm free.

It's like flying—soaring above the city across an endless sea of stars—but a million times better.

I've touched the edge of paradise, and I never want to leave.

But, as the saying goes, all good things must end.

On the fourth morning, I come crashing back to earth with a bang.

It's official.

I have the hangover from Hell.

Literally.

The first thing I realize—when I'm *compos mentis* enough to be aware again—is the pounding in my head.

Pounding.

Ugh.

That's an understatement.

Someone's taken a pneumatic drill to my skull and bared down hard.

I smack my lips, and my fur-lined tongue scrapes against the roof of my mouth.

With more care than I've ever done anything, like peeling the skin off an apple in one go, I prise my heavy eyelids open.

Oh, God.

The light hits my retinas and agony blazes along my optic nerves.

And I thought the guy with the pneumatic drill was bad.

Never, ever again.

Immortal words, uttered by everyone the morning after the night before.

It's only when I roll onto my side I realise I'm lying down.

My skin, where it rubs against the soft sheets beneath me, tingles all over with a sandpaper rawness.

I don't remember the journey from Lancelot's lair to my room three floors above.

I take an experimental sniff.

The space smells shut up and musty.

We haven't left the building since Lancelot gave us our first infusion of shadowmancy.

I glare at the massive window.

The bright sun glares right back.

Why?

Why did I leave the curtains open?

I should do something about that.

Luckily, there are perks to being a witch. At least I don't have to get up. I raise a heavy hand and flick my fingers at the curtains. "*Claudere.*" I wait for the familiar tingle in my chest that signals magic, but it doesn't come. I clench my fist, shake out my hand, and try again. "*Claudere.*"

The curtains refuse to close.

"*Claudere.*"

Nothing.

What the fuck?

Through the dim haze of my lingering hangover, the past three days surface in a disjointed kaleidoscope of images.

The first dose of shadowmancy… the second… the tenth… the fiftieth—each stronger than the last.

I lost track of time after that.

But I'm certain of one thing.

I haven't used any magic.

So, why isn't it working?

It has to be the influx of demonic power.

Has it interfered with my magic?

I close my eyes and cast my senses deep inside myself, finding that place in my chest where my magic lives and… it's there. Not the raging fire I'm used to, just a tiny spark.

My eyes snap open.

Somehow, the shadowmancy has drained my powers. It's as if I've used up every ounce of magic I have, just like when I battled Vex.

Shit.

I collapse back onto the pillows with a groan, and a ten-ton weight crashes into me, pressing me further down into the mattress.

Lancelot's power has made me sick. Like an infection.

It's a dark, malign thing.

Wrong.

Corrosive.

Lancelot has made me weak.

Powerless.

A shudder goes through me.

I never want to feel like this again.

The demon is to blame.

That smug, smirking bastard.

I'll show him just how powerful I am, with or without his precious shadowmancy.

No one should have access to this power.

It's far too destructive.

We should never have conjured Lancelot.

As an MID officer, I know what has to happen now.

I need to protect the world from this.

I need to banish Lancelot—screw the consequences—but first; I need to get my magic back.

So, that's exactly what I'm going to do.

Chapter 27
Christian

By the time the sun sets—after much sweating, shaking, and vomiting, courtesy of Lancelot's foreign power, no doubt—I'm sure I have enough strength to heave myself out of bed.

Is this what John's addiction felt like?

Is that what I am?

An addict?

No.

I'm no addict.

I've only had one dose of Lancelot's power, and I don't intend to have any more.

The last of my dizziness subsides and, when I'm feeling more like myself again, I swing my legs around and drop my feet to the floor.

I stand on my elastic muscles and take a couple of experimental steps.

The worst of it seems to have passed.

My mind turns to what needs to happen next.

Am I ready to banish Lancelot?

A shiver passes down my spine.

I don't have a choice.

There's no way to contact Kate, and no one at Pentacle is going to help me.

The demon might be powerful, but so am I.

I clench my fists.

Besides, Lancelot said it himself when we first conjured him. He's in a weakened state.

Luckily for you, I am not strong enough to stay in this realm without the aid of the circle... for now...

I can do this.

I stride over to my bedroom door, through the apartments and—thank God—don't come across another living soul.

Good.

I won't have to think of an excuse about why I'm sneaking into Lancelot's lair in the dead of night.

I make it to the kitchen, breathless.

Picking my way through the room, I find the cupboard housing the liquid silver syringes I'd seen on my first day here. I pluck out a syringe, uncap it, jab the needle's sharp tip into the crook of my elbow, and depress the plunger.

The familiar cold grips me, quickly thawed by a rush of heat.

Warmth suffuses my chest, and I know the liquid silver has replenished my magic.

Chucking the spent syringe in the waste bin, I exit the kitchen and cross the living area until I'm facing the bare stretch of brick wall that marks the entrance to the basement.

"Here goes nothing," I mutter, placing my hand flat against the cool, rough brickwork. "*Patentibus.*"

The welcome buzz of magic flares in my chest and races down my arm, copper coats the back of my tongue, and the potent scent of ozone prickles in my nostrils.

It's the best feeling in the world.

The lively snap-crackle of magic is warm and natural... and mine.

The spell takes hold, and the solid brick wall slides silently to one side.

I'm only wearing thin clothes, so the cold gust of air that greets me pinches my skin tight.

I consider turning back.

What if Lancelot made good on his threat to expose my true identity before I could banish him?

I could put John and the others in danger.

What if—

No.

It's a far greater risk to leave that thing on this side of the Gates.

The havoc he could wreak if he broke free...

A second shudder rips through me, and it has little to do with the cold.

It doesn't bear thinking about.

My bare foot finds the first stone step, and I grit my teeth against the icy chill.

No going back.

I need to end this.

Now.

I sense Lancelot's presence—dark and unyielding—before I've even reached the foot of the stairs.

I wave my hand through the air. *"Ignis."*

All the candles in the room sputter to life, lit by the violet glow of my magic. As they catch hold, the light flares up, illuminating Lancelot's stony face.

He stands facing me, expectant.

In hindsight, I'm sure he knew I intended to come here.

"I wondered how long it would take you," he says.

A crawling tingle passes over my scalp, like the delicate creep of a spider's legs.

I approach the demon's cage with caution.

His eyes meet mine, pupils bloated.

I force myself to hold his gaze. "It was a mistake to summon you. I'm sending you back."

"Sending me back?" Lancelot's face breaks into a shit-eating grin, and he laces his fingers in front of him. "We both know that is a lie."

My stomach tightens. "Do we?"

His eyes flash. "Do not push me, Christian Winter. Remember what I hold over your head."

I will tell them who you are.

I swallow a hard lump in my throat. "The others aren't here, you can't—"

"Do not presume to tell me what I can and cannot do." Lancelot paces back-and-forth, like a defense lawyer presenting a case to a jury. "The longer I spend in this realm, the more powerful I become."

I suppress a shiver. "How?"

He taps the side of his nose in a 'that's for me to know, and you to find out,' way, a knife-like smile parting his lips. "The range of my Curse is much greater than it was three days ago. I can communicate with Aidan Adedeji and his friends from here."

When I speak, my voice comes out steady. "You're bluffing."

"Are you willing to stake your life on that? Or... your brother's life, perhaps?"

My stomach lurches.

John.

Tori.

Kate.

I need to keep them safe.

"I hate you," I spit at him.

"You might hate me, but you love the power I can give you."

My heart skips a beat. "That's bullshit."

"Have you forgotten my Curse?" He taps the side of his head. "I can read fears and hopes. You crave power more than anything."

"Liar."

He holds up his hand.

I fall silent.

"You are the one lying. You lie to yourself. The more I read, the more I know."

"What's that supposed to mean?"

"You saw what being powerless did to your brother. How it ruined him. You fear an absence of power above all else."

An absence of power.

Sweat slicks my palms, and my pulse hammers at my wrist.

Is he right?

"You enjoy it when people comment on your magical proficiency, because it gives you status among your peers."

Am I that person?

"And that, Christian Winter, is why you do not intend to banish me. I can give you the one thing you crave. More power than you know what to do with. I can end your fear."

As much as I want to scream that he's wrong, to brand him a lying demon bastard...

I can't.

"You..." The words die in my throat.

"I love being right."

Hot coals burn in my gut, rage chasing away my apathy. "I swear on my magic, you smug son of a—"

"What the fuck are you doing down here?" a voice says from behind me.

Chapter 28
Christian

"Are you deaf?" Michelle snaps. "I said, what the fuck are you doing?"

I flinch and twist to face her.

She looks as wrecked as I feel.

Her long red tresses stand away from her head in a mess of tangles, and dark smudges bruise the sallow skin beneath her eyes.

"Um... I—I was just—"

She makes a mocking series of sputtering noises and takes two steps towards me. "Well, spit it out."

Lancelot scuffs his feet behind me. "He came down here to b—"

"I need more!" I shout over him, before he can land me in the shit.

Michelle narrows her eyes, and her smooth brow corrugates into a deep frown. "More?"

"More power," I say.

She sets her jaw. "Ade decides when we get more, not you."

"Actually—" Lancelot's tone is steely "—that decision rests with me."

We both ignore him.

"It's..." I allow just the right amount of hesitation. "I don't want to wait."

She cocks her head to the side; her gaze travelling over my shoulder. "Is he telling the truth?"

My stomach drops.

Lancelot could undo my entire undercover mission based on what he says next.

That is up to you, witch... are you still planning on banishing me?

Fuck.

He's got me.

There's only one way out of this mess.

I direct my thoughts at him. *No.*

You swear it?

I swear.

On your magic?

I hate this demon with every fibre of my being.

His sneering voice chides me. *Well? Do you swear it on your magic?*

I swear on my magic.

Lancelot smiles at Michelle. "Of course he is telling the truth. Demonic power can have this effect on some people. It can be... addictive."

Michelle's eyes scan Lancelot warily.

Those smart cogs of hers are whirring again, trying to figure out if the demon's lying.

The silence stretches on, and on, and on.

Eventually, Michelle's gaze snaps back to mine. "Addictive or not, we wait. Aidan will tell us when it's time."

"I can't—"

"Get your shit together. If you can't, we've got no use for you. Now, come on. I'm hungry, and I could do with some coffee, too."

She turns to leave.

My feet remain rooted to the spot.

"Don't make me tell you again," she says.

I can't afford to make her any more suspicious than she already is. With a last glare at Lancelot, I follow her.

When I reach the stairs, the demon's voice caresses the edges of my mind.

You made the right choice, witch. I will only warn you one last time. Try anything like this again, and I swear, I will tell them everything about you.

There's a tightness in my throat I can't shift.

He's got me backed into a corner.

And he knows it.

I trudge back upstairs, trailing in Michelle's wake.

My cover is still intact.

I should be happy. I'm not, because I hate feeling trapped. But I need to keep the people I love safe. I couldn't live with myself if anything ever happened to John and the others.

Something else nags at the back of my mind.

What was it Lancelot told Michelle?

Demonic power can have that effect on some people. It can be... addictive.

I'd assumed he said that to get me off the hook...

What if he was telling the truth?

Am I becoming addicted to shadowmancy?

An icy cool finger trails down my spine.

No.

I'm no addict.

Lancelot's wrong.

I can resist his power. There's no way—

Something hard thuds into my chest.

My back slams against the wall.

Michelle stalks towards me, her eyes shining with fury.

"What the fuck are you—"

Michelle's lips move and her hand rises, the tips of her fingers curled into claws. "*Pedibus nostris.*"

The binding spell freezes me in place.

Shit.

I'm so stupid.

I'd replenished my magic using liquid silver. It stands to reason Michelle would've done the same thing.

I try to move my feet, but they won't budge.

"What are you doing?"

Without breaking stride, Michelle marches forward until our noses are inches apart. The moonlight streaming through the windows catches her hair, and—even in the darkness—it ripples like liquid fire. "Know this," she hisses. "I don't trust you."

"I haven't—"

"Don't fuck with me. I can't prove it—yet—but you're shady as shit. I'll find out what you're up to, and when I do, you'll be sorry."

With that, she spins away from me and strides from the room.

Snap.

The pressure on my legs eases the moment the binding spell dissipates.

I rub my tired eyes, breathing hard, heart slamming against my ribcage.

Fuck.

I was right about Michelle.

She's had my card marked this entire time.

So much for treading carefully. I'm on seriously thin ice, and it's cracking beneath my feet.

This case had better wrap up soon, because I'm not sure how much longer I can last.

Gathering my resolve, I turn back to the opening in the brick wall and wave my hand across it. "*Claudere.*"

Just before the gap in the brickwork closes, Lancelot's voice drifts through my mind like smoke.

Remember how high the stakes are...

The wall is smooth again.

He wasn't bluffing.

His powers are growing.

Try anything like this again, and I swear, I will tell them everything about you.

Lancelot's threat is clear.

If I make a move against him, he'll expose me.

Pentacle will go after my loved ones.

Damn.

What the hell am I going to do now?

Chapter 29
Tori

I'm alone in the incident room, staring at the board upon which we have pinned all the information we have on Aidan Adedeji, and the other members of Pentacle.

A pen from Christian's desk sits on the table in front of me.

Four times I've tried to cast a locator spell on the pen.

Each time, it failed.

The spell refuses to catch.

Where are you, Cristian?

A slow, creeping dread crawls through my stomach.

I pick up the pen, grip it hard, about to try the locater spell again, when footsteps sound behind me. I turn to find Kate striding towards me.

"Tori," she says, "I thought I sent you home."

I fasten my gaze back on the board. "You did, ma'am."

She comes closer. "He'll be okay."

I shake my head. "You can't promise that."

Her cool hand rests on my shoulder. "I've known Christian a long time. He's a bloody good detective. There'll be a reason he's still with Pentacle."

"I can't track him." I hold up the pen.

Kate's grip firms on my shoulder, and she spins me round to face her. "I'm not surprised. Pentacle will be wise to locater spells. Wherever they're holed up, Adedeji will have warded it."

I make a noise in my throat that might be assent.

"What is it?"

"What if…?" I can't finish the question.

Kate must know what I was going to ask, because she says, "You can't think like that."

"We need to do something!" I brush her hand away and stalk to the other side of the room.

"Like what?"

I pinch the bridge of my nose, attempting to ease the first pangs of the headache. "We should have officers out there trying to locate Pentacle."

Kate stays silent.

Her lack of response sparks a pang of heat in my gut, and I twist to face her. "How can you stay so calm? Don't you want him back?"

She glares at me, fire flaring in her russet eyes.

I brush my hair away from my face. "Sorry. That wasn't fair. I just… I hate sitting on my arse. There must be something we can do."

"I don't see what. I sent some junior officers to the industrial estate. They picked up a faint energy signature, likely left behind by a portal."

A twinge of something like hope stirs in my chest, but the look on Kate's face smothers it.

"They weren't able to trace it back to the source," she says.

My fists clench. "We can't just leave him there."

"We won't. Pentacle are bound to surface eventually, and when they do, we'll be ready."

"And if he... if he isn't with them, what then?"

"He will be. They needed a fifth witch."

I nod, but without conviction.

"He'll be fine," she repeats.

"Sure." The word comes out flat.

"Actually, there is something you can do?"

My head snaps up. "Ma'am?"

"John."

John?

No offense, but what does Christian's brother have to do with anything?

"What about him?" I ask.

"I promised Christian I'd check in on him, but I dare not leave right now."

I open my mouth to argue—

"You wanted to do something. This will help."

I snort. "How?"

"By taking something off my plate."

I sigh. "Fine. I'll check in on him."

"Thank you." Kate turns her attention to the incident board, her eyes locked on the photo of Aidan Adedeji. "We'll find him, Tori. We'll get him back."

"I hope so."

Chapter 30
Tori

I pull my car to a halt outside Christian's house.

The lights are on, so John must be home.

I kill the engine, slide out of the car, and shut the door behind me, grateful I'd decided not to wear a jacket.

Although the moon is high, the night air is still muggy and close.

My footsteps crunch across the gravel driveway and the closer I get to the house, the more my stomach tightens.

I'm nervous… well, not nervous, exactly.

It's a strange mix of apprehension and excitement I can't quite pin down.

When I met John the other night—when we hugged—I felt something.

Some kind of connection.

It makes little sense.

I don't fancy him or anything like that.

He's not my type.

Too groomed.

Way too preppy looking.

But there's something…

I don't warm to people easily, but John instantly put me at ease, like I'd known him forever.

It was like I… recognised him, which is ridiculous, because I'd never met him before.

And now I sound certifiably insane.

Maybe it's because Christian spoke about him so often, or because I've seen his picture above the mantelpiece so many times.

Whatever it is, he feels familiar.

There's another reason for the pinch in my gut, too.

Christian.

Where is he?

Why did he miss his check in?

John is my only connection to Christian right now.

Maybe that's why I'm excited to see him.

When I reach the front door, I raise my fist and rap on the wooden surface three times. I wait, my fingers fiddling with the hem of my top.

Seconds pass, then John approaches the door—his figure distorted by the clouded glass.

The door opens.

John's expression is one of shock, his golden eyebrows raised. "Oh, hey."

"Hi."

He stands back, sweeping his arm in a wide arc. "Come in."

"Thanks," I say, striding over the threshold.

Cooking smells waft up my nose.

Sesame oil, rich and savoury.

Ginger, sharp and spicy.

My stomach rumbles… *loudly*.

I've had a busy few days at work, and I can't remember the last time I've eaten.

John chuckles. "Hungry?"

I give him a sheepish smile. "Starving."

"Good thing, too. I always make way too much stir-fry." He brushes past me and heads into the kitchen.

The deep, *umami* scent of John's cooking is stronger in here.

My mouth waters.

John picks up a wooden spatula and crosses to the wok on the hob, stirring the hissing contents. "If you came to see Chris, he's not here. He's—"

"Working undercover, I know."

John halts, turns, and fixes me with a sharp look. "You're with the MID too, then?"

I nod. "I came to see you."

He places the spatula on a plate next to the stove. "Me? Why?"

"My boss asked me to pop by. She promised Christian she'd keep an eye on you while he was gone."

I don't know why, but I expect him to be annoyed by this, like we're checking up on him or something.

He surprises me when he says, "That's thoughtful, but there's no need. I'm fine." His fingers reach up and find the golden dragon pendant hanging around his neck. He runs it back-and-forth across the chain, and it rasps.

I zero in on the movement. "You sure about that?"

He drops the pendant like it scalds him, crosses to the cupboards and fetches two plates and some cutlery. "Honestly, I've been feeling a bit... off, to tell you the truth."

Off?

Christian's told me all about John's past, and his addictions.

My eyes scan the room for empty vodka bottles and discarded drug paraphernalia.

He laughs. "Relax. I'm not about to shoot up, or anything. It's just weird, being back here."

The back of my neck tingles.

He's holding something back.

Before I can question him further, he says, "Come on, let's eat." He dishes up our meal, and we sit at the kitchen table.

I scoop up a huge forkful of stir-fry and cram it into my mouth.

The flavours explode on my tongue—salty, spicy, with just a hint of sweetness.

Heaven.

I groan.

This makes John grin.

He looks a lot younger—a lot more carefree—when he smiles.

"Good?" he asks.

I swallow the large mouthful. "Good? It's amazing! Who taught you to cook like this?"

His expression clouds over, and he shoves in a huge mouthful of his own.

"Sorry," I say, although I'm not sure why.

He shakes his head and takes a long draft from the glass of water beside his plate. "So, how long have you and Chris been seeing each other?"

He'll be fine.

The echo of Kate's words sounds hollow, and the food—so scrumptious seconds ago—tastes sour in my mouth.

What if something happened to him?

What if—

John's gaze sharpens, his blue eyes freezing into icy pools. "What is it, Tori?"

I swallow, hard.

A shiver runs down my spine.

I take a sip of my drink. "Nothing."

"You're lying."

I pick at the corner of my placemat. "I can't tell you."

"What do you mean?"

"You're not an MID officer. I can't share classified information with you."

He grips the edge of the table. "If something's happened to Chris, I need to know."

"I never said—"

"What's happened?"

I need to get him off this topic.

"What are you hiding, John?"

His face goes blank.

The only sound is the *tick, tick, tick* of the clock mounted on the wall.

"Well?" I arch an eyebrow at him.

He arches an eyebrow right back. "We all have secrets. I'm far more interested in yours."

"What? What are you talking—"

He holds up his hand. "Nothing. Forget it."

A spark of irritation flares in my chest. "No. I won't forget it. What did you mean by that?"

He takes a deep breath. "It's stupid. You'll think I'm mad."

I lean back in my chair and cross my arms. "Try me."

He snorts. "Okay. This is going to sound insane, but... when we met the other night, did you...?"

My heart rate quickens. "Did I what?"

"Did you feel anything?"

A strange mix of apprehension and excitement.

Some kind of connection.

Like I recognised him.

I try to respond, but my mouth is too dry. I take another sip of water and clear my throat. "No."

His eyes narrow. "Now who's hiding things?"

"I'm not."

His fingers find that dragon's head pendant again. "Yeah, you are. I can tell."

I cross my arms and scoff. "How?"

He shrugs. "I'm good at reading people."

My eyes still haven't left the dragon's head. "That's unusual."

"Pardon?"

"That pendant. It's unusual."

He drops it again. "Not really. Picked it up at a flea market. Ten-a-penny."

"Flea market, my eye."

We lapse into an uneasy silence while we finish eating.

When we're done, John clears the plates.

The whole time, I can't stop thinking about that pendant.

There's something strange about it, something that makes the hairs on the back of my neck stand on end, but I can't work out what it is.

When John turns to face me again, I swear the pendant glows, lit from within by a faint golden corona of light.

I'm entranced by that glow.

My legs move of their own accord. I walk towards him slowly, unable to take my eyes off the glimmering dragon's head.

"What are you doing?" he asks.

I don't really know.

My hand rises...

My fingers brush the pendant... and everything breaks apart in a shower of golden shards.

Chapter 31
Tori

Everything here is gold-tinted.

Wherever here is?

The landscape in front of me is craggy, the dark peaks of rugged mountains rising in the distance.

And the sky...

I've seen nothing like it before.

The bloated clouds writhe and twist like tormented beasts, and they're the sickly yellow colour of bile.

My nostrils flare.

The air reeks of sulphur.

What's going on?

What's—

I glance down.

There's someone sprawled at my feet.

A beautiful young woman. She has long, glossy, dark hair, delicate features, and she's clad from head to toe in tough-looking, worn leather, like armour.

The wound in her stomach gushes dark blood.

I stand over her, but it's not really me.

My hands don't belong to me.

They're too big.

The skin's too pale.

And there's a sword clutched in my grip.

Blood drips from the blade and stains the foreign hand.

That's not all.

There's a slight weight around my neck.

My eyes find the pendant.

John's dragon head pendant.

My—John's—lips move.

"Selina," he says.

Chapter 32
Tori

John steps away from me, and the image of the young woman disappears.

I'm back in the kitchen.

My head spins, and when I try to speak, no sound comes out. My heart beats against my rib cage and I taste acid at the back of my throat.

"Tori?" His features crease with concern. "You all right?"

Bile-coloured clouds.

Air stinking of sulphur.

The blood.

So much blood.

Selina.

I back away from him. "What—what the fuck was that?"

"What was what?"

I jab a shaking finger towards the pendant. "*That*?"

His gaze drifts down, then back up to mine. He's staring at me with something like... awe.

"Why are you looking at me like that?" I ask.

He blinks, lips parted. "I knew it."

"You knew what?"

He takes a step towards me.

I flinch back. "Stay the hell away from me."

"Hey." He holds out his hands. "I won't hurt you."

"No?"

The blood.

Sulphur.

"Tell that to Selina," I say.

John sucks in a breath like I winded him, and tears form at the corner of his eyes. "What... where did you hear that name?"

"I..."

What just happened?

John's gaze does that weird thing where it goes all sharp and hard. "What did you See?"

Panic stirs in my chest, spreads down to my core, and leaves me awash with queasy heat. "See? I didn't—"

He darts forward, faster than I've ever seen anyone move, and grips my upper arms.

I struggle. "Get off me."

"This isn't a game. Tell me what you Saw." His grip tightens.

I react the only way I know how. I conjure my magic, prickling pins and needles racing up and down my arms, the sharp ozone scent cutting through the air. "*Pedibus nostris.*"

The binding spell hits John, and his entire body goes rigid.

I prise myself out of his frozen grip and back away.

The muscles in his arms strain against the spell, but it's no use.

I've got him locked tight.

He makes a sound in his throat, like he's trying to speak.

I wave my hand, relinquishing the part of the spell holding his mouth closed.

His lips snap open. "What you Saw. It's not what you think."

I open my mouth, close it again.

Whatever just happened, I can't admit to it.

God, I think I'm going mad.

"I told you, I didn't See anything. I don't know what you're—"

"Has anything like that happened to you before?"

"Anything like what?"

"Anything you can't explain?"

"I—no..."

Wait.

That's not quite true, is it?

What about what happened with Stone last year?

He'd broken into the evidence room, searching for the Cursed Crown.

I followed him inside.

He tried to hide from me using an invisibility spell, when...

Where are you? I know you're here.

Where are you? I know you're here.

Where are you? I know you're here.

The mantra had come from nowhere.

A golden glow had suffused the room, and Stone's invisibility spell had broken, without me having to cast anything.

I told no one because...

Because casting without reciting a spell is impossible.

"Something else has happened," John says, snapping me out of my reverie.

"What?" The room should be stuffy, but the temperature has plummeted, and I have to tense my thighs to stop my knees from shaking. "No. Don't be ridiculous." I can't catch my breath.

"Tori—"

I need to get out of here.

I need to run.

"I—I have to go." The ringing in my ears blocks out John's reply. I spin on my heel, bolt from the kitchen, and sprint to the front door. I yank the door open, racing to my car.

Then I'm behind the wheel.

I shove my key into the ignition and twist.

The engine roars to life.

I jam the accelerator down.

The wheels spin, kicking up gravel, and then I'm speeding away.

I don't release John's binding spell until I'm halfway down the drive.

And even then, his words still ring in my ears.

What did you See?

Chapter 33
Christian

Remember how high the stakes are...
The threat of exposure Lancelot holds over my head hangs there like the sword of Damocles, forcing me to go along with Pentacle's plans—at least for now.

It's been three weeks since my last one-on-one conversation with Lancelot, and during that time, he's been teaching us how to control our borrowed shadowmancy.

The euphoric rush I'd experienced in those first few days has long since vanished, but the addiction hasn't.

The longer I go without an injection of demonic power, the weaker I become.

I need it just to feel normal.

In my 'sober' periods, I'm subjected to the most hideous migraines I've ever experienced. My limbs shake, and my hands are clammy with sweat.

Not long now.
Hold on.

All I need to do is hold on a little longer, then I can go home.

Home.

John.

Tori.

Kate.

I bet they're climbing the walls.

But I can't do anything about that right now.

All I can do now is bide my time.

Aside from its addictive qualities, shadowmancy's having some other, more desirable effects.

I am—as promised—becoming more powerful with each passing day.

We're all gathered in Lancelot's layer now.

He's teaching us how to wield a shadow-strike.

A long table stands at the other end of the basement.

Aidan has placed a row of empty tin cans on it.

"Focus," Lancelot says. "You almost had it last time."

I roll my shoulders and raise my hand for what seems like the millionth time, fingers outstretched in the table's direction.

"You've got this, Carl," Eric says.

"Humph."

Michelle.

Who else?

I ignore the scornful noise, narrowing my eyes at the can in the centre, following Lancelot's earlier instructions.

Take a deep breath.

Empty my mind of everything but my intention.

Exhale.

And...

Strike.

A tingling chill breaks out at the base of my skull.

It's working this time.

Ice spreads down my throat, into my chest, and down my arm.

A thin trail of black smoke curls from my fingers and floats up to the ceiling, before fading away to nothing.

The chill abates.

Shit.

Failed again.

Lancelot shakes his head. "Pathetic."

Michelle laughs.

"Chelle," Aidan chides, but there's no heart in it. He's given up trying to stop us from spatting.

The sound of Michelle's throaty chuckle grates on my last nerve.

I spin round and glare at her. "I don't see you doing any better."

Her lips pinch.

Ha!

That shut her up.

"We have to keep trying," Naomi says. "We can't give up."

Sweat beads on my forehead, and my fingers tremble. "I'm trying."

"Not enough, it seems," Lancelot says.

I grit my teeth. I dare not talk back to the demon.

There's that silent threat again.

Rearing its ugly head.

Remember how high the stakes are...

Lancelot continues, "Summoning a shadow-strike takes precision. It takes an iron will. Again."

I sigh. "I need a break."

"Again," he barks.

I set my jaw.

Arsehole.

I turn back to the row of cans and raise my arm again.

"Remember—"

"I know." Despite my resolve not to snap at Lancelot, my words are sharp. "Focus."

Lancelot glowers at me, his mental voice baring into my mind. *You will mind your manners when you address me, witch.*

I give a tight nod.

Okay.

I've got this.

Breathe in.

Clear my mind.

Exhale.

I command you to strike.

The chill returns, much colder this time, racing through my veins with such ferocity it makes me gasp.

My blood thunders, and my pulse pounds.

It's going to—

Whoosh.

A thick stream of dark shadow rockets from my hand, speeding towards the row of metal cans.

On impact—

The torrent of force slams into the table and sends everything—cans, table, and all—flying backwards.

Smack.

The table collides with the back wall with a thunderous crunch and splits in two. Both halves strike the floor with a loud thump.

My stomach clenches.

I glance from the table to my shuddering hand, and back again.

The raw, freezing power still radiates off me in rolling waves.

Lancelot's beaming one of his trademark humourless smiles. "Not bad, for a first attempt. You will become stronger with practise."

Stronger?

That table snapped in two with hardly any effort on my part.

What the fuck will we be capable of with more practise?

It doesn't bear thinking about.

The light in Aidan's eyes tells me he's having the same revelation.

Unlike me, however, the thought doesn't displease him.

He's smiling like a child on Christmas morning.

"Astounding," he whispers. Then he raises his voice. "Opposing The Witches Council is going to be a walk in the park."

I don't like this.

I don't like it at all.

No? Lancelot's voice echoes through my mind. *Admit it to yourself, Christian Winter. Part of you enjoys having this power. If you stopped fighting it, you would enjoy it even more.*

Despite his earlier warning, I narrow my eyes at him. *Shut up.*

He just lifts the corner of his mouth in a lazy grin.

He's right, of course.

Part of me enjoys how it feels to wield shadowmancy.

Just give in.

Lancelot's voice again.

He keeps doing this.

Whispering to me more and more.

Telling me to give in.

Give in to what, though?

I'm already using shadowmancy when he tells me to.

What more does he want?

I've been fighting the demon's whispers so hard.

But I'm tired.

Lancelot clears his throat. "Time for another dose, I think."

"Again?" There's a hint of apprehension in Eric's voice. "We only topped up two hours ago. Aren't you giving us too much?"

Lancelot shrugs. "The more shadow you take in, the easier it will be for you to control it."

"How long?" Naomi says, a bite in her tone. "How long until we can take on The Witches Council?"

"Not long now. I estimate another few days before you have full control of your new abilities."

"A few days?" Michelle says, her gaze sharp.

The demon's eyes flash black. "Was my meaning unclear?"

Michelle shrinks away from the circle.

"Do what he says," Aidan snaps, stepping towards Lancelot.

I get that now familiar, creeping, sinking sense of wrongness.

We're tumbling down a dark rabbit hole, and I hate to think of what's waiting at the bottom.

I step forwards. "I don't think that's a good idea, Ade."

"It's not your choice. I'm in charge, and I say we take more power."

"I'm not—"

"Don't question me."

I clench my fists. "I just think it's prudent to—"

Aidan marches up to me and jabs a finger into my chest. "Remember why we're doing this? My sister. Your brother."

"I know... it's just... this feels risky."

He waves his hand like he's shooing an irritating wasp. "All power comes with risks. Just think of the rewards."

Equality and justice.

That's what Aidan's fighting for.

His sister.

My brother.

Fairness for all witches.

Is that so wrong?

My job has exposed me to a lot of nasty bastards, and I can't deny improvements need to be made. And the longer I stay here, the more convincing Aidan's argument becomes.

An icy fist clamps around my heart and shakes.

No.

What am I thinking?

Aidan wants to take down The Witches Council.

The story about Naismith and his sister is a lie.

I can't forget why I'm here.

To stop Pentacle.

A new mantra cycles through my mind.

My name is Christian Winter. I'm twenty-nine years old. I'm a Detective Inspector at the Magical Investigations Department.

My name is Christian Winter—

Lancelot's voice scrapes through my mind. *You are not strong enough to resist my power.*

You're wrong.

And you delude yourself.

I can resist.

But you don't want to.

I...

Relent.

Never.

Relent.

I can't.

Relent.

It's like I'm a dam, and the pressure of Lancelot's will is the water pushing against me, straining to break through.

The pressure builds, becoming more and more and more intense.

Until...

The last of my resistance vanishes.

My limbs move as if controlled by a puppeteer. Brushing past Aidan, I glide up to the barrier. My hand rests against the glowing shield of its own accord.

Lancelot's satisfied smile curdles my stomach, but I don't back away. I couldn't even if I tried.

The demon's hand drifts up to meet mine.

Sable smoke rushes out of him and into me.

I close my eyes, floating in a numbing sea of black.

Chapter 34
Lancelot

I relish the thrill of the Ley Line energy flowing through me, and into Christian Winter, because it means I am one step closer to freedom.

Witches.

It appears they never change.

I have not walked on this earth for over fifteen hundred years, and they are still a race of arrogant fools.

Aidan Adedeji and his acolytes believe they control me.

They think the Transference of power is strengthening them and that is true, but I know something they do not.

Something I have intentionally failed to mention.

I am the one growing stronger.

Transference is not a one-way street.

The more energy I give, the more I take.

And the more energy I take, the weaker these witches will become... and eventually, their infernal circle will break.

Christian Winter's will is already crumbling under the weight of my influence. It will not be long until the others follow suit and, when that happens, this pathetic cage I find myself in will malfunction.

I will be free.

A shiver goes through me.

How dare these witches think they can tame me?

I will make them sorry.

I will make them pay.

Look at him.

Christian Winter.

Lost in the throes of shadow.

Heavy eyelids half-closed.

Lips parted a little.

A small smile curving his lips.

How could these witches ever think their bodies could ever contain the incredible power of the Lines?

Like I said.

Pathetic.

I will enjoy watching them fall one by one.

A reckoning is coming.

And it can't come soon enough.

Chapter 35
Christian

The day has finally arrived.

Today's the day Pentacle will march against The Witches Council.

I can't allow that to happen.

I might be drunk on Lancelot's power, but I'm still an MID officer, damn it, and I still know right from wrong.

This is so wrong.

We crowd around the long glass table that dominates the living area in Pentacle's headquarters.

Aidan's eyes flick around the room. "First things first, we Teleport straight into the chamber outside Naismith's office."

"What happens when we get there?" I ask.

"We do whatever it takes to find Naismith."

Whatever it takes...

A bead of cold sweat trickles down my spine.

Voice firm, Aidan says, "If you're not up to this—"

"No!" The word explodes from me. I need to be with Aidan and the others when they make their move. It's the only way I can stop them. "No," I say, more softly. "I know what I signed up for.

Michelle arches a fiery eyebrow at me. "You better not fuck this up."

"I won't."

She snorts and looks away.

Eric shakes his head. "Why so prickly today?"

"Shut up," Michelle snaps.

"If we could stay on track, I'd appreciate it." Aidan points to the blueprints spread across the table—blueprints of The Witches Council. "Naismith's office is here. He stations three guards outside here, here, and here. So, we Teleport in, and take them out, before we advance on him."

Take them out.

A polite euphemism for murder.

I need to be ready to stop this.

Aidan isn't hurting anyone on my watch.

As if reading my mind, Aidan says, "Chelle, Eric, Naomi. I want you to deal with the guards."

The three nod.

I shift from foot to foot. "What about me?"

"You and I seem to have the most control over shadowmancy. I want you with me."

"And what are we going to do?"

"We're going to end Naismith."

I go cold.

My head spins.

There are too many variables.

So much that can go wrong.

I don't know if I'll be able to—

Michelle says, "Every single one of them deserves to die."

Ugh.

Bile surges up my throat, bringing up words that refused to remain unspoken. "How can you say that?"

"Because it's true."

"There are innocent people in there." I turn to Aidan, attempting to reason with him one final time. I should have said something sooner, but we should think this through. Most of the witches on the Council now probably didn't even work there when Jules di—"

Aidan's eyes flash.

I change tack immediately. "When she was murdered. They aren't all to blame for what happened to her."

His nostrils flare, but he says nothing.

I press on. "What happened to 'empowering witches who deserve it, not murdering those who don't'?"

He's quiet for a long time. When he speaks, the volume of his voice is barely above a whisper. "Open your goddamn eyes. The Witches Council is a tight unit, and they're corrupt. Everyone who works there plays a hand in that."

My fists clench. "You can't know that."

"*Enough*!" Aidan hisses.

I fall silent.

"I'll give you one last chance, Carl. Are you with us… or against us?"

Michelle stares at me like a vulture eyeing up a particularly succulent carcass.

"Well?" Aidan asks, his tone deadly.

I don't have a choice.

Remember how high the stakes are…

Play along.

Not much longer now.

I glance away. "I'm with you."

"You sure about that?" Michelle asks.

I straighten my spine, and stare her down. "Yeah. Just a last-minute wobble. I'm over it."

Aidan regards me, lips pursed, for a long time. Then he marches forward and claps me on the shoulder. "Good."

The way he says the word *change* makes my blood run cold. "I just—"

Michelle barges between Aidan and I before I can blink, getting right in my face. "Why are you trying so hard to stop this? From the moment you got here, all you've done is ask questions, pick holes in our plans, and defend The Witches Council. Hardly seems like the Carl Weston I read up on when we recruited you."

The thin ice creeks beneath my feet.

One wrong move and I'll blow my cover.

"I'm not defending them," I say, squaring up to her. "Just trying to be rational. You clearly want to attack first and ask questions later, but that's exactly the sort of thinking we're trying to prevent. It's the kind of thinking that led to vessels being persecuted."

"Carl..." Naomi's tone is thick with warning.

"No. This is how it starts. Someone gets it into their head they're superior—"

"*Superior!*" Michelle's cheeks flush scarlet, a deep frown creasing her brow. "How dare you? Who the fuck do you think you are? You don't know the first thing about me."

"Cool it, guys," Eric says, with a worried glance between Michelle and I.

I round on him. "I don't need to cool anything. It's not me who—"

"Shut up. All of you." Aidan's voice thunders around the room. "I've given my orders."

Heavy silence settles over us.

Eventually, Aidan locks eyes with me. "I know change is hard, but it's for the best."

I give a short nod.

"So, are we ready?" Naomi asks.

"Almost. Wait here." He disappears into the kitchen and, when he returns, he's holding five slim, black cases.

My brow creases. "Are they what I think they are?"

He bobs his head. "Liquid silver syringes."

I accept mine. "What's the point? We've got shadowmancy. No one can touch us."

He shrugs. "You never know when magic might come in handy."

I pocket the syringe, and the others do the same.

"Now we're ready." Aidan grasps my hand, and Naomi clasps his—on and on until we stand in an unbroken chain.

"Concentrate on Teleporting to The Witches Council," Aidan says.

I close my eyes, take a deep breath, and draw on the icy-dark power of shadowmancy.

Take us to The Witches Council.

Black smoke rises, my stomach plummets, and the world dissolves.

Chapter 36
Christian

My vision swims back into focus, revealing a cavernous round atrium with marble floors and wood-paneled walls.

"What the hell?" a male voice shouts.

I spin in place—heart thudding in my throat—and spot Naismith's three guards instantly.

They stand at equidistant points around the walls.

The second guard plants their feet in a wide stance. "Who the fuck are you, and how did you get in here?"

"We're taking over." Aidan's strong voice echoes around the hollow space. "And you can't stop us."

The final guard laughs. "Excuse me?"

"You heard." Eric's tone is unusually stern.

The first guard's mouth pinches tight.

Shit.

Guard number two's gaze flicks at the other two.

The third guard says, "You dare to come in here and threaten us."

Michelle takes a step forward. "We dare to do whatever the hell we want."

Aidan eyes each guard. "Fabian Naismith is corrupt. He isn't fit to lead us."

It's going to kick off.

I need to be ready.

The relevant passage from *Curses & Gifts: The Abilities of Demons and Sorcerers* shifts to the forefront of my mind.

> *Temporomancy: The ability to manipulate time, including slowing time, freezing time, and (in some extremely rare cases) reversing time.*

One guard nods at the other two, and all three conjure fireballs—green, blue, and orange respectively.

I need to freeze time if I'm going to save these people without Pentacle noticing.

The problem is, I've never tried it before.

"You're all under arrest," one guard says. "Come quietly, or we will use reasonable force."

Please let this work.

Aidan smiles a sharp, lupine smile. "Do your worst."

The witches launch their fireballs.

Aidan flings his arms out to the sides, and a dome of dark energy coalesces, separating us from our attackers.

The fire spells explode against the shadowmancy barrier, which doesn't even waver.

Shocked expressions mar the guards' faces.

"How did you do that?" one asks.

"You didn't cast," another says.

A thin smile cuts across Aidan's face. "Kill them."

Eric, Michelle, and Naomi spring into action, darting forward, and throwing their hands out.

It's now or never.

Shadow gathers in my colleagues' hands.

Time slows to a crawl.

With a unified cry of, "*Obstructionum*," the guards conjure rippling barriers.

Three coal-black streams of power erupt from Eric, Michelle, and Naomi, rocketing straight for the guards.

Their shields won't be enough.

Now.

Breathe in, clear my mind, and exhale.

The shadows are almost upon the guards.

Freeze.

Something rocks the room, and a sound like cannon-fire splits the air.

It's like I'm standing on a spinning turntable that slams to a sudden halt. The effect is so jarring; I stumble a few steps backward, but remain on my feet.

My mouth drops open.

Everyone—apart from me—stands frozen in place.

Like waxworks.

I take a few experimental steps.

Weird.

I'd imagined moving through frozen time to feel like wading through treacle, but I move with ease.

More confident now, I stride over to where Michelle and Eric stand side-by-side, their faces set into grim masks of determination.

I wave my hand in front of Michelle's eyes.

Nothing.

No flicker of recognition.

An icy finger trails down my spine.

What if I'm stuck like this forever?

What if I can't get time working again?

No.

I can't think like that.

Anything I can do, you can do, too.

That's what Lancelot said.

I've got this.

The room makes a creaking sound and tension prickles at my temples.

Shit.

Have the shadow-strikes inched forward slightly?

I don't know how long I can keep this up, but I have to make sure the guards are safe, just in case.

Anything I can do...

Telekinesis.

I focus my attention on Aidan's adversaries.

Move them.

The still-frozen guards skid across the marble floor like chess pieces, moved by massive, invisible hands. They end up standing together on the other side of the room, far from the reach of the shadow-strikes.

Thank God for that.

Time to save the leader of the Witches Council.

Take me to Naismith's office.

Chapter 37
Christian

The smoke fades and I'm standing before Naismith's desk.

He sits behind it, looking a lot older than I remember. His previously salt and pepper hair is white now.

A thumping pain booms through my head, but I keep my grip on time.

I need to act fast.

Unfreeze Naismith, and only Naismith.

Snap.

Naismith unfreezes and carries on writing in his ledger—or attempts to—but no ink leaves his pen. "Bloody thing."

I clear my throat.

He flinches, his eyes snapping to mine. "What the—"

"High Councillor," I interrupt, addressing Naismith using his proper title. "I'm DI Christian Winter. We need to—"

"How did you get in here?"

"I don't have time to explain. You're in danger. I need you to—"

"Danger? What in God's name are you talking about, man?"

"There are some bad people on the other side of that door. They've come here to overthrow The Witches Council."

He laughs, a deep, hearty chuckle. "Don't be so ridiculous. My guards—"

"They're safe, for now. But—"

"Was that a threat?" Naismith gets to his feet, lips moving in a chant.

"No. That didn't come out right. You need to listen to me. If we don't leave now, they'll kill you."

"They?"

"I've been working undercover inside a Supernatural Organised Crime Group called Pentacle."

The colour drains from his face. "Pentacle... you mean Adedeji?"

"I... yes, sir."

He shakes his head. "I don't believe you."

I direct my attention towards the closed office doors.

Open.

They spring apart, revealing the scene beyond.

Aidan wears a murderous expression.

Eric, Michelle, and Naomi fan out around him, frozen shadows arcing from their outstretched hands.

Naismith's mouth drops open and his face flushes. He paces back and forth. "No. This can't be happening. It can't."

I don't understand.

Why does he look so afraid?

That disgusting pervert, Naismith, was sexually harassing her. She knocked him back, and he fired her.

Those were Aidan's words back in the library.

He said that 'someone like her' should be grateful for his attention.

The High Councillor knew who Aidan was as soon as I mentioned Pentacle.

He told everyone he fired her for gross misconduct, that she snapped and went on a killing spree.

No.

It can't be...

"How do you know Aidan?" I ask.

Naismith's eyes dart to mine. "What?"

"I said Pentacle, and you knew it was Aidan out there."

The flush in his cheeks deepens. "Well, of course I did. Everyone knows Aidan Adedeji runs Pentacle."

He's lying.

I know he is. I can't...

Was everything Aidan said true?

Did Naismith frame Julianna Caldwell?

My mouth goes dry. "His sister was your assistant."

"Don't talk to me about that woman."

"The Siren."

"She was evil."

I have to find out if he's telling the truth... but how?

How can I?

Anything I can do...

Anything?

I am an Empath. I can read your hopes and fears as easily as a fortune teller reads tea-leaves.

Naismith's still talking. "Well, don't just stand there, man. Like you said, we need to get out of here."

It can't be true.

But I need to know.

I squint my eyes at him.

Naismith cries out. "Oh, my God... your eyes—they're black."

Reveal his fears.

Ice freezes my blood as the borrowed Empathetic Curse takes hold.

A kaleidoscope of images spins before my eyes.

Julianna Caldwell.

A much younger-looking Naismith.

A different office, much smaller than this one.

"*What are you doing?*" Julianna says.

"*Come on. I know you want me.*"

"*No—what are you... stop!*" She slaps him across the face.

"*How dare you? Someone like you should be grateful for my attention.*"

Bile rises in my throat and more snatches of the past whiz past.

Julianna getting fired.

Naismith's bosses putting pressure on him to get results on a murder case.

His blistering rage at the woman who'd knocked him back.

Naismith planting the evidence that framed Julianna.

Her arrest.

The trial.

Julianna knotting a sheet to one of her cell's window bars.

Her legs are swinging.

She's wheezing.

Choking—

"No!" The word explodes from my mouth.

Naismith lies slumped against the wall, knees trembling, teeth chattering. "How did you... do—that?"

My skin itches like it's soiled, like I need a good scrub. I glare at Naismith, breathing hard. "She was innocent."

"I—I didn't..." Naismith says, voice still shaking, "I didn't mean for it to go that far, but once I set things in motion, it was too late. If I'd told the truth—"

Scalding heat rips through me. "If you'd told the truth, she'd still be alive."

"I couldn't. It would've been the end of my career."

"You fucking bastard." *I want to break him.*

The cold tingle of shadowmancy spreads through my mind, a burst of Telekinetic energy tearing out of me.

Crash.

Naismith slams into the wall behind him. He screams, slides down the wall, and slumps on his side.

Shit.

I didn't mean to do that. I didn't mean to—

Why not, though?

He deserves it.

He's scum.

I cross the room and stride round the desk.

Naismith whimpers.

I grab his collar and wrench him into a seated position.

He squeals.

"Tell me why I shouldn't unfreeze them and let Aidan kill you?" I say, in an icy voice that's nothing like my own, pointing back at Aidan.

"Because of all the good I've done since then. You don't understand. I felt sick after she committed suicide. I knew it was my fault. The vessels were my way of making amends. They—"

"That doesn't make it right, you fucking scumbag!"

He's crying now. "I know. God, I know."

As much as I want to, I can't let Aidan kill Naismith. That would bring me down to his level, and I can't go there.

But...

Anything I can do...

Coercion.

The ability to compel someone to take a certain action.

I stare into Naismith's eyes.

Make him do whatever I say.

His gaze goes vacant.

"Listen to me," I say, a strange echo amplifying my voice. "You're going to do exactly what I tell you."

"Okay." The word is monotone.

"Go to the MID, ask to see DCI Kate Denton, and confess to your part in Julianna Caldwell's death. Tell her what happened, step-by-step."

"Step-by-step," he repeats in that same flat voice.

"Leave nothing out."

"Leave nothing out."

"Make sure—"

Fierce agony spikes through my brain, and I cry out.

Turns out, time doesn't like standing still.

The clock above Naismith's desk *tick, tick, ticks*.

Eric, Michelle, and Naomi's shadow-strikes roar back to life, crashing into the walls and splintering the panelling with a deafening crack.

"What the fuck?" Aidan's voice drips with venom.

Naomi furrows her brow at me. "How did you...?"

"How did you get over there, mate?" Eric asks.

The guards shake their heads, staring around in confusion.

Michelle's mouth pinches into a tight line. "You did something. You saved those guards."

"I can explain." My mouth is as dry as salt.

When Aidan speaks, it's through gritted teeth, his eyes glued to a mewling Naismith. "You were trying to get that murdering bastard out."

"Aidan. Listen to me, I've sorted it. I used Lancelot's Curse. He's going to—"

"Lancelot?" Naismith says.

"I'm going to kill you, traitor." Aidan raises his hands.

I get ready to pull on the cold power again. "You don't—"

Icy fingers dig into my skull.

Pain blossoms across my entire body.

I scream.

The ice spreads down my throat, through my chest, and into my gut.

I keep screaming.

The agony's like nothing I've ever experienced, like I'm being frozen from the inside out.

At first, I think it's Aidan's handiwork, and then I hear it.

Lancelot's voice.

You did not truly believe this circle could hold me forever, did you?

No.

Panic sputters in my chest.

He can't be free. He can't—

Foolish witches. Return to me. Now.

The ground beneath my feet shifts and shakes, a whirlpool of black smoke swirling at my ankles.

What the fu—

The smoke swallows me whole.

Chapter 38
Lancelot: Ten Minutes Earlier

I pace back and forth inside this God forsaken circle.

Not much longer now.

My power grows with every second.

Those damn witches.

So arrogant.

Thinking this circle can hold me.

That they control me.

That I am nothing more than a pet they have tamed.

They are wrong.

The link I have created via Transference tethers me to them, even now.

I can sense them.

Aidan Adedeji.

Naomi Adedeji.

Michelle Rees.

Eric Jiménez.

And Christian Winter.

Each of their pathetic, worthless hearts beat in time with mine.

It's a link that cannot be severed.

A link that has allowed me to feed off their magic, pulling its energy into my body, using it to fuel me and make me stronger.

Soon, their barrier will fall, and when it does, I will have my revenge.

And it will be sweet.

In fact...

I creep towards the circle's edge and press my hand against the shining surface of the copper barrier. My skin meets the force field, and a bright copper light flares.

Resistance.

I refuse to give in, not when I am so close to breaking free.

So close to emancipating my brethren.

There is no way in Hell I am going to stop now.

I push harder and harder and harder against the bastard shield.

The light flares so bright I have to squint my eyes.

Remember who you are.

I am Lancelot, the most revered Knight of Camelot.

I do not belong in a cage.

Trapped.

The play-thing of witches.

Enough is enough.

I give one final, almighty shove—

A crack of thunder booms through the room, and a hole opens up in the barrier.

My hand is on the other side, my wrist caught by the glowing bronze light.

A slow, wolfish grin plays over my lips.

Without the barrier to hold my power in check, nothing and no one can stop me from achieving my goal.

Well, almost no one.

There are those who can stop me.

The light to my darkness.

The yin to my yang.

Sorcerers.

I wish I could sense whether there are any close by, and curse the fact they can cloak themselves from demons until they're right on top of us.

A shudder runs through me.

I cannot think about them now.

I will cross that bridge if I happen upon it.

The only thing that matters now is destroying the Gates.

They call to me, even here.

Trying to drag me back to Hell.

I know where they are.

And I know exactly how I am going to get them.

Christian Winter might come in handy after all.

I concentrate on my connection to the five stooges I have set up so artfully.

I see them now, engaged on their fool's errand to destroy The Witches Council.

Aidan is doing this for his sister.

A worthy cause, for sure, but a plan that lacks vision.

Why stop at destroying The Council?

When I am finished—and when my brethren are finally free—it will not just be The Witches Council that falls.

No.

All of witch-kind will bow to us.

I turn my attention back to Pentacle.

They believe they are in control.

Holding all the cards.

Possessing all the power.

"Well, I will show you what genuine power looks like."

I close my eyes and call out to them.

You did not truly believe this circle could hold me forever, did you?

Their fear hits me like a drug.

I drink it in like the finest mead.

Foolish witches. Return to me. Now.

The time has come to end this, once and for all.

Chapter 39
Tori

I'm striding through reception at the MID when the automatic doors at the entrance part.

Fabian Naismith strolls in.

Strolls?

I've never known the High Councillor stroll anywhere.

Odd.

I change course and, when I reach him, say, "High Councillor. What can we do for you?"

He doesn't answer, and his eyes are a little unfocused.

"Mr Naismith," I rest my hand on his arm. "Are you all right?"

"I need to see DCI Denton," he says, his voice flat.

"She's a little busy at the moment. I can—"

"No. You don't understand. I need to see her, and I need to see her now." Sweat beads his upper lip.

I hesitate.

What's wrong with him?

Is he ill?

I bite my lip. "Okay. Follow me, High Councillor."

We take the lift to the top floor, and I lead Naismith through to the briefing room, where Kate's addressing the troops.

She pauses when we enter. "DC Falade, I'm in the middle of a—" she spots Naismith "—High Councillor Naismith. I wasn't expecting you."

Naismith's eyes bulge. "I need to speak to you, DCI Denton."

She nods. "Okay. Let's go to my off—"

He cuts across her. "It was my fault."

My brow furrows.

Huh?

Kate's expression matches mine. "What was your fault?"

He clamps his mouth shut and his cheeks flush red.

It's almost like he's fighting something.

The officers assembled in the briefing room mutter to each other, turning to their neighbours and whispering in confusion.

Kate steps closer. "I think we should talk in priv—"

"Julianna Caldwell." The strangled shout erupts from him.

I flinch.

Jesus.

You don't have to scream in my...

Wait.

Julianna Caldwell.

I recognise that name... but where from?

"The Siren," Kate says. "What about her?"

Siren.

The Siren Murders.

I remember reading the case files during training.

"I—" Naismith claps a hand to his mouth.

He still looks like he's battling something. He's definitely not well.

I turn to Kate. "Ma'am. Maybe we should—"

"I framed her," he says.

Silence blankets the room.

Kate's mouth drops open. "You what?"

The words rush out of him. "I don't know who murdered those men, but it wasn't her. She was innocent. I made a pass at her and she refused. She threatened to tell everyone, and I couldn't allow that. It would've ruined me. I... God, I never meant for it to go as far as it did, and when she killed herself... it was—all my—fault." His voice hitches and he cries.

"Shit," I back away from Naismith.

This is...

Surely, he wouldn't...

Kate moves closer, her fingers inching to the iron cuffs at her belt. "Why are you telling me this now?"

A crease appears on his forehead. "DI Winter told me to."

My heart skips a beat. "You've spoken to Christian?"

He nods.

"Is he... is he okay?"

Another shallow bob of the head.

Relief, sweet and warm, floods my system. "Thank—" my blood runs cold, and my eyes cut to Naismith's "—wait. What do you mean, he told you to?"

Naismith lets out a sudden scream.

Kate takes a step back.

The High Councillor clamps his hands to the sides of his head. "He told me to, he told me to, he told me to."

What the fuck is going on?

Kate crosses to Naismith's side. "Okay, okay. I'm going to need you to come with me."

A fearful look crosses his features. "Where?"

"I need to ask you some questions," she says, voice still soft.

"Questions about Jules?"

"That's right."

"I'm sorry." He slaps his forehead three times. "I'm sorry. I'm sorry."

Kate leads him away. "Fabian Naismith. I'm arresting you for…"

They move out of earshot.

Why are you telling me this now?

DI Winter told me to.

He told me to, he told me to, he told me to.

A shiver runs through me.

Jesus, Christian.

What did you do to him?

Chapter 40
Christian

Lancelot's lair swims into focus.

"What—what happened?" Aidan barks, eyes flying around the room. His gaze sharpens when he realises we're no longer in Naismith's office. He strides up to me. "What did you do?"

I take a step back, drawing my borrowed power close and getting ready to defend myself. But maybe I can still salvage this. "Nothing. Why would I want to pull you away from Naismith?"

Michelle stalks to Aidan's side. "That's a damn good question. I knew it. I knew there was something up with you. Why did you save those guards?"

I round on her. "They were innocent. Naismith is to blame for what happened to Julianna, not them."

When Aidan speaks again, his voice is low and deadly. "They were not innocent. That piece of shit stationed them there to defend him. I'm going back there right now, and I'm going to finish this."

Naomi places a steadying hand on her husband's arm. "I don't think that's such a good idea, Ade."

Aidan yanks his arm out of her grip, a wounded animal look on his face. "What? Are you defending Naismith now?"

She jerks back like he slapped her face. "Of course I'm not. But the MID'll be crawling all over The Witches Council by now. Someone will have called them."

"Naomi's right," Eric chimes in. "We'll never get close enough to him now. It's a suicide mission."

That familiar muscle ticks in Aidan's jaw. "I don't give a shit. I'm too close to let him get away with it now."

"Please—"

I cut across Naomi. "He won't."

When Aidan's eyes meet mine, they blaze. "What?"

Go to the MID, ask to see DCI Kate Denton, and confess to your part in Julianna Caldwell's death. Tell her what happened, step-by-step.

"He won't get away with it," I whisper.

"What the fuck are you talking about?" Michelle asks.

"I... you were right, Aidan."

Aidan's brow creases. "What do you mean?"

I take a deep breath and, on the exhale, the words burst from me in one long rush. "I used Lancelot's Curse on him. His greatest fear was of people discovering what he did to Julianna, and losing his job, his freedom. I couldn't believe it, but he did it. You were right. I... I Coerced him. I told him to go to the MID and confess."

Everyone is silent for a long time.

"He's going to pay for what he did to her," I say.

Aidan ducks his head and, when he glances up again, his eyes shimmer with tears. "It's not enough," he says in a choked voice.

"What? But—"

"My sister took her life because of that fucking wank-stain. I want him dead!"

I shake my head. "The MID will arrest him. They'll make sure he never—"

"Fuck the MID. It's not enough. It's not—"

Michelle—who's remained silent throughout this exchange—butts in, glaring at me. "What I want to know is why you pulled us all out of there."

"I already told you. I didn't pull us out. You can't—"

"Bullshit," she snarls.

"He is telling the truth... for once," Lancelot says from inside the circle.

Oh, shit.

I forgot about him.

Michelle's eyes widen. "What?"

"I said he is telling the truth. Christian Winter did not bring you back here. I did."

My stomach drops through the soles of my shoes.

Fuck.

Lancelot used my real name.

"You did what?" Aidan narrows his eyes at the demon.

"Wait." Michelle speaks at the same time. "Who the hell is Christian Winter?"

Lancelot's face contorts into a mask of mock-horror. "Oh, dear. The proverbial cat is out of the bag. Do you want to tell them, or should I?"

"You bastard," I say.

He just smiles.

Aidan's eyes flick between me and the demon, and back again. "Tell us what?"

I'm going to die.

As soon as they find out who I am—

"Tell. Us. What?" Aidan's voice rings through the room.

"I—" My voice cracks. "I don't know what he's talking about."

Lancelot chuckles. "Oh, come now, Christian Winter. Shyness does not become you."

My cheeks flush.

An icy chill flares at my back.

I spin round.

A swirling ball of shadow floats above Michelle's palm. "Will someone just tell us what the fuck is going on?"

"My, my. You are a feisty one. Fine. I shall tell you." Lancelot winks at me. "Keeping secrets is wrong, after all."

I clench my fists. "You promised you wouldn't tell them."

He smirks. "And you failed to extract an Oath from me like the foolish witch you are."

"Please—"

"This man is not Carl Weston. There is no Carl Weston."

My heart beats so fast it almost hums.

No, no, no.

Confusion clouds Eric's expression. "If he isn't Carl Weston, then who is he?"

Aidan adopts a new posture, shifting his centre of gravity lower and leaning forward, balancing on the balls of his feet.

He's ready to fight.

"Don't do this," I say.

"It is already done." Lancelot casts his dead, empty gaze over the Pentacle members before his eyes land on me. "His name is Christian Winter, and he is a Detective Inspector with the Magical Investigations Department."

My mouth goes dry.

The room is stunned into silence.

Then Michelle lets out a scream of rage. "You fucking treacherous bastard!"

I spin just in time to see her raise her arm and draw more power from the Lines. The shadow-strike's mass doubles.

Fuck!

She launches the strike.

I throw my hands out. Protect.

A shadow-shield rises before me.

Michelle's strike pummels into it with extreme force.

My arms shudder, the power of Michelle's attack driving me back a step.

The barrier holds... barely.

"Finish him, Chelle," Aidan says, his voice a deadly, snake-like hiss.

Michelle advances on me, another sphere of shadow gathering in her fingers. "I fucking knew it. Didn't I tell you, Ade? I knew you were messing with us. But this... a fucking cop!" She spits the word like venom and launches her power again.

I throw myself to the side.

Michelle's ball of shadowmancy whistles past, close enough to chill my skin and raise the hairs along my arms.

The infernal energy rockets past me, slamming into the basement wall, exploding in a black cloud.

The ground trembles.

Eric steps forward to assist Michelle.

"No," she snaps. "This is my fight."

Eric halts and gives a sharp nod.

I have to make her stop. "Lancelot's lying. Please, Chelle, I—"

"Only. My. Friends. Call. Me. Chelle." She grinds out, punctuating each word with a blast of dark smoke.

I conjure another shadow shield, just in time, but—

Crash-Crash-Crash-Crash-Crash-Crash.

Her attack batters my barrier, and on the sixth impact, it shatters.

The strength of that final blow sends me flying.

I tumble through the air in a moment of weightlessness.

My back strikes the floor with a muffled thump, all the air rushing from my lungs in a long wheeze.

Michelle stalks over to where I lay sprawled. She towers over me.

The temperature in the room drops when she plucks another swirl of shadow from the air.

Eyes narrowed to slits, she says, "No one makes fools of us and gets away with it."

Her arm rises.

She's too close.

I'm too winded.

There isn't much I can do to stop her.

This is it.

John.

Tori.

Kate.

I've failed them.

And I didn't even get to say goodbye.

I close my eyes and wait for death.

When my eyelids flicker open, I'm surprised to find I'm still alive.

Michelle isn't moving.

She's... frozen.

Did I do that?

Have I—in my desperation to live—frozen time again?

No.

Whatever's happening, it isn't down to me.

"What are you waiting for, Chelle? Kill him," Naomi orders.

"Ah, ah, ah." Lancelot wags his finger at Naomi. "I cannot allow you to harm him, I am afraid. Christian Winter is integral to my plans."

A dark shadow falls across Aidan's face. "Your plans. *Your* plans. In case it's escaped your notice, you're trapped."

Lancelot glances at the copper ring surrounding him as if he has no fucks to give.

A creeping chill raises my hackles, and—recovered from my winding—I clamber to my feet.

"We control you, demon," Aidan spits at him.

Lancelot's jet black eyes glitter. "Is that so... *witch*?"

My insides plummet.

Lancelot.

It was Lancelot who froze Michelle in place.

Oh, shit.

"We need to get out of here now. Lancelot's—"

I don't have time to finish.

The demon lifts his hand and gives his wrist a sharp twist.

Michelle's head whips to the side.

Crunch.

She crumples to the floor in a ruined heap, her head hanging at an unnatural angle, bones peeking through her delicate white skin.

Bile scalds my throat.

"No!" Eric bellows and sprints towards the circle.

Lancelot flings out his hand, outstretched fingers pointing at Eric.

A torrent of black smoke ploughs into Eric's chest, and he's catapulted from his feet, sailing backwards at high speed.

Eric's body strikes the opposite wall hard enough to leave spider's web cracks in it. He crashes to the floor, bounces once, and lies still. Blood pours from his mouth and his eyes stare at nothing.

Aidan and Naomi have forgotten all about me now.

"Eric! Chelle!" Tears stream down Naomi's face.

"Stop!" Aidan shouts, glaring at Lancelot. "I order you to stop this."

Lancelot shakes his head, slow and steady. "I do not answer to the likes of you."

Aidan stumbles back like the demon shoved him. "You swore an Oath. You swore you wouldn't harm any witches, and you've just—" His voice breaks off in a strangled croak, his tortured gaze drifting between the corpses of his friends.

"You are forgetting something, Aidan Adedeji."

Aidan jabs a finger at the demon. "No. You swore—"

Lancelot sighs, as if Aidan's wasting his time. "You really should be more cautious in your dealings with demons. I swore an Oath not to harm any witches if you let me out of the circle."

My heart sinks.

No.

It can't be.

"But... but we didn't let you out," Naomi says, a tremor in her voice.

My eyes widen. "Fuck."

Lancelot beams at me. "I think Christian Winter has worked it out."

"Worked what out?" A vein bulges on Aidan's forehead.

"Naomi's right. *We* didn't let him out," I say, my voice quiet. "He let himself out."

Lancelot steps forward... and crosses the circle's boundary. "Smart boy. So, as you can see, our deal is off."

Shit.

What have we done?

Chapter 41
Christian

Lancelot rolls his neck, and a sharp pop echoes through the room. "You caged me like an animal, just like your pathetic ancestors. I could not seek revenge against them. I suppose you will have to do."

Aidan sets his jaw in a grim line. "Fuck you. This is for Chelle and Eric."

He exchanges a look with Naomi.

The pair nod, each drawing the slim black case holding the silver syringes Aidan gave us earlier from their pockets and injecting themselves.

Why are they...?

Aidan's earlier words come back to me.

You never know when magic might come in handy.

Ah!

I understand what they want to do.

Banish Lancelot.

And they're going to need magic for that.

I pull out my syringe and use it.

Lancelot's expression is one of amusement. He remains calm as both witches plant their feet in a wide stance and chant in Latin.

Their voices rise and fall in unison.

"*Audi haec verba.*"

Hear these words.

"*Caput nostrum vocationis.*"

Heed our call.

"*Loquimur, et ita est.*"

We speak, and it is so.

"*Ut supra, ut infra.*"

As above, so below.

"*Expellimus te. Expellimus te. Expellimus te.*"

We banish thee. We banish thee. We banish thee.

A light breeze blows through the room and ruffles Lancelot's hair.

He places a hand over his mouth and yawns.

My heart dances a wild jig.

Why didn't that work?

Why is he still here?

Aidan's head snaps round, his eyes finding mine. "Well, don't just stand there. Help us. We might be on different sides, but I'm sure you don't want him to escape any more than I do."

"I—"

I can't move.

I can't breathe.

Vex's words on the night we fought flit through my mind.

Trust me. You're not as powerful as you think you are.

My entire adult life, I've always been the strongest person in the room, but the tables have turned.

Lancelot laughs. "Christian Winter will not help you. He is a coward, paralysed by fear."

Something flickers in my chest, then blazes to life, burning away my terror.

No one calls me a coward.

No one.

I set my jaw and stride across the room, only halting when I stand shoulder-to-shoulder with Aidan and Naomi. "Let's get rid of this thing."

We chant.

"*Audi haec verba. Caput nostrum vocationis. Loquimur, et ita est. Ut supra, ut infra. Expellimus te. Expellimus te. Expellimus te.*"

Another, stronger wind rises.

Lancelot staggers back, a hand going to his chest. He coughs and a cloud of black smoke erupts from his mouth, but other than that, nothing happens.

"It's not working," Aidan says.

"Why?" Naomi's eyes are wide, the muscles in her neck standing out.

Lancelot clears his throat, his steely composure back in place. "Simple mathematics. It takes five witches to summon a demon…"

"And five to send one back," I finish.

"Just so." The demon rakes his gaze over Eric's and Michelle's bodies. "And you are two witches short."

Aidan's face pales.

"What are we going to do?" I ask.

The fight goes out of Aidan. His shoulders slump, and all his bravado disappears. "The only thing we can do," he whispers.

"What—"

He takes three strides towards Lancelot and sinks to one knee, bowing his head. "Please, forgive us, my lord. It's been a trying day, and emotions are running high."

"Ade, what are you doing?" Naomi's tone is half shock, half disgust.

Lancelot slinks forwards until he stands over Aidan. "Rise, Aidan Adedeji."

Aidan does as he's told, standing eye to eye with the demon.

When Lancelot speaks, his voice is calm. "You know, there is one thing I have missed about this realm."

"And what's that, my lord?" Aidan asks.

Lancelot smiles and places a hand on Aidan's shoulder.

What's he doing?

I don't have to wait long for my answer.

Lancelot draws back his free hand.

A column of smoke bursts from his palm.

When it fades, the demon's gripping the hilt of a shining silver sword.

"No!" Naomi screams.

In one smooth motion, Lancelot drives his arm forward, the tip of the sword sinking into Aidan's stomach and bursting through his back.

A groan of pain erupts from Aidan's throat.

Lancelot twists the hilt.

Aidan screams.

"My Shadow Blade," Lancelot says.

Aidan tries to speak, but the small river of blood pouring from his mouth drowns his words. His eyes bulge, and he fights for breath.

"Shush, shush, shush," Lancelot whispers, almost tenderly. "Fighting death is futile. Look at the positives. At least you will see your beloved sister again."

A long, rattling breath escapes Aidan.

Lancelot yanks the sword free.

Aidan drops to the floor at the demon's feet.

"Ade." Naomi's grief stretches her husband's name into a tortured wail.

Lancelot gives his sword a single, sharp flick, spattering the floor with drops of Aidan's blood. He stares at the—Shadow Blade; he called it—with something close to affection. "One of the many perks of crossing fully into a physical realm."

Naomi's still wailing.

Lancelot sighs. "Do not be sad. I shall reunite you soon enough."

"I'll kill you, you murdering bastard." Naomi's hand shoots out, and a stream of shadowmancy barrels at Lancelot.

When the shadow-strike reaches the demon, he sucks in a huge breath, and absorbs the dark power into his chest.

My knees quake.

What's happening?

Lancelot sucks in more and more air.

An anguished scream burst from Naomi, black smoke still pouring from her.

The stream of smoke gets thinner and thinner and thinner... then vanishes all together.

Naomi crumples onto all fours, wracked with fine tremors.

Lancelot expels a long breath.

Naomi pushes back to her knees and throws out her hand again.

Nothing.

I swallow back the tide of vomit rising in my throat.

"What did you do?"

"I simply took back what is mine."

Naomi stares at her empty hand, her face a mask of horror.

Lancelot lets out a short, mirthless bark of laughter. "Surely, you are not arrogant enough to believe you could use my power against me?"

"I don't need your power," Naomi spits at him. "*Mortem.*"

A death-strike.

She's trying the conjure a death-strike.

Her hand remains empty.

"What—" her voice shakes "—what have you done to me?"

"I'm afraid your magic is... inaccessible," the demon says.

Naomi turns her panicked eyes to me. "Do something."

But I still can't move. I stare at Lancelot like he's a nightmare made of flesh.

He chuckles again—the dry sound of sandpaper scraping against wood—and stalks towards Naomi in a predatory fashion. "He cannot help you. Nobody can help you now."

"Don't—"

But my warning falls on deaf ears.

The demon moves so fast, I almost miss it. He crouches low, reverses the grip on his sword, and spins in a half circle so the blade swings out in a wide arc.

Naomi's scream cuts off, and her severed head topples from her body, the open stem of her spinal-cord spurting blood.

The scent of copper hangs heavy in the air.

It clogs my throat, and I gag.

Naomi's body tips to the side with a small *thud*.

Thud-thud-thud, thud-thud-thud, thud-thud-thud.

My heart beats so fast it hurts.

Lancelot fixes his black eyes on me.

Fuck.

Chapter 42
Christian

I'm the only one left.

Those soulless black eyes bore into mine, and a creeping fear so intense my insides liquify passes through me.

My knees tremble and a lump the size of a basketball forms in my throat. I do my best to speak, but my wire-tight vocal cords refuse to work. I have to clear my throat several times before any sound comes out. "You killed them."

My voice is quiet, timid, and so unlike my own.

I sound as powerless as I am.

And I hate myself for it.

Lancelot shrugs. "This is a war. There are always casualties in war."

Something else Lancelot said earlier, right before he snapped Michelle's neck, resurfaces.

I cannot allow you to harm him, I am afraid. Christian Winter is integral to my plans.

"You told Michelle—" My voice breaks.

God.

Michelle.

We might not have been best friends, but—I avoid looking into her lifeless eyes—no one deserves that. "You told her I was integral to your plans. What does that mean?"

The corner of Lancelot's mouth lifts, and he lets go of his sword, still dripping with Aidan's blood.

The sharp blade fades away in a shimmer of black smoke.

"Straight down to business. I respect that."

"I don't need your respect, you fu—"

He speaks across me. "Your question has a simple answer. If enough witches band together, they could banish me in this form. I need a host to prevent that. The only way to banish a demon from a host's body is to kill the host and, where we are going, you are the perfect fit."

I need a host.

A lead weight drops into my stomach.

Possession.

The ability to take ownership of a willing (or unwilling) host's body.

My breaths come in shallow gasps.

The thought of being Lancelot's puppet...

"And you have every right to be terrified, Christian Winter."

Oh, shit.

I'd forgotten about the whole Empathy thing.

I lock my knees in place. "Not happening. I'll never let you—"

"Let me?" Lancelot says. "I am not seeking your permission."

Willing.

Or unwilling.

"You can't do this. I—"

"Lucky, really. When I asked Aidan Adedeji to recruit a fifth, I never dreamed he would bring me someone like you."

Christian Winter is integral to my plans.

Where we are going, you are the perfect fit.

Someone like you.

"I don't get it. Why are you so interested in me, in particular?"

"I am not interested in you, per se." He flicks his fingers in a dismissive gesture. "Your position with the Magical Investigations Department, however…"

"My job. What the hell does that have to do with anything?"

The demon smirks, and a mirthless laugh escapes him. "It staggers me. How ignorant are you?"

My cheeks flush.

His grin widens. "You really don't know, do you?"

Blood pulses in my head, and I clench my fists. "Know. What?"

"Witches and sorcerers erected The Gates of Hell on a Nexus."

Aidan's words from our first conversation about demons float back to me.

The sorcerers were worried they would suffer the same fate as the demons. The most powerful among them created Nexuses—dimensions that exist outside of time and space—where the Ley Lines intersect.

"So… Hell is one place where the Ley Lines meet?"

"Humph. Maybe you are smarter than you look."

"I still don't see what any of this has to do with me."

He rolls his eyes. "Because the Gates stand beneath the Magical Investigations Department. You can get me in there without raising suspicion."

My mouth drops open. "What? No. That's not—"

"True? There is a long-forgotten underground cavern. The Gates are there."

Cavern?

He's mistaken.

"There's nothing under the MID," I say.

"Your ancestors were foolish to allow you to forget your history."

"Our history… what—"

"They were probably ashamed to face the atrocities they committed against my kind."

A spark of anger flares in my chest, and I shoot a pointed gaze at the bodies littered around my feet. "From what I've seen, your kind deserved everything they got."

Lancelot tenses his jaw. "Typical witch. You refuse to see beyond the end of your nose. I am only what treachery and time have made me."

He's pissed off.

That's not good.

I need to get out of here.

Good thing he hasn't taken his power back from me.

I summon the icy chill of shadowmancy, intending to Teleport to the MID.

Take me—

You will stay where you are!

The cold power drains away.

"Return what is mine," Lancelot barks.

Searing heat rages behind my eyes.

Lancelot has hooked metal claws into my skull and he's scraping, wrenching.

The heat builds and builds and—

My mind rips open.

I scream.

Lancelot sucks in a huge lungful of air, just like he had when Naomi attacked him.

A gag cuts my scream short, my stomach lurching.

I heave again.

And again.

And—

A torrent of black smoke bursts from my mouth, streaming towards Lancelot.

The shadow sinks into his chest.

He is still drawing in breath.

The pressure in my head intensifies.

More smoke pours out of me.

I can't breathe—I can't—can't—

The last of the smoke leaves me, and my knees buckle, shins slamming into the concrete floor with a jolting pain.

My hands slap the floor a moment later, and I draw in ragged breaths, heart pounding.

Eventually, my heart rate returns to normal.

A dark shadow falls over me.

Lancelot.

I glance up, tears streaming from my eyes.

"It will be over quickly," he says. "I can promise you that."

"Fuck. You."

A small smile crosses his lips. "I was wrong about you, Christian Winter. You are no coward. It is a shame. At a different time, we might have been friends."

"Go to Hell," I spit through gritted teeth.

He cocks his head to one side. "Tempting offer... but I decline."

"You—"

Without warning, Lancelot's humanoid form explodes outward in a cloud of black smoke.

The dense, roiling storm fills the room. It blocks out everything: the candlelight, the corpses, until nothing but a sea of empty, endless black floats in front of me.

Lancelot's voice fills my mind.

Goodbye, Christian Winter.

The black haze rushes forward and, when it strikes the exposed skin of my hands and face, ice freezes my veins.

What the fuck?

I twist and writhe, but there's nothing I can do to prevent this sinister mist from forcing its way into my nostrils, pushing past my lips and into my mouth, and flowing down my throat.

Cold isn't the word for this.

It's like Lancelot buried me in a snow-drift.

In the Arctic.

Naked.

I have to fight.

I need to hang on.

Lancelot's voice booms again.

It is futile. It will be easier if you surrender.

Never.

I will fight this.

I'll fight with everything I have, even if it kills me.

A low rumble of laughter fills my head and bounces around the inside of my skull.

If possible, the cold intensifies, and my teeth chatter so hard the sound echoes.

You cannot stop me.

My mental defences waver.

No.

Get out of my head.

Lancelot's voice comes again, like he's whispering right in my ear.

But I am already in your head.

The last of my resolve crumbles to ash, and darkness sweeps in.

A vice grips my head, my chest, my entire body.

The ground beneath my feet vanishes.

I am falling...

Falling...

Falling...

And...

At last.

I have waited centuries for this.

Christian Winter is gone.

Lost forever.

I am Lancelot, and I am truly, *finally*, free.

It is marvellous.

I take a deep, cleansing breath and—stepping over the lifeless bodies at my feet without a second glance—stalk over to the basement's entrance, up the stairs and into the living space above.

I roam the Pentacle residence, searching for something very specific.

My thunderous footsteps echo around the space.

I come across my target resting upon a pedestal in a cavernous library.

The crown.

I snatch it off the stand.

Camelot's symbol catches my eye.

Words from long ago, Arthur's words, drift through my mind like shadowmancy floating on the breeze.

Camelot stands united, and nothing will ever tear us apart.

Foolish, foolish boy.

How I wanted to believe in you.

Alas…

The Once and Future King was wrong, but that time has passed, and his crown can still serve a purpose.

If I am to destroy the Gates, I will need the Key to do it.

I place the crown on my head, relishing its weight.

Oh, yes.

I am free now.

And soon, my brethren will stand beside me while witch-kind perishes.

I will relish the sound of their screams.

CHAPTER 43
Tori

I bolt awake and untangle myself from sweat-soaked sheets, struggling into a sitting position. I'd been dreaming, or more accurately, having the worst nightmare of my life.

Blood.

Death.

Snapping necks.

A dark, underground room littered with corpses.

Black smoke rising to choke me in its icy, deathlike grip.

I shake my head to clear the last of the smoke clinging to my consciousness. I know, instinctively, that something's wrong.

Something's wrong with Christian.

What did you See?

I lift trembling fingers to my mouth.

I'm going crazy.

When I touched that pendant—

The stomach wound.

The sword.

Selina.

John.

It's not possible.

I shouldn't be able to See the things I've Seen.

And yet...

Whatever this strange power is, I can't ignore it now.

Christian's in danger.

I fling myself out of bed and dart over to the huge oak wardrobe in the room's corner. Flinging it open, I reach up to the top shelf and pull down one of Christian's spare hoodies.

I need to try the locater spell again.

I have to find him.

Crossing back to the bed, I sink into a cross-legged position on the mattress, clutching Christian's hoodie in a tight fist.

Please work.

I grip the jacket tighter, close my eyes, and chant in a low, melodic voice. "*Ostende, mihi, Christian Winter. Ostende, mihi, Christian Winter. Ostende, mihi, Christian Winter.*"

Usually, when I cast, magic flows easily and without friction. Now, it's as if my powers brush up against something hard and unyielding.

I keep chanting, refusing to give up hope.

Scarlet mist leaks from my pores and sinks down into the jacket.

Despite that, that resistance is there.

What is that?

I scrunch my eyes tight and force more magic into the spell, my forehead peppered with sweat.

Something pushes back against me.

I push harder, and harder and harder until—

Snap!

The spell takes hold.

An image forms in my mind.

The edges are frayed and lined in hazy gold.

There he is.

Christian.

This is strange

I've used a locater spell hundreds of times, but I've never been… transported like this. Never been able to see my target so clearly.

I don't have time to worry about that now. I focus on Christian.

It's like I'm following him from behind.

He's striding along a familiar street, in the city's heart, and I know where he's heading at once.

The MID.

I call out to him, but my voice doesn't work in the void.

My physical body, still sat on the bed, reacts—my brow creasing.

Christian looks different, somehow.

His clothes.

They're… bizarre.

He wears what looks like a leather armour, with interlocking plates—composed of black metal—encasing his shoulders.

That's ridiculous.

Why would Christian be wearing armour? How—

Wait.

Is that… King Arthur's crown on his head?

What the hell's going on?

He rounds the corner, turning down the side road leading to the MID headquarters.

What are you playing at, Christian?

He comes to a sudden, jarring halt.

There's something about the way he stands—predatory, as if poised to strike—that's so unlike him.

It sets my teeth on edge.

What the hell is he doing?

The golden haze of the vision ripples, and a sound fills my mind. It's a low, rumbling laugh that slices into my skull like a rusty scalpel. The hair on my arms stands on end.

What the fuck?

I stare, transfixed, as Christian turns his head this way and that.

When he speaks, his voice is flat, and deeper than usual. The sounds he makes are foreign—the vowels too elongated, the consonants too clipped. "I know you are there, witch. Where are you hiding?"

A hard chunk of ice forms in my stomach.

This isn't possible.

I shouldn't be able to hear him like this.

"Wait." Another rusty chuckle rises from Christian's throat. "Tricky witch. You are not here, are you? You are somewhere else."

My heart is pounding, and I suck in a strangled breath.

Is he...?

Is Christian speaking to me?

He can't be.

There's no way.

Then he turns to face me, and I almost scream.

His eyes are jet-black, the pupils swallowing the iris. "Ah. There you are."

My throat pulls tight.

Whoever those eyes belong to, it's not Christian.

A single word drifts through my mind, so clear.

So startling.

Demon.

I'm not sure how, but I know that's what this creature is.

This monster who's wearing Christian's face.

Demons aren't real.

And yet...

Something uncoils inside of me. Something hot, and vicious, and deadly.

Hatred.

Pure, burning hatred.

I want to hurt this demon, to maim it. I want to hunt it down and kill it, to wipe all traces of it—and anything else like it—from the earth.

The golden mist clinging to the edges of the vision swirls and shifts, obscuring my view of Christian.

What's—

A woman strolls through the mist. She moves with the grace and poise of a dancer, and she's dressed like she's going to a renaissance fair. Green velvet gown flowing to the floor, corset cinched in tight at the waist, a gorgeous gold silk headscarf wound through her thick Afro curls.

She seems familiar, but the mist obscures her face.

A silky voice drifts through my mind.

Kill the demon.

It's the woman in the green dress.

"What... I—"

We must kill the demon. It is our sacred duty.

She lifts her hand, and I spot the symbol from the crown tattooed on her palm in black ink.

"I don't understand. Who are you?"

The woman glides forward, and her face comes into focus.

My heart stops.

She looks like... me, but her eyes—oh my God—her eyes glitter with the same golden light of the mist.

The woman smiles. *I am you. Or, rather, you are me.*

Back in the corporeal world, a cold shiver travels from the crown of my head to the base of my spine. "I don't understand."

The woman turns and sways back towards the mist. *Help the Dragon. Trust him. Slay the demon. It is our duty.*

"Wait. Who are you? What's your name?"

The woman pauses, her back to me. *I have many names, but only one matters.* Then she's walking away again.

"Stop. Please. I don't..."

But she's gone.

The mist recedes.

Christian stands before me again.

The flash of white-hot, fiery anger fades as quick as it came.

What the fuck was that?

Who was that woman?

Kill the demon.

It is our sacred duty.

Trust the Dragon.

Slay the demon.

I have many names.

I don't have time to contemplate it, however, because the thing that looks like Christian is speaking again.

"Where I am from, it is rude to spy on people." Demon-Christian raises his hand and a torrent of black smoke rushes forth.

It obscures my vision.

It pulls me down, down, down.

Smothering me.

Suffocating me.

I scream.

Then the demon's voice, so cold and grating, whispers into my mind.

Rudeness deserves to be punished.

A burst of power explodes outwards and, the next thing I know, I'm lifted off the bed and catapulted into the wall.

Crack.

A sharp, stabbing pain flares up my arm.

I crash to the floor in a heap.

My vision swims, and my arm hangs at a crooked angle.

Shit.

It's broken.

Everything's going dark.

Tears stream down my face and one clear thought races through my mind.

Please, God. Someone help me.

My panic rises to fever pitch and, seconds later, a burst of golden light fills the room.

Chapter 44
Tori

When the light fades, I'm forced to blink my eyes several times to clear the black spots from my eyes.

It's like I've looked straight into the sun.

My vision finally clears.

"John? What—"

All my questions jam in my throat when I take in John's appearance.

Gone are the plain, expensive garments, replaced by... are they biker leathers?

No.

The leather outfit is tough, worn, and well-fitting. Overlapping plates of gold shine at his shoulders, and someone has stitched a small, blazing golden sun into the left breast of the jacket. There's a... is that a—Christ, it is—a sword strapped across his back; the hilt peeking over his shoulder.

Demon-Christian appears in my mind.

He wears leather armour, interlocking silver plates encasing his shoulders.

John's dressed like that thing.

Is John a demon too?

Kill the demon.

It is our sacred duty.

John takes a step towards me. "Shit. Your arm—"

"Stay away from me." I scramble back and fling out my hand. "*Fulgur.*"

Scarlet lightning rockets from my fingertips.

John moves faster than my eyes can track, dodging the lightning strike with ease.

The jagged streaks of energy scream past him, slamming into a glass vase on my desk, which shatters in a tinkling explosion of glass.

John holds out his hands in a placatory gesture. "I won't hurt you. You called for me."

"Called for you? What the fuck are you—"

"You called for help," he says.

"I didn't. I..."

Wait.

After the demon attacked me, a thought had screamed through my mind.

Please, God. Someone help me.

"You... you heard my thoughts?"

He nods.

"This is... what the hell is going on?" I wince and grit my teeth at the sharp pain that sets my arm blazing.

John inches closer and crouches down when he reaches me.

"I said, stay away from me, demon."

"I'm not a..." he pauses, a look of confusion spreading across his features. "How do you know about demons?"

Kill the demon.

It is our sacred duty.

"I..." The words dry up in my throat. I can't tell John about the renaissance woman in my vision. He'll think I'm crazy.

John's eyes flick from my face, to the crumpled hoodie on the bed, and back to me. "You were looking for Chris?"

I bob my head, the moving sending another burst of pain down my arm.

"Let me have a look at that," he says.

I laugh, but I'm not sure where it comes from. There's nothing funny about this situation. "Why? Did you train as a doctor while you were away, too?"

The corner of his mouth lifts. "Something like that." He reaches out.

I flinch back.

Ouch doesn't cover it.

His hand pauses. "May I?"

I set my jaw. "Fine."

John's fingers stop just shy of my arm and he closes his eyes, a small crease appearing between his eyebrows.

A warm breeze caresses my skin.

What the—

"It's broken," John says, eyelids still lowered.

"You think? Wait, what are you—"

A soft glow—the colour of honey caressed by sunshine—lights up John's palm and warms my arm.

The pain ceases all at once.

I let out a long, contented sigh. "How are you doing that?"

"Quiet," he says, voice soft. "I need to concentrate."

A pleasant sensation, like slipping into a hot bath, fills me.

The light gets brighter...

And brighter...

And brighter...

So bright I have to shield my eyes.

Seconds pass.

The light fades.

I uncover my eyes.

John draws his hand away.

My arm's fixed.

That's impossible.

"How did you do that?" I ask, still staring at my arm.

John dips his head.

I rotate my wrist. Not a twinge. Good as new. "You're a vessel. You don't have any magic. How did you..." A creeping sensation sweeps over me, my skin prickling. "What are you?"

He bites his lip. "A Healer."

The way he says the word *Healer* makes it sound significant.

"What does that mean?"

"It's my Gift."

Again, extra stress on the word Gift.

"What the hell are you on about?"

He glances up, sapphire blue eyes holding mine, a frown creasing his brow. "I thought you knew about... everything."

Heat swirls through my stomach, and I clamber to my feet.

John follows suit.

"This Rumpelstiltskin guessing game is really pissing me off."

John's pacing now. "This makes little sense."

"I swear on my magic. I *will* punch you—hard—if you don't tell me what's going on!"

John halts and brushes his thumb over his chin. "I'm... I'm a sorcerer."

I blink—once—really slowly. A warm tickle starts in my chest, spreads up my throat and a loud laugh burst from me. "Don't be so ridiculous. There's no such thing."

He shakes his head, looking a little sad. "I'm not joking."

The chuckle dies on my lips. "Demons and sorcerers aren't real. But..."

Kill the demon.

It is our sacred duty.

The golden light that poured from John's hands when he Healed me is the same colour as the bright glow in the renaissance woman's eyes.

The woman who resembled me.

"We exist," he says. "And I think you're a sorcerer, too."

Chapter 45
Tori

"Excuse me?" The words are out of my mouth before I can stop them.

John's gaze is steady, still locked on mine. "You heard me."

I take a deep breath, forcing myself to stay calm, to keep my voice level. "That's ridiculous. I'm a witch. You've just seen that for yourself."

John wheels round and paces across the room, running his hand through his hair, then turns back to face me.

Why is he looking at me like that? He's not my teacher and I'm not a recalcitrant pupil.

He clears his throat. "I know. It shouldn't be possible, but somehow, you have access to witchcraft and sorcery."

"I'm not a fucking—" I take another deep, steadying breath. Calm. Just. Be. Calm. "You're talking out of your arse."

His eyes flash. "Don't pretend you don't know what I'm talking about."

"I'm not pretending."

John lifts his hand to the collar of his leather jacket, pulls the zip down a little, and plucks out the dragon's head pendant. "You think I don't know what happened back at the house? You think I can't guess what you Saw?"

What I Saw.

The pendant.

Considering recent events, I'd forgotten.

I'd touched the pendant, and then—

Selina.

The woman with the gushing wound in her stomach. And John standing over her, a sword in his grip.

My gaze goes to the sword strapped across his back.

There's a distinctive swirling pattern on the hilt.

The same pattern I Saw in the vision.

Fuck.

It's the same sword.

"You killed her. You killed Selina."

He makes a wounded animal sound in his throat. "No."

"You did." back away from him, eyes glued to the sword at his back. "I Saw—"

When I speak, I hate that there is a tremor in my voice. "You killed that woman."

"No!"

His shout makes me flinch.

"I'm sorry," he says, twisting away from me, but not before I catch sight of the tears shimmering on his cheeks. "That's not what happened. I would never… I loved her."

I know he means it.

No one says, "I loved her," like that—with such desperate, aching need—without it being true.

But then…

The blood.

The sword.

It makes little sense.

"You'd better tell me the truth," I say.

"I can't tell you."

"You—"

"I can show you." He rubs a hand over his face and, when he turns back to me, his cheeks are dry. Drawing the pendant over his head, he takes a step towards me and offers me the gold chain. "Well, your Gift can, anyway."

I bite down hard on the inside of my cheek. "What do you mean, my Gift? I already told you, I'm not..."

"You can say it."

"A sorcerer."

He snorts. "God, you're stubborn."

"Damn right I am when someone's chatting shit about me."

He carries on as if I haven't spoken. "I sensed it on the night we met. Like calling to like."

"Oh, for fu—"

"You felt it, too. You said as much when you stopped by for dinner."

"I..."

"I think you're Clairvoyant."

I wrinkle my nose. "That's... you're crazy."

He arches an eyebrow at me, still holding out the pendant.

"You think I can See the future."

He shrugs, causing the pendant to swing. "Past, present, future, and everything in between."

"Bollocks."

"Prove me wrong."

A strange mix of apprehension and excitement.

Some kind of connection.

The dragon's head pendant swings back and forth, fixing its serpentine eyes on me.

Wait.

A dragon's head.

What had the renaissance woman said?

Help the Dragon...

Trust him...

The Dragon.

Is John the Dragon?

The pendant.

Is he who I'm supposed to trust?

Something inside me shifts, and my fingers itch to reach out and touch the cool metal pendant.

But what if he's right?

What if I am a... sorcerer?

I can't imagine the MID being comfortable with that.

What would it mean for Christian and me?

Shit!

Christian.

"John, I need to tell you something. It's Christian. When I cast the locater spell, I Saw him. I think he's... I think there's a..."

"I know," he says, face grave. "A demon's possessed him."

I point at the pendant. "Then we don't have time for—"

"Yes, we do. This is important. I have a plan to banish the demon, but I might need your help."

"My help? What—"

"Believe I'm telling you the truth. Believe you're a sorcerer. It's the only way you'll be able to help me save him."

"But..." I eye the pendant warily. "I'm a witch. That's all I am."

"No. You're so much more than that. You can trust me, Tori. I promise."

Help the Dragon...

Trust him...

Banish the demon...

The dragon's head pendant carries on swinging.

I have a plan to banish the demon.

Christian.

I have to save Christian.

Whatever it takes.

I reach out for the necklace, freezing when John speaks.

"Focus on Selina."

I nod, set my jaw, and curl my fingers around the gold chain.

Golden mist swallows me.

Then I'm falling.

Fast.

Chapter 46
Tori

Falling—falling—falling—

Flash.

Gold-plated images and sensations swirl through my mind.

John's arms swing at my sides.

I'm with my fellow Guild trainees.

Selina, Stephan, and Amber.

We trudge under the bile-coloured sky, thick black scarves wrapped over our faces to ward off the rotten, sulfurous wind.

Selina's warm fingers lace with mine. "Don't worry, we'll pass the Trial."

"I'm not worried," I say, John's rich voice spilling between my lips.

She jostles my hip with hers, smiling brightly. "Liar."

That smile.

My—no, John's stomach flips.

Oh, yeah.

He loves her, all right.

I wonder—

Flash.

"Watch out!" Selina shouts.

I backpedal, but the demon's sword slices into my collarbone.

Searing pain flashes through me, and I cry out.

Blood spatters my leather armour, but I barely have time to register the hot, slick liquid.

The demon thrusts forward.

Fuelled by sheer adrenaline, I dodge the blade again, putting more distance between us.

"You're dead, sorcerer," the demon growls, black eyes swirling. "You and the rest of your bastard Guild."

I twirl my sword in a tight, figure-eight pattern. "We'll see."

The demon lunges with a loud war cry.

Heart hammering against my ribcage, I meet it with a louder one of my own, rushing—

Flash.

"*Selina!*"

There's nothing I can do.

One of the demon army has plunged his sword deep into her gut.

He wrenches the blade out.

Her blood splatters, staining the dusty, rocky earth.

Stephan flies out of nowhere, the battle axe clenched in his fists, sweeping through the air in a wide arc, and separates the demon's head from his body.

I rush to where Selina lies, blood gushing from the stab wound in her abdomen. The sword falls from my grasp, clattering to the rock beneath my feet. My knees slam into the hard ground. "Selina. Fuck. Can you hear me?"

Her eyelids flutter open, and she gives a delicate cough. In a weak voice, nothing like her own, she says, "You should see the other guy."

I laugh, even though it's not funny. "Hang on. I've got you. You're going to be fine." My hand hovers over the wound.

Heal.

Nothing happens.

"Shit." I shake out my hand. "It's okay. I can do this."

Heal.

Nothing.

I try again.

Heal, heal, fucking heal!

Selina closes her blood-stained fingers over mine. "It's too late for that, Doc."

Doc.

Stupid fucking nickname.

Tears sting the back of my throat. "Don't say that. I can Heal you, I can—"

She shakes her head, tears in her own eyes now. "I'm sorry."

"Sorry for what?"

"I treated you like shit when you first got to the Guild. I should never have—"

"I don't care about that." I brush her hair away from her face. "This is bullshit. I won't let you die."

"You..." When she coughs this time, it's wet-sounding. "You don't have a choice."

I try...

Heal.

And try...

Heal.

And try again...

Oh, God. Please! *Heal, heal, heal, heal, heal.*

Still nothing.

"John..."

My throat is too tight. I can't speak.

"I'm cold," she says, so quiet it's almost a whisper.

A strangled sob escapes me.

"Hold me," she croaks. "I don't want to be alone."

I pull her into my arms.

Her breathing gets shallower, and shallower, and shallower, until it hitches in her chest. She holds something up, hand trembling.

Her pendant.

The dragon's eyes hold me fast.

She whispers something.

I bend my head closer.

When she speaks again, I can barely feel her breath against my ear. "Take... it."

"No. I can't. Kalia gave you that. She—"

"Mother will understand. Please, John. Take it."

Flash.

Amber rests her hand on my shoulder. "You need to let her go, John."

"No." I clutch Selina tighter to my chest.

She stopped breathing a while ago.

"She's gone," Amber says, her voice tear-choked.

No, no, no.

CHAPTER 47
Tori

The golden mist fades.

I'm facing John again, and he's crying, tears streaming down his face.

My own cheeks are wet with tears, too.

You killed her.

You killed Selina.

I can't believe I accused him of that.

I'm such a bitch.

"Believe me now?" John's voice is waterlogged.

"Yes." I let go of the necklace. "I'm so, so sorry."

He shrugs, wiping his face on the back of his hand, and slips the pendant over his head again.

"You didn't kill her," I say, sweeping forward and clutching him to me in a tight hug.

We stand like this for about ten seconds, then he draws back. "What was that for?"

"You needed it."

"Well, cheers, I guess." A sad smile curves his lips. He wipes his face again and rolls his shoulders. Closing his eyes, he takes a deep breath and, when he opens them again, they're dry. "We need to stop the demon that's taken Chris."

A knot tightens in my chest. "I know. But how?"

"Like I said, I've got a plan."

"The demon was heading to the MID."

He nods. "And I know why."

"You do?

Another nod. "Because of what's there."

"What do you—"

"I don't have time to explain." He holds out his hand for me to take. "Here."

"What are you doing?"

"Taking us to the MID."

"I can conjure a—"

"This is faster than a portal."

"O... kay."

"Trust me?"

Help the Dragon.

Trust him.

Banish the demon.

I place my hand in his.

A golden haze rises around us and—

Oh, shit.

My stomach drops through the floor.

Chapter 48
Lancelot

With a last burst of power, the connection forged by the female witch's locater spell breaks, and I know I am alone again.

I pivot on my heel, turning towards the glass and steel building before me.

The witches have tried to hide the building's true appearance behind layers of pathetic glamours and concealment magic.

It matters little.

Their paltry illusions are as diaphanous as the thinnest layer of silk.

So, this is where the so-called Magical Investigations Department conducts their operations from.

I snort.

I am unimpressed by something so fragile.

What has happened to this world?

I remember the grand days of Camelot, when all four races lived in towering castles with acres of land around them. I can still taste the dizzying height and power of my former position as a Knight of the Round Table.

Oh, how I miss it.

If it wasn't for Arthur's fall...

If only witches, sorcerers, and demons—

No.

Sentimental fool.

That is in the past.

Before they conspired against us to erect those damn Gates.

Before they sentenced us all to Hell.

I cannot change it.

I can influence only the present.

My fist clenches so hard my knuckles crack.

I will make them all pay for what they did to my people.

I will free my brethren from their long and unjust incarceration, and when I do...

My footsteps halt on the edge of the vast... I scour Christian Winter's mind for the modern terminology—car park—that borders the Magical Investigations Department's pretend fortress.

I take a deep breath. My nostrils flare.

The earth even smells different.

Where is the green scent of nature: open fields, cut grass, and wildflowers—fragrances so familiar last time I'd walked on this side of the Gates?

Instead...

Christ.

I smell waste.

Pollution.

Decay.

What in the name of the Lines have the mortals done to this realm?

That is a question for another time.

I cast my awareness outwards, mentally scanning the building beyond.

There are twenty witches inside, but that does not concern me.

The magic of a mere score cannot compare to my power.

The corner of my mouth lifts into a smile.

They do not know what is coming.

I stride on, ducking through a rusted hole in the chain-link fence that surrounds the car park.

With every step, my heart beats a little faster.

The Gates of Hell are here.

They want to sink their toxic, malign claws into me. They call for my blood, baying for me.

Well, they can want me.

But they cannot have me.

My host will see to that.

These witches will not banish me if it means killing one of their own.

As long as I Possess him, I am safe.

And once I have destroyed the Gates, Hell will cease to exist.

There will be war.

Rivers of blood will run.

There will be retribution.

I stride on.

I am close to the building's entrance now.

More glass.

I must not enter with my demonic black eyes showing.

With a small amount of will and intention, I force them to mimic the dark brown hue of the host I inhabit.

The doors in front of me slide apart on their own and, after another quick tour of Christian Winter's mind, I realise there is no magic behind it.

It is some kind of technological advancement known as…

Electricity.

My, my, this place really has gone to the dogs.

I yearn for home, where I had servants on hand to open doors for me.

Everything here is so impersonal.

I stalk through the doors and find myself at the farthest end of a wide corridor, opening into a large circular space.

It stinks of pine, the scent too strong and cloying to be natural.

White lights adorn the ceiling.

It is not witch-light, however.

It is the fault of electricity again.

I scan the walls, taking in the strips of glowing glass.

Glass upon glass upon glass.

Well, mortals were always good at inventing things, I suppose.

My gaze flicks to the end of the corridor.

Two witches, one male and one female, sit behind a glass—glass again... by the gods—desk.

The sign hanging above it reads *Reception*.

I expect them to run screaming like the filthy vermin they are, but I am disappointed.

Instead, they smile at me.

"Christian. Thank God you're safe. DCI Denton's been really worried about you," the woman says.

Of course.

They think I am Christian Winter.

I smile back.

This is going to be fun.

I stroll towards the desk. "Safe as castles," I say, the voice pouring from my lips foreign to me.

"Does Tori know you're back?" the man asks.

"No. I have not spoken with her yet."

The pair twitter on, spewing inane pleasantries.

All the while, I cast my senses outward, searching for the exact location of the Gates.

And then...

My awareness brushes up against something cold and unyielding far below.

Interesting.

The two witches behind the desk do not know what they are sitting on top of.

The woman stops talking—at last—and narrows her eyes at me. "Are you okay?"

"I am fine. Why do you ask?"

She shrugs. "I don't know. You don't seem like yourself."

"Well, now that is funny. You are not the first person to say that to me today."

The man's face hardens with suspicion. "Why are you talking like that?"

"Like what?"

With a sudden burst of movement, the male witch leaps to his feet, swiping his hand through the air. "*Revelare.*"

The unmasking spell sweeps over me and a cloud of black mist pours from my skin, then fades away to nothing.

The sight of the black mist makes the woman's eyes go wide. "Who—what—the hell are you?"

"Sound the alarm," the male witch says.

The woman reaches for something beneath the desk.

I raise my hand and twist.

Crack.

Her neck snaps loudly, and she collapses back into her chair, her head bent at an awkward angle.

The male witch lets out an agonised wail.

It is the sweetest, most beautiful sound.

I lift my other hand.

Be. Quiet.

The scream dies in his throat.

Oh, the taste of his fear is like a delicacy. "I would say this is not personal, but that would be a lie."

Twist.

His head whips to the side.

Crack.

Witches.

So breakable.

A flick of both my wrists sends the corpses—still slumped in their chairs—flying towards the walls on either side of the reception area.

The chairs tip and the corpses spill out, landing in a tangled heap on the floor.

I roll my neck, and it gives a satisfying *pop*.

Ah, it is good to be back.

I stroll around the edge of the desk, pacing around its circumference once, twice, three times.

The passage leading to the Gates is right beneath this desk.

Accessing it is a simple matter of blasting through the floor, and then—

"That you, Christian," a voice says from behind me.

I turn.

Another witch.

Pale skin.

Green eyes.

Short, black hair.

No.

His eyes are not merely green.

They are a vivid emerald.

He is Sighted.

The witch's expression morphs into one of relief. "Thank God you're back. Denton's doing her nut in. She's been freaking out ever since we lost contact, and... what the hell are you wearing? Don't tell me you went undercover as a biker?"

This is a complication I could do without.

An irritating one.

I try my best to adopt the modern patois. "Everything's fine. Costume's all part of the cover. Just came in to give Denton an update, that's all."

He says, "Bit risky, isn't it? Coming to the office? Aren't you supposed to be meeting her incognito?"

I hate witches.

Buzzing around like flies and involving themselves in things that do not concern them.

I pace towards him, not wanting him to get too far down the corridor. I cannot have him spotting his broken-necked colleagues, after all. "Yeah, but I had to come straight away. There's been a development."

"Right..." The witch hesitates. "You okay? You seem a little off."

I do my best to keep the tension out of my voice. "I'm fine. Just tired. Now come on. We can see Denton together, if you like."

"Sure, okay." He turns and walks ahead of me, but then he halts, the muscles in his shoulders pulling rigid. "Strange. You never call her Denton."

I should have just killed him on the spot. "That's her name, isn't it?"

His shoulders relax. "Yeah. That's her name."

We walk back up the corridor.

He mutters something.

"Pardon?"

Without warning, the witch spins round and throws out his hands.

A tornado of green tinted wind crashes into me and my boots slide over the polished floor, driven by the gale.

I dig in my heels and skid to a halt.

Sighted or not, this witch is not strong enough to stop me.

He charges forward, stopping dead when he catches sight of one of the dead receptionists. Little green sparks fly from his fingers. "You're not Christian."

The impetuous little shit caught me off-guard. That will not happen again. "No. I am not Christian Winter. Though he is still in here." I tap my temple.

The young witch's eyes widen. "Christian. If you can hear me, whatever this is, fight it."

I laugh. "That is not possible, I'm afraid. His body belongs to me now."

He hesitates.

I can tell he doesn't want to hurt my host.

"Let him go," the witch says.

"Try to make me. I dare you."

Something in the witch's preternaturally green eyes hardens. "*Baculum*." He conjures a glimmering emerald staff composed of magical energy, spinning it round and round. "Well, whoever the fuck you are, I'm arresting you for the murder of—"

I laugh.

I cannot help it.

"You think this is funny, arsehole?"

"Forgive me, but I think it is hysterical. Are you supposed to be threatening me?"

For a moment, he looks nonplussed. "What?"

I invoke my Empathy.

The witch stiffens. "What the hell's that?"

My Curse reveals a great deal about Detective Constable Henry Stone. "Interesting."

"What are you talking about?" His voice quavers a little.

My smile grows wider. "You are afraid of death."

Beads of sweat pepper Henry Stone's temples and drip down his cheeks. "What the fuck are you talking about?"

I narrow my focus. "No. My mistake. You are afraid of a very specific kind of death. The thought of having your throat slit petrifies you."

His face grows paler still, if that is possible. "How do you know that?"

"The how is not important. Can you imagine it? How it would feel? A blade tearing your throat open, parting your skin. Lifeblood pouring out of you."

"Stop it."

"Just like your parents."

"Shut up!"

"I have just the thing to make your fear a reality." I grip the air and, in a burst of black smoke, my Shadow Blade materialises.

Much to his credit, Henry Stone draws himself up to his full height, and says, "I haven't given into fear in years. I'm not about to start now. I'm going to kick your arse."

He spins the witch-staff again.

I trace its swirling pattern with my eyes. "I doubt that."

"Oh?"

"Indeed. Because you brought a toothpick to a sword fight."

"We'll see." He darts forward, staff swinging down.

I dodge.

He drops into a low crouch; the staff sweeping towards my legs.

Crack.

It slams into my leather armour, barely making a dent.

Henry Stone's eyes go wide. "What the—"

I drive my blade down.

He goes to block me with that ridiculous staff.

My sword crashes into it, and there is a sound like breaking glass.

The staff explodes in a shower of green sparks.

Henry Stone cries out in pain.

I lash out with my foot, the top of my boot catching his cheek.

He cries out again and crashes to the floor, but doesn't stay down. He rolls back over his shoulder and springs to his feet.

This one has a fighting spirit I might admire under different circumstances.

"*Mortem*," he shouts.

The death-strike darts towards me, smacks into my chest and... my armour absorbs it.

He staggers back. "That's not possible."

I direct my will at him.

Stay.

Henry Stone's muscles stop working at my command.

I prowl towards him until our faces are inches apart. "Know this, witch. I am sparing your life for one purpose only. I want you to deliver a message to your colleagues. When you wake up, tell them a war is coming. Tell them the demons are taking back control."

At the word *demons*, panic flares in his eyes.

I relish it.

"Tell them they cannot win. I will give you and your ilk one chance to surrender. If you refuse to comply, I will kill every one of you."

With that, I lift my hand and send a shadow-strike pummeling into Henry Stone's chest.

It propels him backwards, and he lands, unconscious, several feet away.

I turn back to the reception desk, all thoughts of Henry Stone forgotten.

It is time to destroy the Gates of Hell once and for all.

Time to set my people free.

I fire a volley of shadow at the reception desk.

My ears ring with the shatter of breaking glass, and the screech of tortured steel.

I blast a hole straight through the floor.

Chapter 49
Lancelot

I stand on the lip of the hole I created in the floor and stare into the darkness below.

The power of the Gates pulses somewhere deep beneath me.

That power will not exist for much longer.

I step off the edge and drop into the black pit, landing in a crouch when my feet strike the floor.

Bones line the walls, all kinds of bones.

Skulls.

Femurs.

Scapulas.

The sacrificial lambs that gave their lives to erect the Gates.

An ossuary for the dead.

This far below ground, the air is crisp.

I can't believe the witches allowed themselves to forget this place. They know nothing of true power. Their spells and incantations are mere party tricks.

Still, their lapse in judgement is a golden opportunity for me.

I can reach the Gates without opposition.

The passage stretches ahead of me, the sightless eyes of the skulls boring into mine.

I stroll along with a slow, unhurried gait.

The floor is hard and smooth, worn by passing time.

Such a dark place to hide something even darker.

I press on, my heartbeat quickening with each step.

The malevolent power of the Gates pulses close by, and I swear I can hear my brothers and sisters screaming for release.

They will not have to wait long.

I am coming to save them.

Eventually, the dark tunnel widens out into a vast chamber made of bones.

My eyes flick to the back of the room.

And there they are.

Sitting atop a wide set of stone stairs on a platform that covers the entire back wall.

The Gates of Hell.

Truly something to behold.

The ivory doors almost glisten.

My insides twist with loathing.

I hate these Gates, two twisted doors of metal and bone that stretch towards the cavernous ceiling.

The mouths of the skulls are wide open and screaming.

I can almost taste their agony, sharp and bitter.

If only these modern witches knew who constructed the Gates, and how.

So much blood and pain.

Would they be so quick to brand me a monster and condemn me back to Hell if they knew?

I catch sight of something that makes my blood boil with fierce heat.

Camelot's symbol—the circular glyph that represents all four races—shines on the doors, but it is a bastardised version of the one I am familiar with.

Blasphemy.

Someone has scorched the crescent moon—the mark of my people. It's blackened and twisted beyond recognition.

A powerful surge of hate flows through me.

When this is over, I will decorate this chamber with the blood of all witches. I will wipe all the other races from the earth, just as the demons had been.

We will take our revenge and claim our justice.

It is time to end this.

I cross the cavern, my footsteps echoing off the barren ground, and climb the short flight of steps to the platform.

With the Gates so close, their power pulses at my temples.

Calling.

Baying.

They are the only thing standing in my way.

Once they fall, we will rise again.

We will be free.

I raise both hands, my sights set on the blistered crescent moon.

Fuck you.

I draw a huge amount of power through the Lines, the cold energy filling me, refreshing me, and fuelling my purpose. I funnel the Ley Line energy from the ground and up through my body until a pinpoint of ice coalesces at my forehead.

The crown's weight is heavy.

I focus on that heaviness and push my power into the crown.

Destroy.

A powerful, focused beam of shadowmancy bursts from the crown's golden glyph and slams into the accursed Gates.

They will come crashing down.

Chapter 50
Lancelot

I sense them before they are even halfway down the tunnel.

Witches.

That Sighted wretch, Henry Stone, is among them, the stink of his crystalline fear almost palpable.

I sigh.

I don't have time for this.

Stop.

The torrent of black smoke pouring from the crown fades until it dies away.

I turn to face them, fixing them with my most baleful glare, and—much to my delight—it has the desired effect.

Several sharp intakes of breath echo around the chamber.

My black eyes find Henry Stone's emerald green ones. "Henry Stone. Did you convey your message to your superiors like I asked?" My gaze takes in the score of witches before me.

A woman steps forward.

She is sharp-featured, angular.

The leader, perhaps.

I call to my Empathic Curse. Show me.

"My name is—"

I cut across her. "I know exactly who you are, Kate Denton."

Her eyes widen, but she recovers in a heartbeat. "Stone delivered your message. You want a war."

"I do."

"That's unfortunate."

I smirk at her. "Unfortunate for you, yes."

Her lips pinch.

My Empathy tells me she's thinking of Christian Winter.

I chuckle.

"What's so funny?" she asks.

"He is in here, you know."

The colour drains from her cheeks.

"Christian Winter. I underestimated him. He fights to regain control even now."

She shouts his name. "If you can hear me, keep on fighting. You can do this. You can beat—"

"No." My voice echoes around the chamber. "He cannot."

She glares at me, her attempt at intimidation pathetic. "Do you have a name, demon?"

"Lancelot," I reply.

Murmuring spreads through the room.

Again, Kate Denton recovers quickly.

Humph.

Mildly impressive.

"What have you done with Adedeji and the other members of Pentacle?"

"What do you think?"

"You killed them."

I bob my head. "You should thank me, Kate Denton. He wanted to destroy your precious Witches Council."

"*Thank you?*" she spits. "You're a monster."

Monster.

The word is like a smoking brand against my skin. "I am the monster? Your ancestors turned against my kind for no justifiable—"

"I'll give you one chance," Kate Denton says. "Surrender. There are twenty witches in this room. You can't win."

I wave my hand in a dismissive gesture. "I see your kind haven't changed."

She arches her eyebrow in question.

"Arrogance. There could be hundreds of witches in this room. Without the aid of the sorcerers, you are no match for me."

"We'll see about that," she says, lifting her hand and chanting.

"Yes, we will." I raise my voice. "*Stay. Where. You. Are.*"

A haze of smoke lifts from my body and spreads across the room.

When it reaches Henry Stone and the others, an icy darkness settles over them and roots them to the spot.

They shift their eyes from side to side, but that's all.

I know what they are thinking.

This cannot be possible.

How is he doing this?

I direct my thoughts to the crowd. *With shadowmancy, anything is possible. Now, you will witness the rebirth of demons, and we will burn your world to cinders.*

I turn my back on them, and let thick black smoke shoot from the crown's symbol again, renewing my assault on the Gates.

Coward.

Kate Denton projects the word at me.

I reign in my power a second time, and turn with deliberate slowness. "What did you call me?"

I said, you're a coward. You claim to be powerful, and yet you freeze us in place. Are you scared of us?

"Ridiculous."

Prove it. Fight me.

I chuckle. "Are you so eager to face death, Kate Denton?"

Like I said… coward.

I release her.

She works her arms and legs.

Henry Stone's eyes bulge.

I know what he would say if he could.

"Don't do it, Kate. He'll kill you!"

He would not be wrong.

Kate Denton dies today.

I let my arms hang loose at my sides. "Give it your best shot."

She fixes a flinty gaze on me, and her hand darts out. "*Torrens ignis.*"

A thick stream of white fire rockets from her open palm.

It gets closer…

Closer…

Closer…

Gather.

The fire halts inches from my face and coalesces into a swirling cloud of white light.

Kate Denton lowers her arm, her face a mask of shock.

I scoop the cloud of fire from the air and, with a coarse laugh, admire it as it dances across my palm. "You realise now how futile it is to oppose me?"

She blinks. "That's not possible."

"Like I said—" I infuse the witch-fire with shadowmancy, the dark power twisting into the element and turning into something hideous "—anything is possible." I launch the dark, swirling cloud balanced in my hand into the crowd.

It strikes the floor with a thunderous boom.

The witches—Kate Denton included—fly every which way.

Their screams are delicious.

I spot her through the smoke.

Time to deal with her for good.

I stroll to the lip of the platform and descend the stairs.

One witch flips to their feet and fires a death-strike at me.

Reverse.

The humming dart of magical power skids to a halt, then rebounds on the witch who cast it.

Crack.

Blood spurts.

The witch falls.

Another prepares to cast.

I send them hurtling through the air.

They slam against one of the ossuary walls, and a protruding shard of bone impales them.

A third slams a kick into my side.

It is akin to feathers tickling my skin.

I punch the witch's nose so hard their septum lodges in their skull. Then I'm towering over Kate Denton, sprawled at my feet. I hold my hand high and she clutches at her throat, body floating up with the path of my arm, legs dangling uselessly beneath her.

Her face turns white, then red, then purple.

I cock my head to one side. "Such hubris. Your kind always think they're the most powerful people in the room. Well, I can assure you, Kate Denton, there is no one in this God forsaken realm with the power to stop me."

Fear leaks from her pores like sweat.

"Goodbye, witch," I say.

Kil—

An invisible force pummels me in the chest with the force of an iron cudgel.

I sail through the air, losing my grip on Kate Denton, and crash to the floor, rolling a few times to absorb the impact.

What in the name of—

I sense it then.

Warmth.

Sunshine.

Sorcery.

Chapter 51
Lancelot

I glance up from my position on the floor.

Two people have materialised out of thin air.

The first is a young woman, dark curls fanning out around her head and falling to her shoulders.

I can smell the ozone stink of her magic—she's a witch.

But there is something else there, too.

She seems familiar.

Calling to my Empathy, I command it to show me her hopes and fears.

An image floats before my eyes. It's the strange woman—only it is not—clad in a green dress and golden headscarf. In one hand, she holds a Light Blade, and in the other...

This cannot be.

The apparition smiles at me, a cold smirk, and speaks into my mind. *We are one. And you will leave us alone.*

Searing pain boils my brain within my skull, and I cry out, withdrawing my power.

The witch stands before me again.

I know who she is now, or rather, who she will become. I would recognise the origins of that brand of sorcery anywhere.

"I can't believe her plan worked," I say.

She flinches at the sound of my voice like I struck her. In a tremulous voice, she says, "Who's plan?"

"Oh... this is priceless. You don't know what you are, do you, child?" I laugh. "You will soon enough. Damn her. Hiding in plain sight."

The girl's forehead creases. "I don't understand. What do you—"

I laugh. I cannot resist. "It is impossible to be both witch and sorcerer, and yet, here you are. By the gods, I knew she was a powerful Clairvoyant, but to engineer a Prophecy that bastardises genetics... such ingenuity. Such power. Then again, I always admired those qualities about Mor—"

And then I spot the man at her side.

While something contains the girl's sorcery—for now—the power of the Lines rages through her companion, as golden as his sun-kissed hair.

He steps forward, the gold-plated armour at his shoulders sparkling. "That's the problem with demons," he says, a self-satisfied smile curling his lips. "The hubris. Your kind always think that they're the most powerful people in the room."

His repetition of my earlier words makes my blood boil in my veins.

I hate witches, but it's nothing compared to the pure loathing I harbour towards sorcerers.

I push off from the ground, on my feet again in an instant. "A sarcastic sorcerer. How very unoriginal."

The sorcerer bends his fair head towards Kate Denton, where she lies on the ground, and offers her his hand.

"You okay?" he asks.

A spark of recognition brightens her eyes. "What are you doing here? It's not safe. Go. Tori, how could you bring him here? What were you thinking?"

The halfling girl steps forward and says, "Actually, he brought me."

Kate allows the male sorcerer to pull her to her feet. "You need to get out of—"

"I can help," he says.

"Help? No offence, but there's nothing you can do. You don't have any power—" Her words break off, and she gazes at the sorcerer. "Something flung that demon away from me. Did that... did that come from you?"

"We have a lot of catching up to do."

She takes him in, as if for the first time. "I don't understand. Why are you... dressed like him?" She tilts her chin at me.

I clear my throat. "You keep strange company, sorcerer."

Kate's eyes widen, and she takes a step away from the male.

I smirk at him. "Oh, they didn't know. Do you see how frightened of your power they are? Like startled cattle. And he should scare you, witches—"

The sorcerer narrows his eyes. "Don't listen to that thing. I'm here to help. Everyone move back. I'll take it from here."

The witches just stare at him, unblinking.

They cannot deny the existence of the other races now.

Sheep.

An apt description.

Our power.

Our strength.

We scare them to death.

I drink their fear in.

"I said *get back*," the sorcerer booms, the influence of sorcery lacing the final two words.

As one, the witches draw back against the walls.

He flexes his fingers, and a wall of golden light rises between us and them.

Interesting.

He's left the girl on our side of the light-shield.

I dare not touch her. If I do, the ancient power lurking just beneath her skin will smite me.

Some things are too powerful to challenge.

Her face pales when she notices my eyes on her.

The male sorcerer says, "It's over."

I deign to look at him. "Ah, the arrogance of youth. Nothing is over, boy. I am Sir Lancelot of The Round Table, one of the most revered demons in the—"

"Yeah, yeah. Save the speech. I get it. You're some kind of big cheese in Hell. What is it with evil geniuses and speeches, anyway?"

"You dare to mock me, sorcerer?"

"No offence, buddy, but I've tackled house spiders scarier than you. The dark armour, the black eyes. Let me tell you, it's not as impressive as you think."

My fists clench, and a muscle ticks in my jaw. "I have not killed one of your kind in centuries. This is going to be fun."

"Yeah, it is." He jabs a finger in my direction.

A warm breeze blows through the room.

I try to move, but I am bound. "You dare to bind me?"

He smiles, a feral grin that sets my teeth on edge. "Oh, I'm just getting started."

"You will—"

He jabs a finger at me. "I banish you, demon."

My chest tightens, but little else happens. "Pathetic."

"This body doesn't belong to you. I banish you back to Hell."

A knife-edged pain plunges between my ribs, and I gasp. "You do not have the—"

"Hear me. I banish you!"

Blazing agony carves a line down my abdomen, and a dark mist rises from my skin.

No.

Christian Winter is mine.

I will not allow this sorcerer to—

"I banish you, demon. I. Banish. You!"

Razors rake through my entire body, blistering fire consumes my innards, and I explode in a cloud of black smoke.

CHAPTER 52
John

The tar-black smoke consumes Christian.

"What's happening?" Tori shouts from behind me.

"It's working. The demon's nearly out."

The smoke writhes and twists, bucking like an out-of-control horse.

"I banish you," I say again, sweat dripping down my face. *I won't let you take my brother, you son of a bitch.*

The smoke drifts slowly back, back, back, and the Gates let off a soft white glow.

Yes!

They're drawing it back in.

It's going to work. It's going to—

An anguished, high-pitched shriek tears through the room, so ear-splitting, I'm forced to clamp my hands around my head.

The sounds morph into something far more terrifying.

Righteous, triumphant laughter.

Thick tendrils of smoke draw back into Christian's body—his eyes, his nose, his ears.

"You did not honestly think that would work, did you?" The demon stretches my brother's arms high and yawns. "This body is mine now. And I am not going anywhere until I have set my people free."

I unsheathe the sword strapped across my back and point it at the Christian's—no, the demon's—chest. "We'll see about that."

"You can't hurt him," Tori says. "It's still Christian."

I don't take my eyes off the infernal creature. "I'm hoping I won't have to."

With a sharp gesture from Lancelot, a column of black smoke rockets from his hand. When it fades, he's clutching his Shadow Blade.

The hilt is black as pitch, the straight lines of the hand guard ending in two wickedly barbed tips. The blade's straight, serrated along one edge.

Lancelot flicks the sword up to guard his face. "You will die here tonight, sorcerer. And when I am finished with you, I shall use your bones to club your witch friends to death." He lunges, swinging the sword in a lightning fast arc towards the crown of my head.

Good thing I'm quick, too.

I bring my sword up and block the strike.

The force of the blades colliding is so powerful, it sets my arm juddering and I almost lose my grip on the sword.

I shove up with my blade, pushing Lancelot off me, then counter with three swift cutting motions.

He blocks them all, each clang of our blades deafening in the wide space.

Repeatedly, our blades meet until sparks fly from both weapons.

Lancelot stabs at me.

I move to defend myself.

He changes direction fast.

A stinging flash of pain sears the back of my hand.

I fall back, blood dripping off my fingers.

The demon grins. "If that is the best you can do, this will not take long."

"You want my best, you got it."

Without warning, Lancelot strikes again, hard and fast.

His Shadow Blade snaps my sword in two, the severed end flying off and clattering into the shadows.

"It is just a regular sword." Lancelot draws back, nonplussed for a moment, then a cruel smile peels his lips away from his teeth. "By the gods, you are but a pup. You have yet to Ascend. You cannot even summon a Light Blade."

From the corner of my eye, Tori takes a step towards the demon and opens her mouth like she's going to cast.

I shake my head. "Stay put."

The demon strides forward, raises the pummel of his sword, and cracks me over the head with it.

I make no move to stop him.

Stars swim before my eyes, and I collapse to the floor.

Blood trickles into my ear.

A shadow passes over me, and I glance up to see Lancelot glaring down, a gloating smirk on his face.

"It is a pity. I was hoping for a better fight."

"Screw you."

He just laughs and raises his free hand, dark shadows gathering in his palm. "You are not very good at this, are you, Pup?"

I can't hold it in anymore.

The laughter I've been straining to contain since Lancelot snapped my sword bursts out of me, loud and clear.

His brow knits together.

That makes me laugh harder.

He's playing right into my hands.

The dark cloud of energy dissipates, and he stares at me askance. "Does the thought of death amuse you?"

"No." I wipe my eyes. "No, it's not that."

"What, then?" The demon asks through gritted teeth.

"It's just... it's just that you said I'm not very good at this."

"Why is that amusing?"

"It's amusing..." I pause, drawing as much energy as I can from the Lines—which is a hell of a lot—until my blood sings with power.

Lancelot's eyes widen. He must sense my strength.

Good.

That makes what's about to happen next all the sweeter.

He steps back.

"... because that's exactly what I wanted you to think," I say, before letting my power loose.

CHAPTER 53
John

The blast of golden energy catapults Lancelot across the room. He flies towards the platform, clears it, and slams into the Gates.

They shudder, but don't fall.

It'll take more than that to breach Hell.

Lancelot's body hits the floor with a bone-jarring thump.

I'm on my feet again.

Heal me.

A soft warmth spreads through my entire body like a balm, and my Gift seals the wounds Lancelot inflicted on me.

From behind me, Tori whoops. "That was brilliant."

I smile, but keep my eyes locked on the demon.

They're slippery bastards, and I have no intention of letting it out of my sight.

"Cheers," I call to her, flicking my wrist.

A flash of gold light arcs from my hand, and the weight of my Light Blade slaps into my palm.

I grip the hilt and a profound sense of peace washes over me like a balm.

The sword is more than just an ordinary blade. It's an extension of my soul, forged from the deepest focus of my intent.

When Selina died, I turned all my rage and hate on the demons who murdered her. In that moment I Ascended, and claimed full command over my sorcery. I ceased being a "pup," as Lancelot calls it.

When a sorcerer Ascends, their Light Blade manifests.

Mine was born that day.

I stare down at the pommel, shaped like a dragon's head, and the curved cross-guard, which gives the impression of unfurling wings.

This is for you, Selina.

Everything I do is for you.

Lancelot regains his feet.

My eyes snap to his.

He comes forward, the tread of his boots neither disturbing the dust on the ground, nor making a sound.

I point my blade at him.

At the edge of the platform he sinks into a low crouch, a classic stalking pose.

This demon might wear my brother's face, but he's nothing like Chris.

"A Healer," Lancelot says. "That makes things harder, but not impossible. Even Healers can die. You are—" His eyes trace the hilt clenched in my fist, gaze landing on Selina's pendant, and his eyes widen. "No."

I grin at him. "Oh, yes."

"The sword. The trinket. You're the Dragon."

I sketch a quick bow. "In the flesh."

I'm gratified when he stumbles back a little. "The legends are true."

"The best ones always are."

He scowls. "When I heard about you—the trainee sorcerer who killed ten Lesser Demons with a single blow, I thought it was a tall tale indeed."

"Well... I'm pretty tall, I guess." I circle my wrist, my Light Blade cutting through the air. "But if you're looking for an autograph, you're fresh out of luck."

Lancelot raises his blade again. "What I want is your head on a pike. The demons that you and your... *associates*... killed were friends of mine. It will give me great pleasure to watch the light leave your eyes."

I don't wait for Lancelot to attack this time. Instead, I Teleport across the room in a flash of light, landing behind him. I slash with my blade, aiming for the demon's torso.

Lancelot disappears in a haze of black smoke, reappearing at the other end of the platform.

"Running scared?" I ask.

"In your dreams, sorcerer."

I rush forward with a booming battle cry.

When I reach him, Lancelot strikes mercilessly, his sword battering mine again and again.

With our blades locked together, muscles straining, Lancelot steps close to me. "You're holding back. Why?"

"I'm not—"

He flicks his fingers and I'm hoisted off my feet, flying off the platform and crashing to the ground below.

Without missing a beat, I roll back over my shoulder and spring to my feet, my Light Blade shining.

Lancelot's smiling now, all trace of fear gone. He narrows his eyes. "What fears are you hiding?"

A presence shunts the edge of my mind.

Lancelot.

Fear.

Shit.

I should have remembered from my studies.

He's an Empath.

If he finds out who I am, who Christian is to me—

I throw up tons of mental barriers, just like Kalia taught me, but I needn't have bothered.

Lancelot slips through my defences with ease.

Oh, this is too precious.

Fuck.

He knows.

Lancelot laughs, but it's cold and cruel. "So, the infamous Dragon is none other than John Winter. What a fortunate coincidence."

"Get out of my head."

"Funny. Your brother said the same thing before I overwhelmed him."

"Listen to me, you stinking sack of—"

"No. You will listen to me. I know your fears now."

The tip of an icy finger trails down my spine. "Is that supposed to scare me?"

He counters with a question of his own. "Is that a tremor in your voice, oh mighty Dragon?"

"You can take your tremor and shove—"

"You fear that everyone you love will abandon you."

I just want the pain to stop.

Don't we all.

Christian's words.

Don't.

We.

All.

"He abandoned you that night, in his own way," Lancelot says.

My sword hand shakes, just a little. "Shut your mouth."

"They all abandon you in the end, don't they?"

"I said, shut it."

"Your parents."

The demon's words are like a knife to my gut, twisting, twisting. "Stop."

"Christian."

My ears ring.

"Selina."

Her face flashes before my eyes, creased in agony.

That's how I remember her now.

The gushing wound in her gut.

A dark shimmer of blood staining her lips.

I'm cold...

I can still remember her scent—jasmine and honeysuckle.

Something inside me snaps.

One moment, I'm standing below the platform, staring up at Lancelot, and the next, I've Teleported to his side.

I land a sharp blow to the demon's elbow.

Crack.

Lancelot issues a keening wail, his Shadow Blade tumbling from his grasp.

Before the sword can vanish in a swirl of shadows, I snatch it from the air with my free hand and drive my knee into the demon's stomach.

The air goes out of Lancelot, and he staggers back against the wall.

I press the demon's own keen-edged sword against his throat, and rest the tip of my Spirit Blade on his abdomen. "Fuck. You."

"John, stop!" Tori screeches. "Christian's still in there."

Christian's still in there.

Those words make my rage drain away to nothing.

"Tori Falade is right." A slow smile spreads across Lancelot's face. "Kill me, and you kill your brother. You may as well just let me finish what I started."

My body shakes so violently I'm surprised it doesn't fall apart, and my grip on both swords tightens...

But I can't do it.

There's no way I can kill Chris.

I glare into those soulless black eyes and say, "Chris, I know you're in there somewhere, pal. Fight this. You can't let him win."

"You still do not understand, John Winter. I have already won."

There has to be a way to reach Chris.

But I can't think of one, and I'm running out of time.

I'd sworn an Oath when I joined The Sorcerer's Guild, an Oath to protect the Gates and keep the demons within trapped, no matter what the cost.

If Lancelot won't leave on his own, then I need to force his hand.

I'll just try one last time. "Christian... If you're in there..."

"Oh, he is in here. And he's screaming in torment."

Shit.

"I'm not going anywhere," the demon says.

I'm out of options.

It's my duty.

"Then you leave me no choice." I take a deep, shuddering breath and whisper, "I'm so sorry, Chris."

I draw back my sword and plunge it deep into Lancelot's stomach.

Chapter 54

John

Lancelot's face, though scrunched in pain, is a picture of shock. "You—you stabbed me."

"It's my duty," I say, drawing back, and yanking my sword free with a swift, sharp tug.

The demon slides down the wall, leaving a bloody trail at his back.

A collective cry of outrage rises from the witches standing at the edge of the room.

They beat against my light-shield, to no avail.

They're trapped until I release them.

Even above the din of the witches, something else tears into my ears.

A cry of animalistic rage.

I pivot.

Tori bolts towards me, her fingers hooked into claws, angry red light shining in her palms. She's shouting at me, cursing, but—amid her fury—her words are unintelligible. Tori reaches the platform steps and makes to launch the crimson light at me.

I steel myself, drawing on the Ley Lines.

Freeze!

The gears of time grind to a halt with a jarring jolt.

I stare around the room.

Faces twisted with abject fury.

They've got the right to hate me. After all, they've just watched one of their own get stabbed.

And, registering the looks on their faces, I realise that—even though I saved them all—I'll never be one of them.

Vessel.

Sorcerer.

Doesn't matter.

I'll always be on the outside with witches.

Something... *other*.

I turn away from the crowd, fastening my eyes on the demon, frozen in time, along with everyone else.

Lancelot lies slumped against the wall, hands clamped against his wound.

A wave of dizziness rushes over me.

It's like history repeating itself.

Selina's eyes hover before mine.

Blank eyes.

Dead eyes.

No.

Demons already stole someone I love.

I won't let it happen again.

Besides, I never expected Lancelot to leave voluntarily.

Stabbing Christian was always Plan B.

I turn to Tori.

Time for her to play her part.

I step aside so I'm not in her path.

Focusing on her, I bring her—and only her—out of the frozen state.

The scarlet spell sails past me and explodes against the wall with a bang.

She readies another strike.

"Don't," I say.

Her eyes simmer with rage. "You stabbed him."

"We can save him. You're going to have to trust me."

"*Trust you*? You're out of your fucking mind."

"It was the only way to get Lancelot to leave. If Chris is in a weakened state, Lancelot won't be able to maintain the Possession."

"Weakened? Is that what you call it. He's about to di—" she breaks off, staring at the immobile witches. "What did you do?"

"Froze time."

"You—you can do that?"

"Yeah."

She laughs, but there's no warmth. "So, what's your plan? Keep Christian frozen forever?"

"No. I can save him."

"Heal him, you mean?" Tori's tone is sharp enough to wound. "Didn't work so well for Selina, did it?"

And wound it does.

Like a knife to the chest.

Unbidden, my fingers drift to the dragon pendant around my neck.

Tori reaches for her pocket and says, "I've got some liquid silver in—"

I hold up a hand to silence her, take a deep breath, and swallow back tears. "That won't work."

"What? Why not?"

"The Possession. It's too recent. His body will be really weak. That weakness will nullify the effects of the silver."

Her searching fingers go still and her face pales. "You're sure you can Heal him?"

God, I hope so.

I nod. "Things are different now."

"Yeah? What things?"

"I've got my full powers for a start."

"And?"

"I've got you."

"Me?"

I nod. "You're a sorcerer too, remember?"

"That's... I don't know how to Heal anyone."

"Like I said, you'll just have to trust me."

I turn my attention back to Lancelot.

Please.

Please, if there's anyone looking out for me up there, make this work.

With a simple gesture, I unfreeze the demon.

Chapter 55
John

Chris is bleeding out onto the floor while Lancelot speaks through his lips. "You would kill your own brother just to be rid of me?"

I move closer to the demon and crouch down beside him. "That's the least of your worries where you're going."

He laughs, and the wound in his stomach makes an odd sucking sound.

My gut clenches.

"Like I said, I am not going anywhere."

"John," Tori says, in a panic-stricken voice. "It's not working. He's going to bleed out. If you don't do something now, he'll die."

"Just wait. The demon has to leave first."

"Foolish sorcerer. Even if you succeed, my return to Hell will be temporary." He points to the crown atop his head. "There will always be those who seek demonic power. The crown—"

"Won't be an issue. Once you're gone, I'm going to take it somewhere no one can find it."

Lancelot loses all composure. His mouth twists and flecks of saliva shoot from his mouth. "You filthy, light-loving bastard. This isn't over. This isn't—" He gasps in pain, his words choking off, then he coughs.

Once.

Twice.

A third time.

I stand and back away.

"What's happening?" Tori asks.

"It's working."

Black smoke pours from Chris's mouth, thicker than tar.

The stink of sulfur scents the air, and a wailing shriek tears through the cavern.

"Heal him," Tori snaps. "Now."

"Not yet."

"Why the hell not?"

"Because of that," I say, pointing.

The last of the smoke leaves Chris's body, swirling up, up, up.

Two deeper spots of darkness stare out at us.

Lancelot's voice forces its way into my mind.

You will not defeat me. I will burn this place to the ground, and all of you along with it. I will—

He screams, and his voice recedes.

The Gates shine, bright white fingers of light reaching for the demon.

No. No. No.

The light entwines with the smoke, and Lancelot issues a deafening, screeching wail.

I clamp my hands over my ears, and the ground rumbles beneath my feet.

A flash of blinding light forces me to shield my eyes, followed by a clap of thunder.

And all is silent.

I lower my hand.

The demon has vanished, and the Gates no longer shine, the silent skulls staring... no, some look like they're smiling.

A shiver passes through me.

"Ugh!"

Shit.

Chris.

I dash to my brother's side—Tori hot on my heels—and crash to my knees.

Chris seems dazed, pale from blood loss, but his eyes are sharp. "John... John, is that you?"

"Yeah, I'm here."

"Listen to me." Chris says, in between quick breaths. "There's a demon. I know it sounds crazy, but there's—"

"I've taken care of that."

"You... but—" His face pales. "I'm cold."

My heart stops.

I'm cold...

Selina.

No.

Not again.

I can't go through this again.

It's—

"Do something!" Tori screams, folding one of Chris's hands in hers.

Dizzying heat steals my focus.

I'm cold...

"Tori?" Chris's voice sounds weak.

"I'm here," she says, shooting me a thorny glare. "John. Snap out of it and do something."

Her sharp command brings me back to my senses, and I clench my fists. "Don't worry, Chris," I say. "You're going to be okay."

"But—" he starts.

I freeze him again, and he falls silent.

Tori rounds on me. "Sorcerer or not, if he dies, I swear on my magic I'll kill you."

I believe her. "He won't. Not if we both help him."

"I've already told you, I don't—"

"You don't need to do anything, just hold my hand."

"Why?"

"I'm going to channel Ley Line energy through both of us. It'll amplify my Gift, and we'll save him together."

She stares at my hand like it's crawling with fleas. "You sure this'll work?"

"It's the best shot we've got."

Tori's hand slides into mine.

"Brace yourself," I say. "This is going to hurt."

"I don't care. Do what you need to do."

I reach out with my mind and draw on the power of the Lines, funnelling it through Tori and into me.

Tori goes rigid. She screams in my ear.

I wince.

Her screams continue.

I draw more and more power from the Lines, more than I've ever called on in my life.

Tori screams louder.

My entire body shudders so violently, I almost lose my grip on her hand.

Shit.

Hold on.

Just hold on.

Bring me more of your energy.

Sweat pours down my back, my leather armour sticking to my skin, and something warm and wet coats my upper lip.

Blood.

My nose is bleeding.

More.

A scream of my own tears from my throat.

My knees shake.

I can't hold any more power.

It's time.

Now or never.

I stare at the wound in my brother's abdomen, reaching out with my free hand.

Please.

Please let this work.

Heal!

Golden light—richer and darker than I'm used to—rockets from my hand with the force of a fire hydrant exploding.

My arms judder, my head pounds, and my heart hammers. The veins on the back of my hand shine with golden iridescence.

The wound in Chris's abdomen stops bleeding.

It's working.

Holy fuck.

It's actually working.

Muscle and sinew draw together, and I stare in amazement as the wound stitches itself closed, and a fresh layer of skin forms.

Nearly there.

Just hang on, Chris.

Nearly there.

I give one last massive mental push.

Searing agony wracks my brain.

The gold light stutters and fades, and the wound has vanished.

I breathe a sigh of relief.

I've done it.

He's going to be okay…

I collapse to my knees, breathing hard.

Chris gasps, his eyelids snap open, and he launches to his feet. "Demon. There's a fucking—" He catches sight of me. "John. What… what's going on?"

I push to my feet, and the room spins. I stumble.

Tori grabs my arm to steady me. "Holy shit," she says, her voice a little shaky. "We did it!"

Chris's brow creases in confusion. "Did what?" His gaze slides away from Tori and me, taking in the room.

The golden barrier.

The time-frozen witches.

"Lancelot wasn't lying," he says when his eyes land on the Gates. "But, I don't understand. Where is he?"

I'm steady now, so I shrug off Tori's hand. "I took care of it."

His eyebrows draw together. "You? But you don't have any… what are you wearing?"

And I tell him.

I tell him everything.

Tori fills him in on her part in it.

When we finish, he's quiet for the longest time.

"Chris—"

He holds up a hand to silence me. "Let me get this straight. You're both sorcerers?"

"Well, I am," I say. "Tori's situation is a little more… nuanced."

"And you stabbed me?"

I let out a heavy sigh. "Um… about that—"

"Then you Healed me?"

I nod.

"Right." He rubs his forehead like he's got the mother of all headaches. "Well, I guess your cagey behaviour makes sense now."

"I wasn't cagey, I was—"

"Oh, you were cagey," Tori says.

"Hey. Us sorcerers need to stick together."

"Like you said, my situation's more nuanced."

"Guys," Chris says. "Not to sour the mood, but what are we going to do about them?"

I turn.

Kate and the other MID officers remain frozen in time, oblivious to everything happening right now.

I sigh.

My power scares them.

And I know what witches do when they're afraid of something.

They either shun it.

Or attack it.

If they attack me, they'll force me to defend myself, and I don't want to hurt anyone.

I spin back to face Chris. "I need to leave."

His face pales. "Leave! You only just got back."

"I don't have a choice. They know about me."

"You don't have to leave," Tori says.

I stare at her, dumbstruck. "Are you kidding me? I saw the looks on their faces. It's just like when I was a vessel, but worse. They'll never—"

"We can wipe their memories."

"What?" Christian and I shout in unison.

"You'll be able to stay."

My gaze goes to Chris.

He scrunches up his face.

It's an expression I recognize—he's conflicted.

"Chris..."

"You want me to lie to Kate? To everyone? Not only that, but you want me to mess with their memories?"

He's hating every second of this, and it's killing me. "I won't force you."

If possible, his face scrunches up even further. Then his expression clears.

He's decided.

"Listen, I get it—"

All the air gets crushed from my lungs when Chris embraces me in a tight bear hug. "You're my brother. I love you, and I'll do whatever it takes to keep you safe."

I love you.

Tears spring into my eyes, and I hug him back.

I never thought I'd hear him say that to me again.

"I love you, too," I say.

He pulls away. "Oh, shit."

"What?"

"The crown."

My gaze flicks up to the crown, the golden glyph glinting at Chris's brow. "What about it?"

He snatches it off his head. "We need to get rid of it. What if someone finds it? We can't—"

"I'll deal with it," I say.

"Deal with it?" Tori asks. "How?"

"I know a place where no one will ever find it." I hold out my hand for the crown.

Chris hesitates.

That stings.

"I know you said you didn't trust me before, but you can, you know."

Chris sets his jaw and exhales through his nose.

Trust me.

Please.

Eventually, he passes me the crown, and says, "I know."

"Right." Tori places her hands on her hips and gazes out at the crowd of time-frozen witches. "We'll sort this lot."

I step away from them, preparing to Teleport out.

"I—" Christian's hand goes to his chest, his brow creasing.

"What is it?" I ask.

"It's…" A pained expression crosses his features. "My magic. I can't feel my magic."

"What?"

"I think—" a strangled sob escapes him "—I think it's gone. I mean, really gone."

The uncertainty in my brother's voice makes me want to cry. "What do you mean it's—"

A sharp pain blossoms behind my right eye.

The witches shift position ever so slightly.

Shit.

"What was that?" Tori asks, clutching her stomach like she's going to be sick.

"Time doesn't like standing still for long," I say.

"You need to get the crown. We'll—" Her cheeks flush, and she can't meet Chris's eye. "I'll handle them."

"Right." I cast one last look at Chris. "Hey. We'll fix it."

"Yeah." He nods, but the movement lacks conviction. "You should go."

I can't think of anything else to say.

I can't make this better.

The room lurches again.

"Go!" Tori shouts.

She's right.

I have to leave.

Now.

Take me away from here.

The heady power of the Lines washes over me.

Gold light rises around me and obscures everything.

It's time to finish this.

Once and for all.

CHAPTER 56
Christian

After John leaves, my hand remains planted against my chest... my empty chest.

Somehow, I know my magic is gone, not just exhausted. When magic is exhausted, it's still there—the spark of heat out of reach until the energy replenishes, or until you give it a boost with liquid silver.

But this...

This is different.

I'm hollow.

A shell.

There's nothing there.

Nothing.

The realisation smacks into me like a meaty fist sporting knuckle-dusters.

I have no magic.

My stomach lurches, and the room lurches with it—time desperately trying to reestablish itself—but I barely notice.

All that power I prided myself on for so many years...

Extinguished.

A strangled sound works its way from my throat.

Tori's at my side in an instant, her soft, warm hand squeezing my arm. "Are you okay?"

My gaze fixes on the place where she touches me.

She's so strong.

And I'm so weak.

I'm not worthy of her touch, so I shrug her off. "No. No, I'm not."

"We'll fix this."

Hope flares in my chest… pointless.

My powers have deserted me.

Tori says, "Kate's bound to know how to—"

"Don't." The word comes out harsher than I intended. I soften my voice. "Please. This is hard enough as it is."

"Sure…" She bites her lip. "Christian."

"What?"

"You were going to ask me something before the case, weren't you?"

Oh.

Right.

I was going to ask her to move in with me.

But I can't now.

Not when I'm…

Not now, when my magic is…

"The answer's yes," she says.

My head snaps up. "Excuse me?"

She smiles. "You've been carrying that spare house key round for ages."

"How did you…"

"I'm a detective. I detect. Think I wouldn't notice."

That poisonous feeling of hope is back again and, when I speak, my voice cracks a little. "You—you still—want me?"

Her brow creases and she takes my hands in hers. "Of course. Why wouldn't I?"

"Even... like this?"

"Like what?"

"My magic. I'm not... I'm weak."

She squeezes my hands. "You're an idiot is what you are. I don't love you because you're a powerful witch. I love you because you're the most caring, kind person I've ever met."

I snort. "Yeah?"

She drops a light kiss on my lips. "Yeah. So, I'd love to move in. If you'll have me?"

I touch my forehead to hers. "Thank you."

She laughs, but it's tinged with sadness. "What for?"

"Not abandoning me."

"Never."

We stand—pressed together—for the longest time...

Until time starts again, in fact.

There's a loud *crack*.

The sound of Tori's watch *tick-tick-ticking* fills the silence.

Kate and the others stare around the room, looking a little bewildered.

Injecting more confidence in my voice than I feel, I say to Tori, "You'd better cast the memory spell."

She gives my hand one last squeeze and shoots me a sad half-smile before turning to face the room, her voice spilling out in a low chant.

Kate and my other colleagues will forget what they know about John.

Lucky them.

I wish I could forget everything that's happened to me.

Chapter 57
John

The woods are dark and, despite the warmth of the summer night, I shiver beneath my sorcerer's armour.

I can't believe I'm going to do this. I swore to myself I wouldn't contact anyone from the Guild until I was ready.

My grip tightens on the crown, and the golden glyph winks at me.

Bloody crown.

More trouble than it's worth.

Just thinking about what could've happened if Lancelot succeeded...

He wouldn't have stopped at exterminating witches, either.

No.

He would've hunted mortals into extinction next.

Then he would've come for us.

Still can't believe I'm about to do this.

Even if it *is* the only way.

The vault back at the Guild is the only thing that can contain the crown.

I can't go there myself.

Too many ghosts.

But I have to reach out to someone.

With trembling hands and a fast-beating heart, I take a deep breath.

The rich, loamy scent of the woods fills my nostrils, but does little to soothe my nerves.

I hate feeling this way.

Uncertain.

Swamped by loss.

I didn't just lose Selina that day. I lost everything.

Kalia.

Stephan.

Amber.

I lost everything, even my sense of belonging.

I couldn't stay with them anymore.

Her presence filled the entire dimension. Her clothes. Our room. Her smell.

Jasmine and honeysuckle.

I couldn't stand it.

The guilt.

She was so much better than me in every way. More kind, more witty, more self-sacrificing.

It isn't fair.

Why should she lie dead, buried under six feet of cold earth, while I get to live?

It's a question I'll never stop asking myself.

But the crown...

This needs to happen.

I close my eyes and reach out across the vast distance—through time, through space, through the Lines and into the Guild's Nexus.

Amber. It's John. I need your help.

When my eyelids drift open, I'm still alone.

Sorcery is nothing but intention made real, but to have true intention, you really have to want what you're asking for.

Do I really want to see Amber again?

To see that look in her eyes?

Pity.

The worst.

The last thing I need is anyone's pity.

But...

Needs must.

I concentrate on Amber, conjuring a clear image of her in my mind.

Serene smile.

Chestnut hair.

The way she balances on the balls of her feet, like a bird preparing to take flight.

Amber. Please. If you can hear me, I really need you.

A golden glow suffuses the air, accompanied by the rush of speeding wind and—when it fades—Amber stands before me.

I brace myself for the pity, but it doesn't come.

Instead, she breaks into a wide smile, sea-green eyes sparkling. "It's good to see you."

"You too," I say, but I'm not sure I mean it.

She rushes forward and throws her arms around my neck, burying her face in my shoulder.

I stiffen.

She squeezes tighter.

I relent, hugging her back.

"Missed you," she says, pulling away from me. The smile falls from her face, her eyes flicking to the dragon's head pendant resting against my chest.

Still, there's no pity there, only sympathy.

It's a fine line.

She reaches out and brushes her fingers over the pendant. "I miss her, as well. Every day."

"I know."

Amber takes a step back and glances down at the floor, scuffing the dirt with the point of her shoe, biting her lower lip. "I didn't think we'd hear from you so soon. After she di—" she catches herself "—after you left."

I remain silent.

She glances back up. "Does this mean... are you coming home?"

"No," I say, a little too quickly.

Her expression darkens. "You should be with family."

"It's too soon." The hot prickle of tears stings the corner of my eyes. "Besides, I *am* with family. I'm staying with Chris."

She arches an eyebrow. "Your brother?"

I nod.

"The same brother who abandoned you?"

"He didn't abandon me. It was hard for him, and—"

"He'll never understand you."

"Amber..."

"I'm sorry, but it's true."

"Please, Amber. I can't come back. Not yet. It's... it's too soon."

She gives a shallow nod, sensing the finality in my voice, and says, "If I'm not here to bring you home, then what am I here for?"

"This," I say, holding up the crown.

Her eyes widen. "Shit. Is that what I think it is?"

"Yes. Arthur's crown."

She closes her eyes. "I can't sense anything demonic. Thank God no one had the chance to use this. It's a—"

"Someone's already used it."

"Shit. We need to summon Kalia and Stephan. We need to tell them—"

"Hey. Relax. I've dealt with it."

"Dealt with it?"

"I sent Lancelot back to Hell where he belongs."

"*Lancelot*?" Her eyes nearly bug out of her head and she punches my arm hard enough to bruise.

"Ow. What was that for?"

"You tackled a demon lord on your own. Have you gone insane? He could've killed you."

I shrug. "But he didn't."

She paces left and right. "You're such a dick."

"I know," I snort.

"When Kalia hears about this—"

"You can't tell her."

"I have to. She needs to know."

"It's not a request."

Her eyebrows rise. "What?"

"It's an order. You wouldn't disobey a direct order, would you, soldier?"

"I…"

"Amber."

Her shoulders droop, then she pulls herself up to her full height and fixes me with a look of steely determination. "No, sir."

"Good." Then, to soften the blow, I add, "Sorry to pull rank."

That earns me a half smile. "You're more like Kalia than you realise."

"So you and Stephan keep telling me."

She chuckles.

"How is he?"

"Same as ever… you know Stephan." She rolls her eyes, but there's no disguising the fondness in her tone.

"Annoying as an itch you can't scratch," we say in unison.

Then we stand in companionable silence.

Eventually, Amber hugs me again, whispers, "Please come home soon," and lets go.

"Don't forget this." I hand her the crown.

"Goodbye, John."

"Bye, Amber."

Another flash of golden light… and she's gone, taking the crown with her.

Alone in the all-consuming darkness, I cross to a fallen tree and perch on the thick trunk like it's a bench.

I place my head in my hands and take a huge breath.

The fragrance of the night air resembles damp moss, and it carries the subtle flavour of earthy peat.

The silence is like a soothing balm to my sense.

Shit.

So much has happened.

Selina.

My battle with Lancelot.

Nearly losing Chris.

Tori.

Ah, yeah.

Tori.

Somehow, she can wield witchcraft and sorcery.

That's not possible, or at least… it shouldn't be.

Lancelot said something to her before I banished him.

Something about hiding in plain sight, and a Prophecy, and bastardising genetics.

I have no clue what he meant by that.

And it's not like I can ask him now.

Tori will need training if she's going to master her sorcery... if she even wants to.

I should tell Kalia and the others about her, but I can't.

She is someone who shouldn't exist.

I'm not sure how the Guild will react to her.

I've got a feeling it won't be good.

I'll just have to train her myself.

But that's a problem for another day.

Right now, all I want to do is go home, make sure Chris is okay—even though I know he won't be, with his magic absent—and attempt to tell him about everything that's happened to me since I left.

I clutch Selina's pendant in my fist.

Telling Chris my story is going to be about as much fun as water torture.

But I promised.

And I keep my promises.

No matter the cost.

EPILOGUE
Christian

Two months have passed since John defeated Lancelot.

My magic still hasn't returned.

John finally told me everything.

Here's how that went...

John and I sit across from each other in my lounge.

He's fiddling with that dragon's head pendant again.

I catch his eye. "You need to tell me what happened to you."

He drops the pendant, gnaws on his thumbnail, then says, "I know, but... I've never told anyone before."

My lips pinch. "You told Tori."

He shakes his head. "I showed her. That's different."

"Can't you show me?"

"No. You're not a Sorcerer, and you don't have Tori's Gift."

Tori's Gift.

I'm still getting used to that.

John doesn't know why, but Tori has sorcerer and witch powers. Something which, according to him, shouldn't be possible.

I clear my throat. "Please, John. I need to know."

He exhales a heavy breath, pushes to his feet, and crosses to the mantlepiece. "I'll try."

I wait.

John picks up the family photo of the four of us—me, him, Mum, and Dad—and stares at it. After a long period of silence, voice strained, he says, "Do you ever wish we could go back to this?"

"All the time."

He replaces the photo, turns to face me, and crosses his arms. "That night... before I left. The night we rowed..."

The words I launched at John like daggers that night pollute the air between us.

I want the pain to stop!

Don't we all.

Don't.

We.

All.

"I never should've said that," I blurt out. "I didn't mean it. It was—"

He holds up a hand. "No. You were right. I needed to sort myself out, but..."

"But?"

He hesitates, biting his lip.

The seconds tick by.

John rubs the back of his neck, stealing himself for his next words. When he speaks, his voice comes out quiet. "When I slit my wrists, I wanted to die. I wanted it more than anything I'd ever wanted up to that point."

A sharp ache punctures my chest, but I say nothing. I don't want to interrupt John, in case he clams up again.

He walks back to his chair and sinks into it, hunching over. "As soon as I'd done it, I knew I'd made a terrible mistake. I tried to stop the bleeding, but nothing worked until…" his words trail off.

I can't resist this time.

"Until?"

He flinches, like he forgot I was there. "I slapped my hand over the cut and prayed it would Heal. My Gift must've kicked in because it worked. It Healed my wrists… even removed my tattoos… then again, they are a type of scar, I suppose."

Although I don't intend them to, my next words come out bitter. "Then you ran away."

"Yes… and no."

"What does that mean?"

"I told you a little about Kalia?"

"Yeah."

A small smile caresses his lips. "She sensed my power, and Teleported to me, right there in the bathroom. I nearly shit myself."

"She's a sorcerer, too."

He nods. "She's the head of The Sorcerer's Guild."

"Hang on, the what?"

He exhales a curse. "I shouldn't have said that."

I rise from my chair. "John—"

He stands, too. "I swore a Sorcerer's Oath. If I tell you any more about the Guild…"

"You'll die."

He bobs his head.

I hold my hands out in a placatory gesture. "Fine."

We both sit again.

"What happened next?" I ask.

"Kalia told me about sorcerers." He pauses, then explains, "All vessels have the potential to become sorcerers. We can use the empty place where our magic should go to siphon energy from the Lines into our bodies and convert it into sorcery."

A thought comes to me. "What about demons? Were they vessels, too?"

"No." He laces the word with venom. Then his tone softens. "Sorry. We don't like to be compared to them. Nobody knows where demonic power comes from."

"The Guild doesn't keep historical records?" I ask.

"We do, but we can't possibly know everything. Demons channel the Lines like we do, but as to the mechanics of shadowmancy, or what creates a demon… it's a mystery."

Ha!

You can say that again.

Funny how my life has got a lot more mysterious since my brother showed up.

"Sorry," I say. "I interrupted you."

He waves his hand like it doesn't matter. "Kalia offered to train me, to teach me how to be powerful… I accepted because… because I was so jealous of you."

The wounded tone in his voice brings me up short. "Mate…"

He brushes past this. "Anyway. She Teleported me to the Guild straight away. It's inside a Nexus… oh, a Nexus is—"

"A place existing outside of time and space. I know."

"Guess Lancelot taught you a thing or two, huh?"

"Actually, Aidan taught me that."

We fall silent.

A thought strikes me.

A place existing outside of time and space.

I'd never really considered what this meant.

Outside of time and space.

Time must stop in a Nexus.

John's been gone for four years, but—from what I can gather—he's spent most of that time inside a Nexus.

But that means...

"John..."

"Yeah?"

"How long were you in the Nexus for?"

He makes a huffing sound, half laughter, half scoffing. "A long time."

"How long?" I press.

"Just over a decade."

But time has passed in the "real world", so that means...

"You weren't there the whole time, though."

"No. Kalia was adamant we shouldn't lose touch with Earthside."

Earthside.

Interesting term.

He continues, "She wanted us to do all the things we never had the chance to do. Learn to drive, go to uni—"

"Hang on? You went to uni?"

He chuckles, and it's a genuine laugh this time. "Don't sound so surprised."

I can't help but grin back. "What did you study?"

"Classics and mythology."

"Really?"

He rolls his eyes. "Really."

"Whatever tickles your pickle, I guess."

He's playing with the pendant again.

The smile slides off my face. "What about Selina?"

His fingers go still, his face creasing in pain. "Tori told you."

"Yeah."

John scrubs a hand across his mouth. "She's—she *was*—Kalia's daughter."

"Another sorcerer."

He sniffs. "Yep. A far better one than me."

I hold my tongue.

John heaves himself to his feet and paces back and forth. He makes a choked sound. "I loved her so much."

Something inside me cracks. "It wasn't your fault."

He snorts, tears spilling over. "I couldn't Heal her. God, I tried. I really tried… if I hadn't been so weak, she'd still be—"

I'm on my feet and next to my brother in a flash, crushing him in a bear hug. "No. Demons killed her. You did everything you could."

His entire body stiffens, then he relents and his arms go round me. "I missed you, bro."

"You too."

No wonder my brother's a different person.

I'd challenge anyone not to be affected by everything he's been through.

Guess I have to stop treating him like a fucked up twenty-two-year-old. Sure, he still has a few scars, both physical and psychological, but who doesn't?

The point is, he's powerful now.

In every sense.

Self-assured.

Purposeful.

Unlike me.

My magic still hasn't returned, and nobody knows why.

Kate assigned an entire team to fix me.

They've tried all sorts—various amulets, many foul-tasting tinctures, and a shit-load of liquid silver injections.

Nothing's worked.

Kate assigned me to desk duties for the foreseeable future, which means I'll never return to active duty. Oh, speaking of Kate, she managed—God knows how—to convince the Witches Council everything that went down when I stormed their headquarters with Pentacle was under her authority, and necessary to my undercover case.

I kept quiet about Coercing Naismith to confess to framing Julianna Caldwell.

If Kate's worked that out for herself—which, knowing Kate, she has—she hasn't mentioned it once.

She says she's hopeful I'll get my magic back and, despite the team she has in place to help me recover it, I can tell she's humouring me.

Everyone thinks I should accept it and move on.

But I can't.

I'll never give up.

I'm getting my powers back, whatever it takes.

I've waited until the house is empty, and now it's time to test my latest theory.

This has to work.

I cast my gaze down to the chalk circle at my feet. I stand in its centre, our family grimoire open in my hands.

Candles—placed along the circle's edge—glow softly, their cheery light muted by the bright afternoon sunshine pouring through the windows.

I've recreated the Manifestation ritual, and tweaked the incantation a little. Normally, a Potential's parents cast the spell, but I—for obvious reasons—am going solo on this one.

I want my life back.

My job.

After all, what good is a MID officer without magic?

Kate denies it, but the only reason I still have a desk is because she pities me.

Well, I don't need pity.

They all think I'm powerless.

I'm going to prove them wrong.

I recite my version of the Manifestation.

Nothing.

Not even a flicker of power.

I shake my hands out. "Come on. I can do this."

I try again.

Zilch.

Again.

Nada.

Again.

Sweet fuck all.

I cast the spell so many times my throat goes raw and the sun dips below the horizon...

And still nothing.

I let out a primal bellow of rage and pitch the grimoire across the room. It smacks into the wall with a loud thump and crashes to the floor.

Breathing hard, I address the empty room. "There has to be a way."

Think, think, think.

Nothing comes to me.

I've tried everything.

My powers are gone.

There's nothing I can—

A sharp pain stabs the space behind my eyes.

"Ah! What the—"

Another stab.

I cough and taste copper.

Blood.

I lift my fingers to my lips and they come away scarlet.

The temperature plummets, and my breath mists in front of my face.

I know this cold.

The icy, dark chill associated with demons.

Shit.

I need help.

My hand slips into my jeans pocket, and I whip out my phone.

Agony tears through my chest, my abdomen.

I double over, winded by the assault.

What the fuck is happening?

I tap my phone open and bring up my contacts list.

My vision blurs.

Another hacking cough.

More copper.

A wave of dizziness sweeps over me.

My knees buckle.

Everything goes dark.

Can I ask you a cheeky favour?

Thanks for reading *The Demon's Shadow* and joining Christian on his quest for power. I hope you enjoyed the book.

Reviews are really important to authors. They help other readers—like you—discover our work.

If you liked the book, and have a couple of minutes to spare, it would be great if you could leave a short, honest review on the book's Amazon or Goodreads page.

Happy reading!

Cheers

Shane

Want More From The Myth & Magic Universe?

DOWNLOAD YOUR EXCLUSIVE PREQUEL SHORT STORY, THE THIEF'S MAGIC (MYTH & MAGIC, BOOK 0.5), FOR FREE!

Want to read Geek's origin story and follow his journey to COVEN? You can download *The Thief's Magic (Myth & Magic, Book 0.5)* today!

Visit: https://bit.ly/thethiefsmagic

Acknowledgments

First, foremost, and always, thank you to my family and friends for being part of my life. I am truly lucky to have each and every one of you.

To my editor—aka The Rock Star—Alexa Padou from *Luna Imprints Author Services*, thank you for championing my work, and challenging me to become a better writer. Here's to fine-tuning many more novels together.

Thank you to Damon and the team at *Damonza*. Just when I think you can't top the previous book cover, you go and smash it out of the park.

To my writerly mentors. You are brilliant humans. Thank you for teaching me, even when I'm reluctant to be taught.

To all the writers I know (whether that be on Instagram, or from one of the writing communities I'm part of), I can't thank you enough. I won't name individuals (because I *will* miss someone out and feel bad about it), but you are my people, and the author journey is much easier because of you.

As always—and last but by no means least— thank you to my readers. Every time I get a review, a social media shout out, or a thoughtful email from one of you, it brightens up my day. You make what I do worth it, and for that, I will always be grateful to you.

ABOUT THE AUTHOR

S. W. Millar is the author of the *Myth & Magic* urban fantasy thriller series. He is also a *Fictionary Certified StoryCoach*, and is currently working on a series of craft guides for writers.

Shane holds a BA in journalism and is a member of *The Alliance of Independent Authors (ALLi)*. He lives in Buckinghamshire, England.

He has taken too many writing courses to count and enjoys reading as much as possible. Shane is obsessed with five things: the writing craft, mythology, personal development, food, and martial arts movies.

Connect with Shane on Instagram

https://www.instagram.com/swmillarauthor/

Visit Shane's Website

https://swmillar.com

ALSO BY S. W. MILLAR

Myth & Magic

The Thief's Magic # 0.5 (FREE prequel short story)
The Witch's Revenge # 1
The Coven's Executioner # 2
The Fury's Vengeance # 3 [Novelette]
More *Myth & Magic* coming soon...

Milton Keynes UK
Ingram Content Group UK Ltd.
UKHW010123210224
438187UK00005B/371